Love
on the
Island

After several very happy years as a bookseller, Jessica Gilmore moved into the charity sector and now works in the Arts, living out her Noel Streatfeild dreams by walking through the Stage Door every morning. Married with one daughter, two dogs and two dog-loathing cats, she lives in the beautiful Chilterns where she can usually be found with her nose in a book. A lover of a happy-ever-after, Jessica loves to write emotional romance with a hint of humour and a splash of sunshine.

JESSICA GILMORE

Love on the Island

ORION

An Orion paperback

First published in Great Britain in 2023 by Orion Fiction,
an imprint of The Orion Publishing Group Ltd
Carmelite House, 50 Victoria Embankment
London EC4Y 0DZ

An Hachette UK Company

1 3 5 7 9 10 8 6 4 2

A CIP catalogue record for this book is
available from the British Library.

ISBN (Mass Market Paperback) 978 1 3987 1554 7
ISBN (eBook) 978 1 3987 1555 4

Typeset by Born Group
Printed and bound in Great Britain by Clays Ltd, Elcograf S.p.A.

MIX
Paper from
responsible sources
FSC® C104740

www.orionbooks.co.uk

For Dan and Abby, love always

Chapter One

Indi

There was nothing India Drewe loved as much as a well-laid plan.

And today might just be the week when not just one but two well-laid plans came to fruition. Which was why, despite standing in what must be 100-degree heat and humidity, her nose alarmingly close to someone else's less than fragrant armpit, she couldn't keep from smiling – a breach of tube etiquette which was getting her more than a few concerned looks from fellow commuters. But for once India didn't care what other people thought. All she had to do was rock this interview and then, on Friday night, Will had planned a special dinner at their favourite restaurant. The one they had gone to on their very first proper date, for every anniversary and to celebrate on the day they had decided to move in together.

Indi took as deep a breath as she could manage while squeezed into a tiny vacuum of standing space, twisting her neck to avoid inhaling any more armpit, trying to calm the dizzying excitement dancing through her. Will had looked uncharacteristically nervous this morning when he had suggested the evening out, when he had said that he wanted to discuss something important with her . . .

Her smile widened and one of her neighbours shuffled back a nervous centimetre. She didn't need to be Hercule

Poirot to work this one out. There was only one logical conclusion – Will was going to ask her to marry him! After all, her thirtieth birthday was just a few weeks away. She had always been clear with him that her life plan included getting engaged by thirty and married by thirty-one. And here was Will planning to propose right on time. He was so *dependable*. Just one of the things that made them so compatible.

A proposal! If Indi wasn't so hemmed in – and so public – she would break out into a happy dance. It totally explained his recent odd behaviour: the hastily closed laptop whenever she came into the room, the abstraction, the obsession with travel documentaries, the mooning over old Facebook memories of his trek to Machu Picchu and his old apartment in Sydney. He wanted a destination wedding, or a really exotic honeymoon! He was always saying how much he would like to show her some of the places he had visited on his gap year, maybe he thought *this* was the perfect time. And she was completely on board – as long as he planned on recreating his backpacking days from the comfort of a five-star hotel, of course. Indi wasn't high maintenance, but she had definitely aged out of dorm rooms.

The train shuddered, jamming Indi's nose straight into the suited armpit she had been trying to avoid, but for once she didn't care, even though surely one of the few upsides of being five foot ten in flat shoes was avoiding inadvertently exploring other people's intimate areas. She didn't care that she was just one of the many human sardines jammed into the hot, sweaty tube carriage, nor that they had been paused outside Russell Square for what might have only been one minute but felt like eternity. No, she was too busy visualising her future with every positive vibe she could muster. Visualise the interview going exactly to plan, visualise the proposal (would he go down on one knee? Hide the ring in her champagne glass?), visualise celebrating her thirtieth birthday as both head of department and a *fiancée*.

After another, harsher judder, one that sent her far deeper into the armpit than any other human should ever need to go, the train started to move with obvious reluctance. Planting her heels firmly on the floor, Indi managed to twist away, lifting her face up to breathe in air that was far from fresh but a significant improvement on her previous situation, bracing herself for the fight through the packed bodies as they finally stopped at her platform.

By the time she reached the exit, Indi felt, as usual, that she had just navigated a particularly testing assault course, the kind saved for the most elite of soldiers. Anxiously, she checked her appearance in a shop window, relieved that all was as it should be. The low bun she had coerced her thick curls into was perfectly in place, not one tendril daring to escape, her discreet make-up hadn't melted, her favourite – and most expensive – light grey suit was miraculously unwrinkled. Best of all, thanks to her careful planning, even the slight delay hadn't derailed her timetable. Of course, she *had* built in a delay contingency. *Lateness*, her father had always said, *was simply the result of bad planning*. And today of all days, punctuality was key.

Indi patted her tote bag, feeling the reassuring outlines of her printed and bound presentation, one for each of the panel. Three internal applicants, including herself, and five externals had made the first round of interviews, this second round was down to just two: Indi and an unknown external candidate. Which suited her perfectly. No external candidate could know the role as well as she did, surely? Victory was so close, she could taste it.

Pulling out her phone, Indi checked her timings. *Oh yes, timetable running to plan.* She had more than enough time to walk to her office, check that her presentation was accessible on her memory stick, in her inbox *and* saved onto the cloud and to grab a very much caffeinated coffee to make sure she was suitably peppy. All nicely on schedule.

This was why she liked a plan. It took all the unnecessary drama out of life.

As Indi went to put her phone back into her bag, a message from her sister flashed up and she paused, eagerly swiping open the full message. It was lovely to know that although Jade might be thousands of miles away (2,115 to be exact, according to Google) and an hour ahead, she had still remembered how important today was.

Although, to be fair, it would have been a surprise if she *had* forgotten after last night's lengthy FaceTime when Indi had practised her presentation three times. She was grateful for video calls, but they were by no means a substitution for Jade's actual, physical presence. The sooner her sister returned home, the better.

Good luck today, you are going to ROCK IT!!! We need to celebrate 🍾🥂🎉🍾 *in person! I MISS YOU!!* 💜

Thank you, I'm a little nervous . . . Indi sent back and the reply was immediate.

You've got this!!! 🍀🍀🤞

Indi bit her lip. How she missed her little sister. She'd expected her to return home at Easter after a few months working on a yacht in the Caribbean, only for Jade to head to Naxos for another seasonal job instead, without even a weekend home in between.

Things hadn't been easy for Jade since the accident that had killed their father when she was just eight, and Indi was glad to see her be more independent. But the two of them had always been so close, it made spending six months apart difficult, even if they did speak nearly every day.

And although the Greek island looked beautiful and Jade seemed happy, Indi couldn't help but worry. At twenty-two, Jade really needed to think about her future, about a career and qualifications. Not that Indi could complain too much, as Jade had suggested that Will and Indi come and stay for free at the fancy resort where she was working. Maybe she should book some holiday and accept the invitation. Not only would she get to see her sister – and check out Nico, the man she had followed to Greece – but a luxurious island resort was, after all, the perfect place to celebrate an engagement – and to celebrate her thirtieth as well, although she didn't want to ruin whatever Will was planning. She'd given him plenty of hints, after all, for how to make her day really special, just as she had done for him almost a year ago.

Indi hesitated, wondering whether to tell Jade about her suspicion that Will was intending to propose or if doing so would tempt fate. Maybe she should wait until the proposal was safely accepted and the ring actually on her finger? She could see the message now – a photo of her left hand, ring sparkling, with a pithy caption. *I said yes!* Or maybe, *Put the champagne on ice.*

Still considering, Indi stepped forward, eyes on her phone, only to let out a high-pitched noise, somewhere between a squeal, a groan and a curse, as she collided with a man rushing past, sending his coffee cup flying as she did so. Time slowed down as, with a sense of impending horror and helplessness, Indi watched the cup drop, bounce off her shoulder and onto her tote bag, leaving a trail of hot latte over both her and her bag.

'No!' Her cry became an anguished wail as the liquid began to soak through the bag and onto her precious paper presentations.

'Watch where you are going,' the owner of the cup snapped and Indi glared at him furiously.

'Watch where *I* was going? You walked right into me. Look at me.' Indi held up her bag, her fury intensifying as she took in the state of it. 'Look at my *presentation*. It's ruined!' She pulled out the top copy and stared at it in dismay; the beautifully bound document was stained and soggy, the paper disintegrating in her hand. 'What am I going to do?' She tugged at her jacket as the spreading dampness seeped through her sleeve and onto her skin. Thank goodness the coffee wasn't newly bought; the heat was uncomfortable but not scalding.

'You should be offering to buy me a new coffee as you're wearing mine,' the man snapped back and walked away, leaving Indi standing there damp and smelling not of the Dior perfume Will had bought her for Christmas, but of soy latte.

Think, Indi. Possible permutations ran quickly through her brain. She would just have to email the presentation to the panel after the interview and be grateful that her three backup plans meant this debacle was just a setback, not a disaster.

But she had congratulated herself too soon; as Indi unbuttoned her jacket to assess the damage, she realised with a horrified yelp that the coffee had soaked through more than just her sleeve and that her blouse was also saturated, no longer crisp, white and smart but crumpled and stained brown. She looked around wildly, but there were no clothes shops between here and her office, nowhere she could pop to without making herself late.

'It's fine,' she muttered, frantically replanning and strategising. Some of her colleagues kept changes of clothes at work, surely someone had something she could borrow? A strategically placed scarf might work. Besides, she had no choice but to carry on, that half-an-hour margin of error had dwindled down to twenty-four minutes and counting. 'You still have several electronic versions of the presentation and you can fix the outfit. You've got this.'

She continued to repeat positive thoughts as she walked at a brisk pace through Bloomsbury until she reached the narrow street of terraced Georgian town houses long since turned into university offices where she worked, heading into the house which was home to the operations department and making her way up the stairs to the project management office. The large first-floor room had once been a prestigious drawing room and still boasted fancy cornicing and an ornate fireplace, but it was now painted a faded industrial shade of green and housed desks and filing cabinets, not sofas and occasional tables.

The office was still empty, apart from Priya who liked to arrive early and have a peaceful coffee away from the demands of her two children before starting work.

'Indi! What's happened?' Priya's look of horror did nothing to help Indi's frayed nerves. 'Isn't your interview this morning?'

'It is. Do you think I can rinse the coffee stain out?' Indi dumped her bag and jacket onto her desk and pulled her blouse out of her waistband as she tried to assess the damage.

'If you don't mind presenting in a see-through damp shirt. Oh, your jacket is ruined too.' Priya took the jacket and held it up, forehead creasing in concern. 'What a shame. I love this jacket on you, it makes you look like a total boss babe.'

'Worse, my presentation has turned to papier mâché . . .' Indi held up the still dripping tote bag at arm's length and Priya took a hurried step back. 'Thank goodness for PowerPoint, I can salvage this at least, but that's more than I can say for my appearance!'

'We could swap clothes?' Priya offered, and despite every-thing, Indi couldn't help but laugh. Priya was a petite five foot nothing and size six, a pixie beside Indi, who was a statuesque and curvy size twelve. She would look even more ridiculous in Priya's red skater dress than she already did. It probably wouldn't cover her bum!

'That's very kind, but I'm not sure I could get a leg into that dress, let alone my boobs. I was wondering if I could do some kind of fancy drapey thing with a scarf or something?'

'That shirt is beyond saving,' Priya said sympathetically but practically. 'Apart from anything else, it reeks of burnt coffee. You get your laptop plugged in and I'll do a raid in the cupboard and see what I can find.'

Indi threw an anxious glance at the clock on the wall. She had just fifteen minutes now. This was supposed to be her calm final prep time; she should be *drinking* coffee not washing it off her, reading her presentation through not dumping it in the bin. Hands shaking, she pulled her laptop out of her rucksack and plugged it in as Priya returned, her expression rueful, three tops in her hands.

'Slim pickings, I'm afraid. I'm sorry, Indi. I could go next door and see if Lou has anything?'

'No time.' Surely, they couldn't be *that* bad. 'Pass them here, one of them will simply have to do.'

'Hello, India, thank you for coming in today.'

'Thank you for asking me back.' Indi smiled at the three people sitting opposite her, trying to look as if she had purposely chosen to team her smart grey linen trousers with a pink T-shirt sporting all five Spice Girls on it. Her other alternatives had been a sweatshirt with a unicorn in sequins above the word '*Believe*' or a neon-green cycling top emblazoned with the name of an energy drink. She noticed all three pairs of eyes flicker to her top and straightened, shoulders back, head up, ready to style it out. 'I'm really excited to talk through my presentation with you.' She put her laptop on the table, touching her trouser pocket to make sure the memory stick was in there; she at least had managed to check that it was ready to load if the presentation, safely saved onto her laptop, should fail at all and the often dodgy Wi-Fi should go down, leaving her email and cloud backups useless. 'I'll just plug this in.'

She quickly connected up her laptop and pressed the remote to switch on the presentation screen. It remained resolutely dark. She pressed it again. Nothing. She attempted a smile, although what she wanted to do was stamp her foot and ask the heavens what she had done to be tested like this?

'Ah, it looks like the remote is out of batteries.' Why hadn't she thought to bring some? A contingency she hadn't even considered she would need to cover.

She pressed the button for a third time, hoping for a miracle.

No such luck.

What was happening? How, despite all her fail-safes, was she standing here in a Spice Girls T-shirt with a painstakingly prepared presentation no one could see?

Indi blinked rapidly, eyes and throat hot.

Keep it together, Drewe.

'Oh, dear.' Maggie, the university's chief operating officer, joined her in pressing several buttons on the remote, but it made no difference. 'I'm sorry, India, but we only have this room for an hour. Can you manage without the screen?'

An hour ago, she would have said a confident 'yes', but an hour ago, she still had her beautifully bound paper copies, which were now taking up half the recycling bin.

Think, think . . . Her laptop screen? No, that was far too small to present from, the interviewers would be so busy peering at it they wouldn't be able to concentrate on what Indi was saying. She stood there for a moment, panic coursing through her. This job was everything she wanted. She was so tantalisingly close, she couldn't give up now.

Turning the laptop towards her, to give herself a framework at least, Indi took a deep breath. How was she going to manage without her pie charts and graphs, her data and examples, while dressed like a twelve-year-old from 1996?

When all else fails, her dad would say, *fake it*.

She could do this. She had to.

'Being a successful project manager is very similar to being a Spice Girl,' she began and saw three pairs of eyebrows instantly shoot up. 'You have to be full of energy like Sporty Spice, channel your inner child like Baby and don't be afraid to keep asking why, carry yourself with poise just as Posh Spice would, and always have a plan B. And, of course, never be afraid to be scary when the situation demands it . . .' Were they actually *buying* this? By the smiles and the nods, it seemed as if they were. But how on earth was she going to work Geri into it? 'Last but not least, you need the confidence of Ginger Spice to push ahead . . .'

Chapter Two

Jade

Jade sat back and looked out across the endless sea. It was a sight that usually left her practically vibrating with happiness. The sunset was spectacular, the sun itself glowing red as it started its descent below the horizon, casting a fiery path along the purpling water, the sky a kaleidoscope of oranges and pinks and gold. No wonder the first people to enjoy this view had worshipped the sun as a god. On a night like this, Jade could almost believe the gods were guiding her fate. After all, they had brought her here, to the small, perfect island of Agios Iohannis. To Nico.

She shifted her gaze from the sunset to the man sitting opposite her. She must have been very, *very* good in her previous life to have got so lucky. Tall and broad with olive skin darkened by weeks of working outside, dark curls falling over his brow, darker eyes heating her through every time they rested on her, a mouth made to kiss and a body made to touch, it was as if Apollo himself had jumped down from his fiery chariot to seduce her. Now she understood how all those mythological women had succumbed to showers of gold. She'd never wanted anyone so desperately in all her admittedly inexperienced life.

And, best of all, he seemed to want her just as much.

But even so, she wasn't sure how he would react to her

news. She wasn't sure how *she* felt about it, after all, and she had known herself for twenty-two years longer than she'd known Nico.

'You look miles away,' Nico said in the perfect English that always put her to shame. She had gone as far as downloading Greek onto her language app, now she all she needed to do was to start actually learning it.

Jade reached out and took his hand. It still seemed unreal that she could just do that, just reach out and touch him, be touched. She sometimes worried their relationship was all a very long daydream and she'd wake up to find herself back on the yacht where they'd met, stepping onto the deck only to be stopped in her tracks by the shirtless Adonis in front of her. The last thing she'd expected when she'd taken a three-month job as a third stewardess for a yacht charter season was to find herself falling head over heels for one of the deckhands. Let alone that he would seem to fall just as hard for her.

More than seem, she reminded herself. After all, he'd asked her to come back to Greece with him at the end of the charter season, had found her a job at his cousin's new resort. They shared a room, a bed, a life.

He talked about forever.

But did he mean it?

There was only one way to find out.

Jade inhaled, searching for the right words, still not sure what she was going to say, just that she had to say *something*. She tightened her grip on his strong, capable hand, threading her fingers through his.

'Nico, I went over to Naxos today.'

'I know.' He sounded slightly surprised, probably wondering why she had mentioned her trip. After all, she visited the bigger island several times a week. Naxos was home to the main company office as well as shops and the post collection point. 'I'm sorry I couldn't take you myself, I hope Antinous took good care of you.'

'Of course, although no one sails like you,' she reassured him. 'Anyway, I've been feeling a little under the weather, so I went to see the doctor while I was there. You know how tired I have been lately.'

'No wonder with the hours you work, I'm always telling Mikhos you do too much,' he scolded, but his eyes darkened with concern. 'Is everything OK?'

'Yes, I mean, I'm not ill. But he did a test and, the thing is . . .' Another deep breath. 'Nico. I'm pregnant.'

Jade had an overwhelming urge to squeeze her eyes closed as if she were a child hiding from something scary, not sure she wanted to see Nico's first reaction, but she forced herself to keep looking at him. All the concern faded until his face was completely expressionless, his hand slackening under hers as he pulled it slowly away. She felt cold without his touch.

'Pregnant?' There was no discernible emotion in his voice and, despite the warm evening, Jade shivered.

'About eight weeks, he said.' She looked down at her hand still stretched out alone in the middle of the table. 'I should have guessed, I suppose, but I'm on the pill and don't always take breaks so didn't realise . . .' She flushed. This shouldn't feel so awkward. After all, they had been intimate enough to make a baby – to make hundreds of babies. 'He said it was probably when I was ill, those bad prawns, remember? Apparently being sick can make the pill less effective. I didn't think. I'm sorry.'

'You're *pregnant*? We're going to have a baby?' Nico was on his feet, running his hands through his thick dark hair until it stood up on end.

'Maybe. It's still early. I might not . . . and we could . . .' Damn, she couldn't manage a single sensible word. 'What I mean is that it's still early days, there's a reason why people wait till three months before they tell people. And *as* it's so early, we have options.'

He stilled. 'Options? Is that what you want?'

'I don't know,' Jade said honestly. 'I am here on a temporary visa, my home is hundreds of miles away, I am only twenty-two, we met just a few months ago. Most people would say having a baby together at this point in our lives is absolutely crazy.'

Her sister for one; his cousin – and her boss – for another.

'But what do *you* say, Jade? You're the only person whose opinion matters here.'

'Not the only one. You matter too.'

'OK.' He sat back down, straight-backed, determined-looking, and some of her tension dissipated. He hadn't run, that was a start, although she had never really thought he would. She'd fallen for the film-star looks but stayed because he was a good, caring man. But their still-fledgling relationship had never been tested like this before. 'You're right. We *have* only been together for a short time. You are supposed to be leaving at the end of the summer. We have very busy jobs, our days are long and intense, tourism is not just seasonal but unpredictable, we are at the start of our careers. A baby will complicate things.'

Jade swallowed. He was only saying everything she had been thinking. It was just that hearing it out loud made her realise how impossible keeping this baby was. And how much she wished it wasn't.

'But . . .' It was Nico's turn to take her hand. 'I love you. I want to make a life with you. We *could* have a baby, Jade. Be a family.'

Wild hope filled her. 'But how?'

He shrugged. 'How does anyone? One day at a time. My parents are close by. I have a job, an apartment, that's more than many people starting out have. We have the sun and the sea and ambition. We're young and strong. We love each other. We could do this. If you wanted.' His eyes gleamed. 'It might be fun. A little girl with your eyes.'

'Or a boy with yours.' Jade hadn't allowed herself to head down this route, to imagine the multiplying cells inside her as an actual *baby*, but suddenly she could see it, a blend of her and Nico, bright eyes and a mass of dark hair.

Was it really possible?

She forced herself to stay calm and channel Indi. In the extremely unlikely event that Indi would ever have an unplanned pregnancy, the first thing she would do would be to look at every option and plan accordingly. So that's what Jade needed to do. She took a sip of water and forced herself to think coolly and without emotion, to go over the options for the umpteenth time since she had left the doctor's office just a few hours ago.

Her first, and the most obvious, option was to *not* have the baby, to return to London as planned at the end of the summer, back to her childhood home, to find a career that she wanted to do, whether that was taking up the teacher-training place Indi had cajoled her into applying for or staying within the tourism and hospitality sector she was thriving in.

She shivered despite the balmy temperature. Jade might be full of conflicting feelings about this sudden curveball life had thrown her, but whenever she tried to visualise her future looking so similar to her past, she froze inside.

Secondly, she could return home and have the baby there. Indi might – would definitely – disapprove, but she would still support Jade with everything she had, that was a certainty. As for their mother, she would happily house Jade and the baby and dish out the same blend of distracted love she'd given Jade and Indi. It would be lonely at times but doable.

Or she could stay here . . .

Here – *Nico* – felt right in a way that nothing had ever felt right before. Jade loved her family and her home, but she sometimes felt that she was defined by her position as the youngest sister, the baby of the family. Defined by her past, by a childhood filled with operations and convalescence. Confined by Indi's dreams and ambitions for her, her sister's need for her to be safe, stable.

And for so long Jade had gone along with Indi's vision, but over the last year she had started to feel stifled, like she was failing. No matter how she tried, Jade couldn't seem to live up to her sister's expectations – disappointing A-level results, no university degree, several jobs, none with prospects. Now here she was with an unplanned pregnancy.

There was no way Jade could fool herself that Indi would be anything but worried. Worse, bitterly disappointed.

But it wasn't Indi's life. It was hers.

Nico tightened his grip on her hand. 'Look, Jade. It's only May, I thought that we had months ahead of us still, but I want you to know that I was hoping, planning, to ask you to stay here with me when the season ended, not because of a baby but because of you, of us.' Nico looked uncharacteristically unsure. 'I was thinking of asking you to marry me.'

Jade could only gape at him, breathless. 'You were *what*?'

'Every day, I feel more and more sure that we belong together. I have had relationships before, some long, some short, but nothing like this. Nothing that feels so right. I can't explain it, I wasn't looking for it, but here we are and I would be a fool if I let you just walk out of my life at the end of the summer, baby or no baby. So yes, I was thinking of asking you. No – I was *planning* on asking you.'

Before she could think better of it, Jade said exactly what was in her heart. 'I was thinking of saying yes.' And as she uttered the words, she knew they were true. Six months wasn't a long relationship, but she and Nico had been together every single one of those days, living and working together. And now they were potentially having a baby together. 'I love you,' she said, more strongly this time. 'Marriage, babies, they seem inevitable, so why wait?'

His dark eyes sparkled and her heart contracted with love and excitement. 'I should have a ring, get down on one knee, do something special. You deserve it all.'

'I don't need any of that,' Jade said and she meant every word. 'I just need you.'

'Then we're engaged? Getting married, having a baby?' The happiness in his voice, in his smile, warmed her through, filled her with certainty; they *could* make this work.

'I think so. Yes! Let's do it!'

It was amazing how right her decision felt. Maybe it wasn't planned or thought out, but wasn't that the joy of it?

'This is amazing! I can't wait to tell people!' Nico was back on his feet, pulling her up to join him, holding her close. 'I want everyone to know you are going to be my wife. To start celebrating with my parents, my cousin, your family.'

'I don't know, do we have to announce it just yet? It feels so romantic keeping it just between us,' Jade pleaded. 'We'll never have this time again, you know? As soon as people find out, they will start asking questions about wedding planning and where are we going to live and what will I do for a job. They'll say we are too young and it's too soon and we'll end up letting them know about the baby. I haven't fully processed how *I* feel about it all yet. I'm not ready to hear everyone else's opinions. Not yet.'

'You think your family won't approve?' His smile faded.

'My mother will approve of anything that makes me happy. And you do. Make me happy I mean,' she added softly as she squeezed his hand again, needing the reassurance of contact. 'Happier than I ever thought possible.'

'And my parents already adore you.' His clasp was warm, reassuring.

'But Mikhos will definitely think it's too soon. I can't imagine he'll be happy when he hears I'm pregnant.'

'Mikhos thinks you're great.' Nico immediately sprang to the defence of his cousin.

'As an assistant, yes. As a member of the family? Doubtful. He'll say we're rushing into things. Indi will say the same.' Jade sighed, feeling some of the certainty ebb away. 'Maybe they are right.' Indi usually was, after all.

'Hey, look at me.' Nico's hand tightened on hers and Jade did as he asked, her whole body heating at the mingled desire and warmth in his almost black eyes. 'I love you and you love me. That's all that matters.'

Jade lost herself in his gaze. How could it be barely six months since she'd boarded the yacht to see Nico on deck, bare-chested, coiling a rope, sweat gleaming on his body, muscles corded with the effort, an appraising, approving grin on his face as he looked her up and down. Jade didn't believe in love at first sight. Lust, sure, but love? Not in real life. But in that moment, as her eyes met his, the world seemed to shift and rearrange, with him at the centre. And he had stayed there over the months that followed.

'You're right. This is what I want. You, me, forever.' And it was. She didn't want to follow in Indi's footsteps, eyes so firmly glued on some mythical future she didn't have time to enjoy the sunset. Jade wanted to see where life led her. 'OK. Let's tell our families about the engagement, but keep the baby between us for now. Just for a few weeks, until we hit the twelve-week mark. I don't want people thinking I've trapped you, after all.'

'Oh, but you have. You trapped me the first moment I saw you, but I am a very willing prisoner. You won't regret this, Jade, I promise that I'm going to make you so happy.'

'You already do.' But although she meant it, Jade could hear the hesitation in her voice, reality intruding on her island idyll. 'And when Indi realises that she will be the first to give us her blessing.'

Who knew, maybe she would. After all, her sister always said that all she wanted was Jade's happiness.

But that feeling of unease stayed with Jade and when, the next evening, she picked up her phone ready to share the news of the engagement, instead of selecting her sister as planned, she pressed on her mother's name instead, although she was fully aware that all she was doing was putting off the inevitable.

She nestled into Nico as the phone rang, a little homesick when it connected to show her mother looking confused, like she always did when accepting a video call. Tabitha was sat outside in their small flower-filled garden, the magnolia tree in full bloom behind her. As always, she held the phone at arm's length, staring at the screen suspiciously.

'Mum? It's Jade.'

Tabitha blinked, then her face lit up with a smile. 'Darling, your backdrop looks glorious, how wonderful to be within a heartbeat of the sea.' One moment later: 'Whereabouts in Italy are you again, darling?'

'I'm in Greece, silly!' Jade rolled her eyes in Nico's direction, glad that she'd warned him that facts slid from their mother's mind like Prosecco down a hen party's throat. It drove Indi mad, their mother's inability to remember anything about their lives when she was in the middle of a creative phase, but Jade had never minded. It was just part of what made Tabitha Drewe unique. 'About fifty minutes from Naxos. I've been here for two months now,' she added pointedly, even knowing that the point would go well and truly over her mother's head.

'Greece, of course. Oh, you lucky girl.' Her mother's voice deepened dramatically. 'I adore Greece. Did I ever tell you about the summer I spent island hopping? I will never forget those long, lazy days communing with the gods. There's a particular cove I found where nobody ever seemed to go. I would shed my clothing as I stepped down the path until it was just me, gloriously nude, feeling the sun on my body, just as nature intended . . .'

'Mum!' Jade's cheeks heated. Only her mother would talk about getting nude before asking how she was. 'You're on loudspeaker.'

'Am I? Why?'

'Because Nico is here. My boyfriend, remember?' she added hastily before her mother could ask who Nico was. Jade had mentioned him multiple times, sent photos, FaceTimed her mother with Nico in the background, but if her mother had forgotten her location, it was unlikely she would remember her companion.

'Of course I remember Nico.' Her mother looked indignant. 'How could I forget such a beautiful young man? Would he like to model for me? Adonis? Or maybe Apollo, does he play the lyre?'

'No, Mum, it's the twenty-first century. He plays the guitar.' She grinned at Nico, silently laughing beside her, warm in the shared camaraderie. 'Look, Mum, I'm calling for a reason. I wanted to tell you our news. Nico and I are engaged. We're getting married.'

'Darling. That's wonderful. I will make you a gift of one of the sculptures I made back when I was in Greece, it will bless your home.'

'That's very generous, but there's a lot to figure out first, we have a long way to go before we can think about art.'

'Oh, darling. Art always comes first. Remember that.' And for Tabitha Drewe that was the unvarnished truth. Jade adored her mercurial mother, but if – *when* – she and Nico had kids, she wanted to be a very different kind of parent, the sort that always turned up to school events and remembered what was going on in her children's lives. 'Married. How wonderful. I shall pour a libation for you both to bless your marriage.'

'Thank you.'

Beside her, Nico shook as he tried to hold in his laughter, but as she finished the call, the humour drained away from Jade, instead she just felt tired. Because, of course, someone *had* turned up to school events and signed her homework diary after making sure all her homework was done. Just as someone had enrolled her in and taken her to swimming lessons and dance classes, ensured her clothes were washed and a hot meal was always on the table. And as for remembering all those hospital appointments, the endless physio and check-ups . . .

Where would she have been without her sister to take care of her? It was Indi who had organised her life, her mother's, the whole family. No wonder she had headed into project management. From the moment their father died, the Drewe family had become Indi's to manage.

It still was.

Jade knew that she owed her sister all her happiness – and that she was about to break her sister's heart.

But as she looked over at Nico, his eyes lit up with laughter, his arm warm around her waist, body solid and real behind hers, inviting her to lean in, to trust him, be with him, she also knew that she had no choice. She didn't want the kind of life Indi had mapped out for her, she wanted Nico and this baby and it was time she told her sister so.

Chapter Three

Indi

Friday 19 May

'That was delicious, but I can't manage another bite.' Indi pushed her *sambal goreng* to one side and picked up her water instead. Her tension levels were wired up to the highest degree, killing her appetite.

So far, there hadn't been a hint of a proposal, just small talk, mainly about their close friends who had recently moved to Australia and who seemed to be having an amazing time according to the WhatsApp messages and gorgeous photos they shared. Indi was really happy for them, although she missed them, but she was less keen on the impact their new life was having on Will, who had been reminiscing about his own Australian adventures ever since the move had been announced until Indi felt she had lived them alongside him.

And much as she liked Lara and Kwame there were other topics Indi would prefer to pursue. The absolutely amazing news about her successful interview for instance! Indi had no idea how she had managed to seize triumph from the coffee-covered jaws of disaster but somehow she had, although it wasn't until she saw the offer in writing that she really believed it. But rather than join her in celebrating, Will seemed to actively want to avoid discussing her new job. OK, he had *said* all the right things when she'd called him with the good news earlier this morning but his reactions had seemed off somehow, as if his mind was elsewhere.

But then again, if he was planning to propose, it was no wonder he was distracted.

'Are you sure you've had enough? In that case, do you mind?'

Before Indi could do more than nod her agreement, Will had taken her plate and was tucking into the tofu. Clearly *he* wasn't suffering from nerves. But then, why should he be? They both knew she would say yes. The asking was just a formality.

If only he would hurry up and actually *do* it. Between waiting two torturous days for the phone call about the job and this, she had reached stratospheric heights of tension this week.

'Of course, the opportunities are amazing,' Will continued, a one-man Australian tourism board. 'A better work-life balance . . .'

Indi didn't mean to tune him out, but she'd heard this symphony far too often recently. A mixture of turning thirty and their friends' emigration seemed to have resurrected all his old travel memories and dreams, but tonight she wanted to look forward not back.

'You know, Priya was just amazing before my interview.' Indi took advantage of a momentary silence to try to redirect the subject. 'I couldn't have kept my cool without her. She said I should get the T-shirt framed as a memento. Who would have thought a childhood of learning every Spice Girls' lyric possible would serve me so well? I even managed to get a line from "Spice Up Your Life" in there. I still can't believe I pulled it off. I thought they spent the last two days laughing at me, that's why I hadn't heard. I ended up asking them to repeat the offer I was so geared up to hear a refusal.'

'Why? You were practically doing the job anyway.' Will didn't look up from her tofu as he spoke.

'I guess so but it's still a big jump up pay and responsibility wise, even without coffee-gate. There were no guarantees I'd get it.' Indi bit her lip. She didn't want to make the evening all about her – she wanted it to be all about *them* – but surely Will could be a little happier for her? Come to think of it he had been somewhat disengaged throughout the whole application process. She knew he was feeling bored and frustrated with his job as a data scientist. Like her, his days were long, his work intense, but recently he seemed to resent how much time he spent at the office, getting increasingly depressed as Sunday evening drew in. She'd tried to help him make some plans for a next step, a new job, some training, but he'd brushed them – her – away. Maybe this new role of hers would help him kick-start *his* next step.

'You know,' she continued. 'I was thinking, this might be a good time to start my MBA. I don't want to get complacent, it's important to keep learning – and I'm in the right place for it. I might not work in higher education forever, so it's good to get the most out of it while I can. The discount is amazing and it would be nice to get my MBA finished while I am still child-free.'

Some people might think a new job, an MBA and a wedding would be too much stress; after all, planning weddings seemed to take up some people's every waking moment. But Indi knew exactly what she wanted: Will's local church, a marquee on his parents' lawn, close friends and family only. She already had a spreadsheet and budget set up ready to go. Maybe tomorrow she could finally get started implementing it!

Will had finally finished clearing her plate and he sat back, his beer in his hand as the waitress cleared their plates. Indi had hoped for champagne, but maybe he had a bottle ordered for after he'd done the deed. She'd been careful to make her own beer last just in case. 'An MBA? You never stop, do you, as soon as one goal is ticked off, you're onto the next.'

Indi shifted uneasily. There was something unnervingly unreadable about Will's tone, his expression equally inscrutable. Maybe he *was* nervous, after all.

'No point in wasting time!' she said brightly.

'No. That's what I've been thinking too.' He tried for a smile, but it was more of a grimace, and Indi realised with a shock that the shadows under his blue eyes were a little more pronounced than usual. Will was usually the picture of glowing health, a work-hard, play-hard fitness fanatic who thought nothing of jumping on his bike for an easy fifty-mile Sunday ride, and who still turned out for rugby practice twice a week. Tall and broad, with dirty-blond hair and an easy smile, Will came from the kind of traditional family who always went to church on Christmas Eve, kept their outdoor clothes in a boot room and who got very competitive over board games. Indi adored visiting them and hoped to persuade Will to buy a house as close to his parents as possible. 'How much time we waste on this treadmill we're on.'

Right. That was unexpected. 'Are you OK?' Her unease deepened. Maybe he *hadn't* brought her here to propose, maybe he was going to tell her he was ill? But surely nobody with a serious illness could eat two large plates of spicy Indonesian food in one sitting? Plus starters.

'I'm just tired. Work has been a lot. Again.' He picked up his beer and then set it back down without taking a sip, instead taking a visibly deep breath as if steadying his nerves.

Was this it? She sat up taller, trying not to look too eager.

'Indi, I am really happy for you, I am. Your ability to get things done, to think on your feet, to go after what you want is impressive.'

That was better. It wasn't exactly poetry, but then again she hadn't actually expected something overly romantic from this moment. Will knew that she wasn't the kind of person who wanted a flash mob or a scoreboard proposal. Priya's husband had written a proposal song and sang it to her at an open mic night and every time she related the story, Indi came out in hives of horror. She looked around just to make sure, no, not a mic in sight!

'Thank you. You're not so bad yourself.' She smiled at him encouragingly. Bless him, he was just nervous! 'I do love you.' Will made her feel so *safe*. He was dependable. Focused.

'And I love you. But . . .'

Indi froze. *But* was not a proposal word. Not with one *or* two ts.

Will leaned forward and took her hand in his. 'Indi, is this really what you want? The promotion, then slogging for an MBA? What then? Another promotion? Isn't it a bit endless?'

What? 'I don't just want those things,' she said carefully, trying to figure out where this unexpected conversational turn was taking them. 'Eventually I want a family as well, I've always wanted children, you know that.' She had been clear from the outset. What was the point of dating someone with incompatible goals?

But Will shared her goals. She'd even shown him her life-plan spreadsheets before they'd moved in together. She'd felt more vulnerable than the first time he'd seen her naked, but although he sometimes gently teased her about them, he had also been obviously impressed, had suggested modifications and amendments so that she had now factored in two children, not three, had agreed to a dog someday as well as a cat. They were *their* shared goals now.

Or at least she'd *thought* they were. But much as she'd tried to dismiss his abstracted mood as a blip, she couldn't deny that ever since they'd waved Lara and Kwame off, Will had seemed to lose focus. Did he want to move to Australia too? Was that what this was about? He knew she could never live so far away from Jade and her mother. Was that an issue for him?

'What about adventure?' Will's voice was low as he avoided eye contact, his own gaze fixed on the place where his plate had been. 'Do you want that?'

'Adventure?' Indi's chest tightened. All excitement and anticipation had ebbed away, replaced with an almost painful anxiety. Whatever Will was about to ask her, marriage didn't seem to be in the running anymore, if it ever even had been.

'Travel, new experiences, discovery. Indi, we work twelve-hour days and for what? Expensive rent, tedious commutes, repetitive days. Where's the fun?'

'Fun? I thought we *were* having fun. This is fun, isn't it? Eating at a nice restaurant?' She stopped, her voice wavering uncontrollably.

'I don't want to sit in north London and eat Indonesian food, Indi, I want to eat it *in* Indonesia, I want to eat brigadeiros in Brazil and pho in Vietnam, have a Christmas Day barbecue on Bondi Beach and surf in Hawaii. I want to see the world, Indi, to have adventures before settling down to a mortgage and a four-by-four and wellies outside the door.'

Bondi Beach? This *was* about Australia. And now she knew the problem she could find a solution. That was what she excelled at after all. 'Is this about Kwame and Lara emigrating? Because it's different for them. Her parents are out there and—'

'No. At least not exactly. Look, Indi. When we got together, you seemed to have all the answers.'

The past tense wasn't lost on Indi. She gripped her water glass tightly, trying not to react, to see exactly where he was going. 'I wouldn't say *all* the answers.'

'Twenty-five and you knew exactly what you wanted and how you were going to get there. I didn't know anyone with your drive, your certainty. You made everything seem so easy. I just had to follow your lead.'

So she was driven, what was wrong with that? 'I didn't see it that way, as me in the lead. I thought we were partners, that you were happy with our life.'

'I was, but recently – with work being such a slog, turning thirty, seeing our friends start new lives, *better* lives – it feels like there's something missing.' Will ran a hand through his hair. 'I've tried to talk to you about how I feel, but you seem to think a new job will fix it. It won't. I need more than a different office or the next step up the ladder. I need a complete change. Look, Indi, it's not you, it's me.' *That old chestnut.* 'But, Indi, sometimes I think that before I know it, I'll be my dad, complaining about the commute, about mowing the lawn, that a pint in the local will be the most exciting part of each week.' He looked anguished at the prospect. Indi didn't understand it; his parents lived an idyllic life; they had given him a perfect childhood. Why was replicating that so horrific?

It wasn't, of course. This was probably a simple case of cold feet. She just needed to re-strategise. Make sure Will felt heard.

Some of the tension seeped out of her. 'But we can make sure that doesn't happen. We can still have adventures, lots of them. And I was just thinking aloud, I don't have to do an MBA now, it can wait. Look, why don't we go and visit

Lara and Kwame for a start? They're always encouraging us to come and stay.' Long-haul holidays weren't in the budget, but they could be, it was a simple case of revising their plan. After all, they didn't have to be engaged *by* thirty, she'd just hoped to be. They had time, as long as it happened at some point in the next year. A trip to Australia might just be the romantic adventure they needed, some quality time together.

But Will didn't look enthused by her concessions – in fact, he looked decidedly mulish. 'I want more than just a couple of weeks here and there, Indi. I want a whole different way of living. There's a world out there and I want to see every part of it. In fact . . .' He took a visibly deep breath. 'I'm going to go and see it. I've decided to hand in my notice and use my savings to travel.'

For one long moment Indi was frozen in place, even her brain seemed to stop working as his words echoed round and round. *Travelling?* Not simply a long haul holiday or even a job abroad as she had feared.

'But . . . What about us?' What she meant was *what about me*, but she couldn't bring herself to sound that needy. That vulnerable. Her role was to be strong, no matter what.

Finally, he met her gaze, his expression and tone equally unreadable. 'You could always come with me.

Indi stared at Will in total disbelief. This evening was supposed to be a celebration of her *new job*, instead Will was asking her to give it up before she had even started!

And if she didn't then he would go anyway and leave her behind.

She searched for the right words, but for once she had no idea what they were. Had no idea how to feel. The room seemed to have faded away, as if she were completely detached from the whole situation. She was totally numb.

She forced herself to respond, to play for time as she tried to disentangle her thoughts, to feel something, anything. 'I don't know, Will, taking time out to travel isn't something I have ever considered.' He knew why. He knew just heading off had never been an option for her. She had responsibilities, people depended on her.

He leaned forward eagerly. 'But we've talked about it, about where you would go if you could go anywhere. You have always wanted to visit Costa Rica, haven't you?'

'Well, yes,' she conceded. 'And we've talked about what superpower I would have, and what our dream jobs would be if we didn't have to earn actual money, and which house in Hampstead we'd own if we won the lottery and whether we'd rather be an eagle or a dolphin. It's talk, Will. Make-believe. I would love to go to Costa Rica one day, but on a holiday, not with a rucksack and always moving on.'

Will sighed. 'Indi, you never *take* holidays. Not really. Getting you away for a long weekend is an effort. Every annual leave you do take, you line up some kind of project. You spent a week repainting Jade's bedroom at Easter and she's not even here.'

'I wanted to make it more grown-up for when she comes home, you know that. And anyway, not every annual leave! What about when we went to Rome? Or Paris? What about Vienna?'

'OK, you will do a long weekend, but when have we gone away for longer?'

'Bordeaux. That week on the Île de Ré.' She sat back and folded her arms. She couldn't believe this complete rewriting of history.

'With your family. And you never stopped all week, organising the travel, day trips, food. We never go away properly, just the two of us or with friends.'

31

Indi watched Will fiddle with his spoon, her numbness morphing into frustration. One of the things she loved about him was how he understood her commitment to her mother and sister. 'You know how it is for me. Jade needs me, but I know that can be limiting that's why I am always happy for you to go skiing with your family or on cycling holidays with your mates. But things have changed, it's easier now Jade is starting to live her own life. I can do more. *We* can. So, why don't we look at spending a few weeks travelling around Australia?' It seemed like the perfect compromise. Maybe she had been too focused on her life plans, her family's needs, but there was time to put that right. There had to be.

'The thing is,' Will said carefully, 'a holiday won't cut it. Not now. I don't want to settle, to compromise anymore. I want to take off and see where the world takes me. I've been thinking about this for some time, Indi. I need to do this.'

'And if I don't?' Her voice was small.

He looked down at his plate. 'Then we want different things for our future. It's up to you.'

How was *any* of this up to her? This wasn't what she wanted. This evening she had expected a celebratory dinner and a proposal, not an ultimatum. It wasn't *fair*.

But Indi knew better than anyone just how unfair life could be.

She had no idea what to say. Didn't want to utter the words that called time on four years. On the future she had so confidently looked forward to. On Will. How could this be happening?

At that moment, her phone screen lit up. She glanced down. 'It's Jade.' She didn't miss the frustrated roll of his eyes as she got to her feet. 'I'll be right back.'

She grabbed her phone and fled the restaurant to the safety of the busy, bustling street outside, glad of the escape. She was usually the one who provided the advice and counsel, but right now she didn't mind admitting she needed help – and nobody knew her better than her sister.

'Jade!'

'Indi, congratulations on the promotion. I knew you'd do it!' Her sister's beloved face filled the screen, tanned and glowing. 'I hope you are celebrating suitably.'

'Will booked a restaurant.' Indi was about to fill her sister in on the rest when Jade pulled back from the screen to reveal that she wasn't alone and Indi swallowed back the words. 'Oh, hi, Nico.'

She was sure Nico was nice enough, but he always seemed to be around. She'd been pleased for Jade at first, that she seemed to have clicked with someone, but she was going to have to warn her against getting too attached to an extended holiday romance. Not that she was in any position to be dishing out relationship advice. Pain struck her, right in the solar plexus, and it was all she could do not to double over.

Will was leaving her.

She forced herself to push the pain away with years-long practice as Nico waved. 'Hi, Indi.'

Jade pulled Nico close, so they were cheek to cheek, beaming into the camera. 'Indi, we have news! You're not the only Drewe with something to celebrate!'

And somehow Indi knew exactly what her sister was going to say before the words were said. The glow, the excitement, Nico's presence all added up to one thing.

On the evening Indi should be announcing her engagement, her little sister was doing so instead.

Chapter Four

Indi

Indi's father had taught her one very important lesson: a well-laid plan was the key to happiness.

What he hadn't taught her, however, was what to do when all her well-laid plans were suddenly redundant. It didn't matter how organised her life plan was if she hadn't put in a contingency for 'massive curveball incoming just before my thirtieth birthday'.

And more fool her, she hadn't. She had been so sure of Will, of them.

Or had she been wilfully blind? Refused to see the signs he was changing? She'd dismissed the job grumbles and romanticising of his gap year as nothing to worry about. Instead, she'd had everything to worry about. But it was hard to reconcile the man last night who had dismissed the life they had built together, dismissed their future, with the man who had liked to tell his friends about her life plan with affectionate pride.

This stranger-Will had issued her with an ultimatum. Had asked for a decision by the end of the week, because he wanted to hand in his notice on his job and their flat and book a plane ticket. Wanted to start his new life, even if it was without her.

Not that it mattered how much time she had to decide, because *of course* she was going to say no. Her life was here,

34

her responsibilities were here, her hard-won new job was here. And even if she didn't have any of those things, she didn't *want* to stuff a sarong into a rucksack and launch herself into the unknown. She never had. Will knew that. But by offering her the option to come with him, he got to be the good guy. She was the one who would end up pulling the plug on them, not him. No matter that he was the one who had just thrown their four years together away.

Indi swallowed, her hands curling into fists. She couldn't think about it, not yet. Couldn't visualise a future with no Will in it, an uncertain future. Back to square one, single, no nearer the contented family village life she dreamed of. In fact, she was further from it than ever.

But if she wasn't going to think about Will, then she would have to think about Jade and that was even more painful. Will wanting to leave her behind while he jetted away on a new life was bad enough but *Jade*? How could her sister want to settle so far away?

Indi was still having trouble believing Jade's news. Believing that her little sister wanted to stay in Greece and get *married*. Clearly, several months of sun, sea and sex had gone to her sister's brain. Twenty-two was far too young for marriage, especially marriage to someone Jade had known for all of five minutes.

It should be *Indi* announcing her engagement. She was the one who was nearly thirty with four years of a sensible relationship behind her. This should be *her* time.

Indi stopped, reaching out to the wall to steady herself. It was too much.

OK. Deep breath. She couldn't resolve both problems, so she had to prioritise. Her own would have to wait. Jade always came first and Indi knew she needed reinforcements to figure out what to do about her sister's unexpected news. Admittedly, when it came to proactive allies, Tabitha Drewe was a long shot, but right now their mother was all she had.

The Islington flat Indi shared with Will was just a couple of miles away from her childhood home. The Drewes had moved to Stoke Newington long before it was trendy. Tabitha had taken one look at the park, the pretty high street, the atmospheric cemetery and firmly resisted any attempt to persuade her to consider any other London borough or, worse in her artistic eyes, a suburb with good schools and rail links.

When Indi had been a girl, their street had been a mix of homes that had been in families for generations, terraces converted into flats and fixer-uppers bought by other young families. Now, the whole street had an identikit feel. Flats had been converted back into houses, all brickwork sandblasted, front doors painted dark grey, railings restored and painted, new sash windows reinstalled. Only one house broke the mould, the front door a cheerful pink, the railings rusty, patterned curtains, rather than the ubiquitous shutters at the bay window, allowing anyone who walked by the opportunity to peek in. Indi turned in at the gate and despite all her inner turmoil felt at home in a way she never did in the new-build flat she rented with Will. Although that might not be her home for much longer. *Not now*, she pushed the thought away.

Indi didn't bother with the bell – it was unlikely her mother would take any notice of it – instead she fished her keys out of her bag and let herself in.

'Mum?' she called out as she made her way through the hall, a long wide corridor filled with antique hatstands, bureaus and several plinths displaying her mother's sculptures. The walls were buried under pictures, some familiar,

36

others new, and Indi paused to look at a couple she hadn't seen before, lingering by one stark landscape, taking in the texture, the deft brushstrokes, the clever use of shadow.

'Beautiful, isn't it?'

Indi hadn't heard Tabitha approach and jumped as her mother appeared at her shoulder, her richly floral scent sweeping over Indi, familiar and faintly exotic all at once.

'I guess.' Discussing art with her mother always made Indi uncomfortable, like it was a language she should know but had forgotten.

She didn't miss her mother's knowing look before she turned away. 'Come on through. I went to the shop and bought Greek wine so that we can toast your sister's happiness.'

She'd already realised it was unlikely that their mother would see things the way Indi did, but this statement proved how futile that vain hope had been. Indi swallowed, feeling more alone than she could remember, even during those long difficult months after her father died, as she followed her mother into the kitchen, desperately trying to figure out how to get her onside. She'd already decided not to mention Will's plans and what was beginning to feel horribly like their inevitable break-up. She was the grown-up in this family, the caretaker. She wasn't sure how to play it any other way. She needed answers and a full plan before drawing her mother into her confidence.

The large square room at the back of the house had the usual kitchen units, a generous dining table and chairs, and two battered sofas by the French doors, the shelves above filled with an eclectic collection of books. As always, a fresh loaf sat on the table, flanked by a lump of cheese and a bowl of apples and tomatoes, Tabitha's habitual diet. Jade wouldn't have starved if Indi hadn't cooked every night, but her diet would have been very restricted; Tabitha liked food she could graze on without preparing. A very fluffy and very fat tortoiseshell cat snoozed on a sofa, bathed in the last of the sunlight, barely deigning to half open an eye to greet Indi. There was no television here, nor anywhere in the house, Tabitha said they dulled creativity, although Indi knew her mother, completely oblivious of her hypocrisy, spent her evenings bingeing box sets on her laptop.

'Here you are.' Her mother handed Indi a silver goblet liberally filled with wine. 'Let's make a libation before we drink.'

Indi had long since stopped protesting the gesture and dutifully stepped out into the garden, making her way to the statue centred in the middle of the lawn. It was one of her mother's sculptures, a young Dionysus, sculpted in her trademark style mingling the ancient and modern. He was, apparently, a statement about corporate greed.

Both women tipped some of their wine at the god of wine's feet, then raised their goblets to the sun-filled afternoon sky before sipping. There was no point attempting any kind of conversation with Tabitha until the ceremony was done and so Indi waited until they were back inside and seated at the battered wooden table before she spoke.

'What did Jade say to you?' Her own conversation with her sister had been short, she'd used Will waiting for her in the restaurant to give her an excuse to end the call and process her shock at the news in private.

'That she was in love.' Tabitha half closed her eyes. 'Are there any more beautiful words in the English language – or in any language? I wonder what love is in Greek? I hope it's as beautiful as Italian. *Ti amo* . . . Oh, it sends a thrill through me. I fell in love for the first time in Florence, did you know that?'

'You mentioned it once or twice.' Indi took another sip and looked at her mother with her usual mix of fondness and exasperation. Now in her late fifties, Tabitha was as eccentric and yet as elegant as ever, today in a bizarre yet very 'her' costume of yoga leggings and a crop top from an expensive lifestyle brand, topped with a kaftan picked up from a local vintage shop. Her curly hair was still a dark brown, almost black, if liberally streaked with grey, and piled up in a precarious bun at the back of her neck. Willowy and elegant, her mother had the gift of making whatever she wore look like couture.

'Falling in love is always wonderful, but falling in love in a beautiful country is something very special indeed. Your sister is a very lucky girl.'

'But, Mum.' Indi repressed an exasperated sigh. This was, after all, a usual pattern in an unusual situation: Indi the voice of reason, Tabitha the expressor of dreams. 'Jade can't just *stay* in Greece.'

'Why not?'

'Her home is here! And even if it wasn't, she's been working as a yacht stewardess and a receptionist – what will she do in the winter? She doesn't have any qualifications, she doesn't speak Greek.' Indi took a brief second to keep her voice level. 'What do we even know about this boy, anyway? How old is he? Does he have a proper job? Where will they live? Look, Mum, I get it's all very romantic, but it's not very practical, is it?'

'Oh, my darling, you do remind me of your father. What is practicality without romance, life without dreams? Jade is a very intuitive person. If she says Nico is the man for her, then we must trust her, India.'

Indi put down her glass and looked at her mother, biting back sharp words. How did *she* know what Jade wanted?

She hadn't attended a single parents' evening after all, hadn't sat over homework, helped with revision, tried to help Jade decide on a career path. When it came to pouring wine, gossiping about love lives or the mysteries of the universe, or storytelling, there was nobody better than their mother, but she'd always left the day-to-day parenting first to her husband and then to Indi, even though Indi had been only in her teens when her father died.

It was Indi who kept Edward's memory alive, telling Jade bedtime stories about their father, how he could scoop Jade up with one hand and balance her on his shoulder. How when she was a baby he would walk up and down the landing with her in the middle of the night, singing pop songs to her as if they were lullabies. How he would take them to his top-floor corner office where everyone would stop and tell them how proud they must be of their daddy, and Indi would glow with pride because it was clear he was a very important man indeed. How he knew the name of every one of her friends. How he encouraged her to reach high, to dream big. To keep her eyes on the path in front of her. To always plan ahead.

Their mother loved them, Indi knew that, she loved them fiercely. But she wasn't interested in the minutiae of everyday life. Even *their* everyday lives.

Indi took another sip of the wine, suddenly profoundly tired.

'And, of course, Greece is a very romantic place,' her mother continued. 'It's made for lovers – the scenery, the seas, the food, the wine. I envy Jade. No wonder she's been swept away. What wonderful adventures await her! It's been far too long since I filled my well of inspiration on its shores. I must visit her there.'

'But . . .' Indi stopped as she absorbed her mother's words. *Romance, swept away, adventures.*

Will thought she was incapable of taking a proper holiday. Thought she couldn't be impulsive. That she had no sense of adventure. She would show him! Why should she hang around waiting for him to turn their lives upside down? She wasn't officially due to start her new role for some weeks yet and she had barely touched her generous annual leave allowance. Why didn't she use some of it to visit Jade?

After all, if she were in Greece, she'd be much better placed to figure out the best way to help Jade realise that summer romances were just that, a seasonal moment. If their father was still here, he would be on the first plane over to talk sense into his daughter, not waste his time with libations and toasts. Although, it *was* very good wine.

And maybe having some time out would help her to start planning her own next steps. To get the courage to face what came next if Will didn't change his mind. Maybe she could even persuade Will to come with her before he made an irrevocable step, could show him that she *was* capable of spontaneity, of change.

And if not, then at least she wouldn't have to be around as he dismantled their lives.

A holiday in Greece. The more she thought about it, the more right it felt. She missed her sister so much, and for once she didn't have the courage to face up to her current reality. Time away would fix both of those things.

Indi immediately felt a load lift. She had a plan, if not a solution.

And that meant that India Drewe was back in business.

Chapter Five

Jade

'Of course. No, it's not an imposition, silly. You're welcome here any time. Yes, I'll expect Will too. Yes, it would be fab if he came. You're right. I'm sure it's just what you both need.'

Jade was glad she was just on speakerphone and not a video call so that Indi couldn't see the look of disgust she pulled at the mention of Will's name. She hoped he *didn't* come with Indi, he absolutely wasn't welcome the . . . the *weasel*! How dare he drop such a bombshell on Indi? The timing couldn't have been worse either, with Indi's birthday just around the corner, as well as taking the buzz off her new job. Ugh.

Oh, Indi was putting on a brave face, as usual – God forbid she actually show any kind of negative emotion or reach out for comfort, that wasn't Indi's way. But Jade knew her sister inside and out and she could tell she was utterly crushed by this unexpected ultimatum. After all, everyone knew Indi wanted to be married in her early thirties, to start a family sooner rather than later. Everyone *including* Will. Poor Indi had been expecting him to propose, not indulge his Kerouac fantasies.

Jade bit her lip guiltily. Her own engagement news could have been timed better. She would just have to make it up to Indi. Spoil her rotten. Help her wash every trace of Weasel-Will not just out of her hair but out of every part of her body. It wasn't that Jade disliked Will – at least she hadn't before now – but she had always wondered if Indi had settled rather than finding someone who challenged her, who really got her. Now she felt guilty for her hidden doubts, her sister was certainly finding Will challenging now.

'OK, let me know your travel arrangements. Actually, let me have your dates and I'll sort out travel. Yes, I'm sure, it's part of my job and I know the ferry times and transfers. Yes I know I've only been here a couple of months, but I have booked several journeys. Trust me.' She rolled her eyes at her computer monitor. Typical Indi to think she was the only one who could organise anything. 'Yes, let me know about Will. Bye. Love you.'

Jade disconnected the call and sat back in her office chair, mind whirring. She'd asked Indi several times to come and stay at some point over the summer but had never really thought her sister would take her up on the offer. Indi didn't really do rest and relaxation. Her idea of a holiday, if she could be persuaded to take one, was a few days somewhere cultural with a meticulously planned itinerary, not chilling and just going with the flow. Agios Iohannis was, in Jade's opinion, paradise on earth, but there wasn't an awful lot to do here *but* relax. When she'd suggested Indi visit, she had thought she and Will were solid, had expected they would make the island their base while they explored this gorgeous corner of the world. Dealing with a heartbroken single Indi was very different to dealing with an independent couple, especially with the first guests due to arrive very soon and Jade correspondingly busy.

Heartbroken. Was that the right word? Indi had sounded bewildered, hurt, a little lost. Shocked. But not utterly devastated. Of course, she and Will had been a steady couple, but even at the beginning, they hadn't exactly set the world ablaze. If Nico walked away from her, then Jade didn't know what she would do, just the thought of it made her gasp, caused her whole body to tense in pain. Indi had sounded pissed off, but functioning. Maybe she was in denial.

There was another complication to Indi's impending visit. Jade didn't want to tell her sister that she was pregnant, not yet. She didn't want Indi to think the pregnancy was her reason for staying in Greece, for the engagement. She needed her sister to see her as an adult, someone who made her own decisions, not the screw-up younger sister who needed managing. If Indi knew about the baby, she not only wouldn't take the engagement seriously, but she'd also map out an alternative path and do her best to whisk Jade down it. Jade knew this time she would resist, was sure that she was doing the right thing, but she didn't want to have that battle. Not just yet.

But, on the other hand, this holiday would give Indi the opportunity to spend time with Nico, to see how much he loved Jade, to see for herself what a good person he was. She would fall in love with this perfect part of the world, start to understand why Jade wanted to make her life here. Then, when Jade announced the pregnancy, Indi would be reassured that even if it was earlier in the relationship than ideal and unplanned, Jade was where, and with whom, she needed to be.

OK. It was a long shot. But it was possible.

Now all Jade needed to do was organise the visit.

She dragged her attention back to her screen and her inbox, answering a few questions and forwarding a couple more to Aurelia, the PR consultant Mikhos had hired to help launch the exclusive island resort.

Jade still couldn't believe her luck that Mikhos had not just given her a job but had entrusted her with the role of getting the new resort ready for the first guests. Her usual day included various administration tasks, dealing with queries from prospective and booked-in guests, acting as an in-person assistant to both Mikhos and Aurelia and also being a hands-on maid of all work when needed, helping the interior and exterior designers get every one of the twenty villas ready for their first guests. It was exhausting work, but she loved every moment, even now with the added queasiness and tiredness.

She also loved her office, set on the ground floor of Mikhos' gorgeous villa, the opposite side of the island to the resort. On one side, she had views out to sea; on the other, she could see through internal glass doors to the plant-filled internal courtyard, her eyes never tiring of the gorgeous views. She was also far too fond of the mouth-watering snacks available at all hours from the kitchen as Demeter, the housekeeper, perfected her recipes. Jade was willing to be her guinea pig forever as long as she kept dishing up crispy pastry-covered treats.

But, for once, the afternoon dragged and she found it hard to stay focused, too many what-ifs and what-abouts swirling through her brain. Had Indi and Will *really* split up? They had seemed so perfect . . . Although, if she was being honest maybe *too* perfect, verging on dull. Old before their time. But, then again, Indi *was* old before her time and Jade knew why; after all, she had been catapulted into adulthood as a teenager. Which was why Indi deserved better than Will weaselling her about!

What Jade needed to do now was make sure it really was OK for Indi to stay. Mikhos had told her she was welcome to invite her family to the villa at any time, but the two to three weeks Indi had mentioned was less of a holiday and more of a short-term let! Jade got up from her desk. No time like the present she supposed.

It had become part of the daily routine for the occupants of the villa to meet in the courtyard after work to talk about any problems that had arisen that day and plan for the following day. It was eye-opening for Jade to be part of those conversations, to get a ringside seat to see how Mikhos operated.

A decade older than Nico, Mikhos had turned a small family-owned bar on Naxos into a multi-hotel empire spanning most of the Cycladic island region. The resort here on the tiny island he had inherited from his grandfather was set to be the jewel in his five-star luxury crown – and she was part of it. A very small part, but very much in the heart of it all.

Jade stepped into the lushly planted courtyard, the sky blue overhead, the low evening sun glinting off the marble pool at the other end. At first, she thought she was alone, but the sound of voices alerted her to Nico and Mikhos standing at the far end of the space. Mikhos had been away for a few days, which meant it was the first time she had seen him since the evening they had announced their engagement and her stomach twisted with nerves. Oh, he had *said* 'Congratulations', but there had been a reserved chill in his voice when he did so, almost imperceptible, but there.

But then she had heard the same chill in Indi's voice whenever she mentioned Nico or alluded to her engagement and future here in Greece. It would be easy to assume that Indi's own emotional drama wouldn't have left her with the bandwidth to worry about anyone else's relationship status, but Jade knew better than to underestimate her sister. But then again Indi underestimated Jade, which gave Jade the upper hand. She would do everything she could to ensure that Indi would leave here completely won over.

Jade headed over to the two men, so deep in conversation neither had noticed her. It was clear that Nico and Mikhos were related, the same curling dark hair swept back from high foreheads, the same strong jawlines. But Nico was more endearingly boyish, warm humour softened his dark eyes, a smile never far from his eminently kissable mouth, whereas there was something harsher about Mikhos. His smile was more sardonic, his gaze unnervingly direct. Jade always found herself wanting to impress him, but often came away feeling like a fool. Like she was trying too hard.

Indi would know how to deal with him. It took more than a handsome self-made millionaire to discombobulate her.

Jade paused, not sure whether to make her presence known. The cousins were engaged in a fierce low-voiced conversation in fast Greek. A conversation which for all its low tones was getting more fiery by the second. A conversation Jade was pretty sure was about her. She may not understand Greek, but she *did* know her name when she heard it.

Teetering on the edge of indecision, she started to back away, but slipped and knocked a water bottle off a small side table and it fell to the tiled floor with a large clatter. She froze as both heads whipped round to look in her direction. So much for a stealthy exit.

'Hi.' She picked up the water bottle, her cheeks hot. 'Good to see you, Mikhos. How was Athens?'

Indi would probably demand to know what they were talking about, but Jade wasn't good with confrontation – she didn't have much practice. Indi ran their household, even now she'd moved out, and Jade usually went along with her decisions, whatever her own thoughts. Until the last year that was.

'Jade.' Nico's eyes brightened as if he hadn't seen her for days, not just a few hours. 'How was your afternoon?'

'Good. I spoke to Indi.'

'How is she?' Nico turned to Mikhos. 'Jade's sister has split up with her boyfriend. I think it was a shock.'

'They haven't exactly split up yet. Will went to his parents to give Indi some space to think about what she's going to do, but it feels inevitable that they will end things.' Jade turned to Mikhos. 'It's so sad; it turns out Will has changed his mind about their future,' she explained. 'Poor Indi was completely oblivious until he dropped it on her.' She stopped, aware that Mikhos was regarding her sardonically.

'How long were they together?' he asked.

'Four years.'

He turned to Nico. 'You see?'

'See what?' Jade had no idea what the subtext was here, she just knew there definitely was one.

Mikhos shrugged. 'Just that your sister was with her boyfriend for *four* years and it hasn't worked out.'

'Mikhos!' Jade had never heard Nico sound so curt before and she stared at him in confusion.

'What have I interrupted?'

'Mikhos has just been telling me that I – that *we* – are making a terrible mistake,' Nico bit out, his jaw tense.

'Oh.' Jade had known that Mikhos wasn't exactly over the moon about their engagement, but she hadn't realised that he was so hostile.

'It's nothing personal, Jade,' Mikhos told her, clearly not the smallest bit embarrassed by Nico's statement. 'You seem like a very nice young woman. But you and Nico have been together for just a few months, you are barely in your twenties. Nico has a career to think of, and so do you. Why rush things?'

There were several things Jade wanted to say, most importantly *What business is it of yours*, but not only was she not great with confrontation, Mikhos was her boss. She needed to stay on good terms with him.

She managed to produce a smile. 'I know it seems quick, but we love each other.'

He rolled his eyes as if she were still an annoying teen. 'Love! You barely know each other. It's been what? Six months? Barely even that.'

'Yes, but we have been together for every day of those six months. Worked together, lived together,' Nico interrupted, his jaw set in stubborn lines. 'I know her, she knows me, but you know what? Even if we were making a mistake – which we're not – that's our problem, not yours.'

'It's OK, Nico,' Jade said quickly, not wanting the argument to get more heated. 'Mikhos is only being honest. He cares about you. It's understandable he has doubts.'

'I get it, Jade.' Mikhos carried on as if Nico hadn't interrupted. 'You're in a beautiful place, you think you're in love, of course you don't want to go home. You're not alone. That's the dream we sell. The dream *I* sell. Paradise. Everyone wants to extend their holiday into a life, their holiday romance into the real deal, but the truth is that behind the sunshine, the landscape, life is hard. The winters here are tough, one bad season can break a business. Look.' His tone gentled. 'My mother is English, she fell for the dream, but she found reality really tough. Nico is still starting out in life. The two of you are in for some hard years. Are you really prepared for that?'

Nico's lips pressed together mutinously. 'Our decisions are ours, they have nothing to do with you.'

'I am your cousin, Nico. Family. I am Jade's employer. Of course it has something to do with me. All I am saying is that if you are right, you really love each other, then you have years ahead of you. You don't need to get engaged now, rush into marriage. Wait until you are more secure. That's more important than romantic feelings.' He spread his hands wide. 'If you still feel like this in two years' time, when you're in a more stable place, then I'll give you both my blessing.'

'Well, that's very big of you.' Nico's eyes sparkled with fury. 'But even though you are the successful one, you are *not* the head of this family. Jade and I don't need your permission to marry. And you are wrong. Love is more important than anything.'

Jade wished she had never interrupted them; this argument would be a lot less uncomfortable if it was still in Greek and she still oblivious.

'Which just shows how unready for this you really are. Is love more important than savings, security, a job? You have big dreams, Nico, but you're not there yet. You don't want to come in and find Jade sobbing in the kitchen after another eighteen-hour day and you still don't know how you'll manage to pay the bills through the winter. You don't want to find yourself having yet another drink earlier and earlier to cope with your guilt.' Mikhos stopped. He hadn't raised his voice, the words were measured and calm, but there was a dark knowledge behind them which struck Jade hard.

Was that his story? She knew his father had died when he was a similar age to Nico, that he had taken on the family business and in just over a decade created one of the Cycladic islands' biggest employers and most prestigious brands. She didn't know what had driven him to that success, what kept driving him. Was it his childhood? His past?

Even so, that didn't have to be an omen for her future. Her baby's future. Despite herself, her hand stole protectively to her still flat belly.

'I have a job. Jade has a job. Or are they dependent on your approval of our lives?'

'Nico. You have a seasonal job because that's what you wanted, you spend the winters away by choice. You don't want to be in an office but out on the sea. And Jade is here on a seasonal visa. There might not be a job for her when the summer ends. I have my core team, I can't guarantee there will be any vacancies. Look, marriage is a grown-up business, Nico. That's all I am saying.'

'You and my sister both,' Jade acknowledged. 'Not that she has actually said so. Yet. But she will. Which reminds me . . .' She needed to ask Mikhos if Indi could stay and she needed to change the subject before Nico blurted out she was pregnant and turned a heated disagreement into a full-blown argument. 'You did say she was welcome to come and stay any time. Is that still OK? With the break-up, she needs some space.'

Mikhos' nod was curt, but at least it was a yes. 'When is she thinking? For how long?'

'As soon as she can get leave for a couple of weeks, I think. I'll confirm as soon as I can. She's usually super-organised, but this week has really knocked her.'

'Fine. She can have the corner suite. Excuse me, I must find Aurelia.' And he was gone, surprisingly light on his feet for such a tall, broad man.

Jade turned to Nico, crossing the distance between them to fall into his arms.

'I'm sorry you had to hear that, *asteráki mou*,' he whispered against her hair and Jade felt a momentary frustration with his protectiveness. It was bad enough her sister swaddled her in good intentions and worry, she didn't need the same from her fiancé.

'No, it's good I know what Mikhos really thinks. I guessed he wasn't best pleased, but I didn't realise he was *that* disapproving.' She looked up at Nico. 'Is that true? About his parents?'

'Yes,' he admitted. 'His father did drink too much, his mother found life here difficult as a result, but *Theia* Hannah still lives here, you know, on Naxos, she's never returned to England.' He blew out a frustrated breath. 'But he's not completely wrong about the seasonality of this place. Even if I do buy a boat and start my own tours, we need the money I make between Easter and October to last us all year. One bad season and things can be very tight. Maybe I need to rethink my plans, take that office job he's always offering me.' He looked dejected at the prospect. Nico was a true sailor, more at home on the sea than off. Jade would never forgive herself if he found himself stuck at a desk because of her.

'It's not all on you.' She touched his cheek. 'I can and will work too. I just need to prove to Mikhos I am so indispensable he can't help but offer me a job at the end of the season. Even if he doesn't approve of us, we'll manage.'

'As long as we're together.' But as Nico pulled her to him and kissed her, Jade couldn't help but remember every one of Mikhos' words. This was no romantic fairy-tale, the summer couldn't last forever. If she and Nico were going to do this, get married and become parents, then they needed to face up to reality. It was time she grew up.

Chapter Six

Indi

Indi hadn't seen Will for a week. She'd returned from her mother's to an empty house and a text telling her he needed some space. He might not want to relive his childhood, but it hadn't taken much for him to return to the sanctuary of his childhood home, where he would be fed and coddled and his ego restored. He'd never really understood that home wasn't like that for everyone. It was easy to dismiss what you took for granted.

Their flat was small, a one-bedroom new-build overlooking the canal, but it felt cavernous without him, every framed photograph a reproach to Indi that she had failed to make Will happy.

She still couldn't believe she hadn't seen it coming. She'd been ploughing blithely on to the next thing in her life plan, her eyes fixed on her happy ever after, without realising she was leaving Will behind, that his eyes were on a totally different horizon. Oh, he'd talked about travelling again one day, but it had never sounded like something he *had* to do, more a nice thing to do, one day, maybe much later in life. When had that changed and why had she not seen it? More importantly, when had travelling become more important than her? Than them? Was he really going to throw everything they had away?

Indi knew she should be heartbroken, cry, eat ice cream, drink a bottle of wine or two, cut up his shirts. Something. But instead she was numb. She hadn't even told anyone what had happened, not properly, playing down the separation. She'd even suggested to Jade that Will would accompany her to Greece.

Who was she kidding? The truth was, he'd been gone before he'd even asked her to come with him. He'd moved on while she was standing still.

But the battle wasn't over just yet. She'd had a week to plan, to replan, to consider all that Will had said and her reaction to it. Life wasn't linear, she knew that, and surely successful relationships were all about compromise, about growing together even if the expected direction changed. It had been a week of painful self-examination but at the end of it Indi had come up with some alternatives to Will's ultimatum. She just needed to actually *talk* to him.

It wasn't like her to put things off, but somehow, she'd not been able to find the courage to reach out to him. Maybe because if he didn't go for her alternatives then it really was all over.

Wearily, Indi stomped up the stairs leading to the flat, a ready meal for one in her tote bag. She usually enjoyed cooking, but it turned out she didn't like cooking for one. She misjudged the portions and the remainder sat in the saucepan, a mocking reproach that she wasn't worthy of love, of a future.

She pushed the bland fake wood door open and stared at the shiny laminated hallway floor. She didn't even want to step inside, but what was the alternative? Go home? It was her thirtieth birthday in less than a month. She was beyond running back to her mother.

As she stepped inside, her gaze snagged on a pair of trainers lying haphazardly across the hallway. Will never lined up his shoes, leaving them for her to trip up. It always drove her mad, like his inability to hang up the bathmat and his belief that pots put themselves in the dishwasher. She'd put all his shoes on their designated shelf on the shoe rack when she'd spring-cleaned last Sunday in a desperate bid to keep herself busy. How did they get there?

Hope rose in her. He was back! He had changed his mind!

The sound of footsteps in the bedroom were all the confirmation she needed and so, setting her bag down carefully on the small table put there for that purpose, Indi pushed open the bedroom door.

For a moment, she couldn't move. There was Will, looking disgustingly relaxed and healthy. *He* didn't seem to have lost his appetite or the ability to sleep through the night.

He turned as the door creaked and smiled. It was sheepish, a long way from the wide, disingenuous grin she was used to. 'Hey.'

'You're back.' But even as she said the words, Indi noticed the suitcase wide open on the bed and froze. 'Or not.'

'How are you?' He sounded oddly formal, as if they were strangers making polite conversation not partners, lovers. But then again right now they weren't either of those things.

'Angry, upset, confused. Did I mention angry?' It wasn't the placatory answer she had meant to give. Nor, judging by the shock on his face, was it the answer he had been expecting – probably he was hoping she would do the right thing and make this – whatever *this* was – as easy as possible for him. Just, as she was beginning to realise, she always did. For him, for Jade, for her mother. For everyone but herself.

'Ah.'

'Are you moving out?'

'It seemed sensible. Under the circumstances.'

'The circumstances. You mean you taking me out to dinner and issuing an ultimatum out of the blue? That set of circumstances?' She watched him gape like a stranded goldfish, but the satisfaction was fleeting and as it ebbed away she felt only tired. 'Oh sod this, I need a glass of wine. Want one?'

Will's nod was wary, but he stopped shoving his clothes into his suitcase and followed her into the combined living and dining room. Indi poured them both a generous glass of the expensive rosé she had bought herself but not felt like touching and opened the doors to the balcony, letting the warm evening air and city noise in. It made her feel less alone.

'How long have you been planning this?' She didn't turn to face him but stared out at the canal view. She had been filled with such hope and happiness when they had signed the lease. The rent was high, especially when she had set herself such tough saving goals, but she hadn't been able to resist the bright, central flat right in the heart of Islington. After all, she had stayed home so much longer than any of her friends, she felt she deserved to live somewhere nice. Even with her new job and higher salary, would she be able to afford the rent on her own? Would she even want to?

'Planning? Not long. But I've been thinking about it for a while now.'

'Since Kwame and Lily started talking about Australia?'

'Around then, yeah.'

'And you didn't say anything because . . .?'

'Because every time I mentioned the future, you immediately took over – should you apply for a promotion, was I looking for a better job, look at these houses we could afford if we upped our savings. There was no space for me to say anything and after a while I just stopped trying.'

Was that right? Was that *fair*?

'You *should* have tried. I'm not a mind reader, Will.'

'I know. I'm sorry.'

She swallowed, forced herself to turn and face the man who just a week ago had been her forever and her heart twisted. He had seemed like the whole package when she had met him, the hearty confidence, ambition that seemed to match hers, handsome in a floppy-haired public-schoolboy way. All her friends, except for Priya, were full of dating-app horror stories, while she and Will just seemed to work from day one. She hadn't been able to believe her luck. But clearly it had all been too good to be true.

He looked the same, but there was a defiance in his expression she had never seen before. Worse, he looked like this was a formality, that he had already moved on, while she was standing here wondering what was happening. It was almost as painful not being in control of the situation as the situation itself.

But she still had a card to play. Her plan dreamed up during those long sleepless nights. She set her glass down and took a deep breath. 'Look, Will. How about we find an alternative to backpacking. I was thinking we should apply for work visas instead. There's a thing with Jade I need to sort out, but by the time the visas come through and we have sorted out jobs, she will be back home and settled.' Hopefully. Indi couldn't have all parts of her life going rogue all at once. Jade would see sense and return home unengaged, wouldn't she?

'Work visas?' Will's forehead creased.

'Yes. I was thinking we could go and work in Australia too. Or New Zealand. Not worry about marriage or kids or buying a house for a few years yet.' She smiled at him hopefully, but he just frowned.

'You want to live abroad?'

'I don't know if I *want* to, but I am willing to try.' Indi had been so closely bound to this part of London, to her family, especially since her father died, that she couldn't imagine being anywhere else. But then neither could she imagine starting again at almost thirty.

Was *that* what was upsetting her? The starting again or losing Will? She wasn't even sure anymore. All she knew was that she wasn't just going to give up if there was any chance of salvaging their future. 'It would be an adventure,' she added. 'Which is what you want, but a bit more focused which would suit me. A real compromise.'

'Wow. I wasn't expecting you to say that.' He sat down on the sofa they had picked together and took a large sip of his wine. 'That's quite the offer.'

She pressed her hands together tightly. 'It's a genuine one. Look, Will, I am taking leave before I start my new job, from next week for a couple of weeks to stay with Jade in Greece. Why don't you come with me? We *do* both work too hard, you're right. Let's take some time out, re-evaluate. Talk properly. Both of us. I'll listen to everything you think, you feel, I promise.'

'And at the end of it, you hope I'll realise that our lives are fine the way they are and get back with the programme?'

She flinched at the hardness in his voice. 'No. Just a holiday with no expectations as to the outcome. Just some quality time to find *us* again.'

Indi felt backed into a corner. She was sure Australia was lovely, but she didn't want to move there, leave her family, the job she had worked so hard for. But relationships were about compromise, weren't they? Give and take? And if there was any chance of this relationship surviving then she had to learn that. Better now than in ten years' time when children might be involved.

But did she want this relationship to survive if she was the one making all the compromises? Was it worth the cost?

She pushed the negativity away. Of course she did! That was why she had done her best to find a way forward and not just give up, even if it meant leaving her hard-won new job, her family.

Will's expression softened and for a moment Indi felt hope. 'Indi, don't think that I don't know what it cost you to make that offer. I know you don't really want to move to Australia. But I need more than getting on the same treadmill in a different city. I want to use my scuba-diving qualifications, to see more of the world. I always did but felt that I was being indulgent, that I should grow up. Then I reached thirty and I *was* grown-up and I realised I felt . . .' He stopped.

'What did you feel, Will?' She had to know.

'Trapped,' he said at last. 'I felt trapped.'

Ouch. 'I see.' She walked over and sat down in the chair opposite him. 'No, actually, I take it back. I *don't* see. I didn't set out to trap you, Will, you pursued me, remember? I thought we wanted the same things, because you *said* you did, you said you wanted marriage and babies and a house in a village one day. You knew my timetable, you even said it was cute. That you liked knowing where we were heading. I know I can be a bit overbearing, that I like to take charge, that I'm not good with change. But you said . . .' Her voice wobbled and she struggled for control. 'You said you loved everything about me.'

Will stared down at his glass. 'I did. You made life so easy. All that stuff felt inevitable, like the path I had to follow anyway, I just had to follow your lead. But over the last few months, I've realised it doesn't have to be inevitable, that I don't need to live according to other people's expectations. Not even yours.'

Indi couldn't answer for a long time, aware her whole body was trembling. Every part of her hurt, inside and out, a bone-weary pain. For the first time, she understood why it was called heartache, it was almost unbearably physically painful, this unravelling of a relationship.

She tried to find the words to ask the question she wasn't sure she wanted an answer to. 'Have you felt trapped the whole time, Will? Has there been no fun at all? What about Paris? Or St Ives? Or the night at the opera? The snow . . . the day we got the keys to the flat.' They hadn't got out of bed for the whole day. A welcome anger relieved some of the pressure building up inside her. 'I'm not letting you rewrite our history because it suits you.'

'No, Indi. I'm not. We did have wonderful moments, days, weeks, years. You are an incredible woman, driven and bright, and at times I couldn't believe my luck, couldn't believe a woman like you would choose me. But I don't see a future for us anymore. I'm sorry. I didn't mean to change, to leave you behind, but it happened and I can't change back, not even for you.'

And Indi knew there was no more to be said or done. 'When are you going?'

'At the end of the summer. After I've worked my notice.'

'You've handed it in?' Without even giving her a heads-up?

'Yes.'

'Wow, this is really happening, Will.' The tears she had tried her best to keep back were running freely down her face and for once she didn't care.

Tears were sparkling in his eyes too. 'I am so sorry. I can't imagine my life without you, Indi, but I know that I have to try.'

Indi blinked hard, wiping her face. No more crying. Not for Will, not for the life they could have had. If anyone knew how to pick themselves up and plough on it was her.

'We have the apartment until September,' she said, proud of the steadiness of her voice, her ability to think. 'You can have it until then. I can stay with my mother when I'm back from Greece. Just give me this week to pack. But I want you to go now. There's no more to say. Not right now.'

He sat for a moment, then put his glass on the table. 'I really am sorry.'

She nodded, still frozen in place as he walked out of the room, out of the flat and out of her life. She would process how she felt later. For now, she was going to concentrate on Jade. Her life might be falling apart, but at least she could prevent her sister from making a huge mistake.

Chapter Seven

Jade

Sunday 4 June

Nico lounged against the door and sighed dramatically. 'Half an hour, you said.' He clasped his hand against his heart even more dramatically, his dark eyes filled with laughter. 'I'll be no time at all, you said. That was three long hours ago and I miss you.'

'I miss you too.' Jade walked over to him and pressed a kiss to his stubbled cheek, unable to resist nibbling her way down to his perfect, petulant mouth. She lingered there, as he returned her kiss with interest, pulling her close, one hand slipping to her hip, curving around to cup her bottom. Desire pooled deep in her belly, but she made herself step away. She couldn't afford to be distracted. 'I'm sorry it's taken so long, but I want everything to be perfect.'

'I know, but this is for family, surely a wrinkle here or there is fine.'

'You don't know Indi. Everything she does is perfect.' She picked up the steamer and once more swept it across the freshly made bed, even though there wasn't a wrinkle in sight. 'So this has to be perfect in return.'

Nico continued to watch her, eyes narrowed. 'Jade, it's a good thing your sister is coming here. You've missed her – you message her at least ten times a day, call her all the time. And she needs you, needs this holiday. Why are you suddenly so anxious?'

Jade continued to press the bed, keeping her gaze fixed on the pristine sheet, unsure how to articulate the myriad emotions stirred by Indi's imminent arrival. For Nico, family was easy, even with Mikhos as cousin, friend and employer, and currently disapproving patriarch. You loved and fought and made up again, celebrated each other's successes, commiserated failures. How could he understand the complicated ties that bound Indi and her? The debt Jade owed her big sister? How much she hated to disappoint her?

To be fair, how *could* he understand when she had never really spoken of it? Part of the attraction of going away had been the opportunity to reinvent herself. No more poor Jade, tragic Jade, invalid Jade, but grown-up, independent, fun Jade. She'd found herself over the last six months. Made her own way, her own life.

But soon now Indi would be here in her idyll, and while part of her couldn't wait to see her beloved big sister, another part of her wished she'd never suggested she join them here on Agios Iohannis but suggested she stay on Naxos instead, with a handy forty-minute sea journey separating them.

Apart from anything else, there was no way she would be able to keep her pregnancy secret for long, not from the person who knew her better than anyone.

She looked up at Nico, who was clearly wondering why his usually happy-go-lucky fiancée had turned into a martinet, scrubbing every inch of the already pristine villa until it gleamed. 'I just want her to be happy for us,' she said at last.

'She'll take one step onto the island and fall in love with it, just as you did. Just wait and see. Of course, she must be wondering about me, about us, but when she leaves here,

I know she will give us her blessing. How could she not, when she sees how much I love you?'

'You're right, I'm probably worrying about nothing.'

But Jade knew her sister. It was far more likely that Indi had a whole plan ready to persuade Jade to come home as soon as possible – and Jade had no idea how she would react when Jade stayed firm.

She looked around the room, needing something else to do, to find something to clean or fix or make, anything to keep her mind occupied until her sister's arrival.

But she had done everything and more.

The corner suite Mikhos had allotted Indi was a light and airy room on the first floor, with sliding glass doors on two walls, both with stunning sea views and a wraparound balcony terrace connecting the two. It was simply but luxuriously decorated and furnished with gleaming wooden floors, white walls hung with abstract paintings reflecting the blue of the sea and handmade wooden furniture. The huge bed was made up with crisp white linen, the floor covered in thick blue rugs, the same colour echoed in the two sofas invitingly grouped around a coffee table at the far end facing the television. One door opened into a sumptuous bathroom with a walk-in shower, two deep sinks and a free-standing bath in front of the window, another into a dressing room with ample wardrobe space, a dressing table and a cream chaise placed in front of the window, perfect for afternoon naps. Vases filled with flowers adorned the bedside tables and coffee table, freshly laundered towels and robes hung in the bathroom. The whole was scrupulously clean, not a speck of dust left to mar the perfection of the room. There really was nothing for Indi to find fault with.

Jade inhaled, pressing her hand to her stomach, trying to quell the faint but persistent nausea that dogged her waking minutes. She was no longer a lost little girl who needed her big sister but a grown woman who made her own choices. A woman who would soon be a wife and a mother, as well as a sister and daughter.

The radio Nico always carried on his belt when he was on duty beeped and he pulled out his phone to read the message. 'Antinous is on schedule to collect your sister,' he said. 'So we have a couple of hours until she arrives. I have a good idea how we can use it . . .' His smile was suggestive as his eyes swept over her, leaving a tingle in every nerve ending, her whole body clenching with need. Despite the nausea, sensitive breasts and tiredness, Jade hadn't found pregnancy affecting her libido, although they were both being extra careful, their lovemaking taking on a new, sweet tenderness as a result.

But the last thing Jade wanted was to meet her sister straight from her fiancé's bed, to give Indi any proof in her suspicion that she was merely hopelessly infatuated.

'Me too, I've been inside all day. I fancy a walk,' she counter-suggested.

'To the hidden cove? Excellent idea.' His smile widened.

They had enjoyed many memorable moments in the little cove, accessible by one hard-to-find path or boat and so nearly completely private.

Jade wavered, longing for the feel of the sea on her skin, Nico's body on hers. But there wasn't time.

'Maybe later,' she promised as she unplugged the steamer and took one, last slightly desperate look around the room and conceded there was nothing else she could do here. Her sister would have no cause to complain about her surroundings at least.

Nico took the steamer off her as she reached for the door. 'You work too hard.'

'I don't mind. Besides, I want Mikhos to see how indispensable I am. If he could offer me a job in the main office once the summer is over, that would solve everything. I know the booking software backwards and no one knows this resort like I do. I'm not due until December and could be back at work by March. I don't want to be a burden to you.'

Worse, she didn't want to head home while Nico went back to the Caribbean for the winter. Nor did she want him to use up his savings on her – he'd spent the last six winters working the lucrative winter season in the Caribbean in order to buy his own boat and start running luxury excursions. The previous winter was supposed to be his last.

His jaw set stubbornly. 'It's my job to take care of you.'

'We take care of each other. And the baby.'

He kissed her. 'Luckily, Mikhos knows how brilliant you are. He'd be a fool to let you go.'

'Hardly brilliant, especially with the need to take maternity leave by the end of the year. Still, at least I know it's not personal. It's *us* he disapproves of, not me in particular.'

No doubt Indi would find a kindred spirit in Nico's cousin. After all, Mikhos Angelos was equally ambitious, equally formidable and equally convinced Jade and Nico were making a mistake as her sister.

She managed a smile. 'I get it. He thinks I'm wrong for you, that I think life here will be all yachts and cocktails and leisure, that I don't understand how demanding tourism is.'

'But you *do* understand and you *are* perfect for me.' Nico took her hand and squeezed it firmly. 'We'll make sure he sees that and if he doesn't, then we'll find you something else. All that matters is that we're together.'

'You're right. That is all that matters.' She kissed him again, this time slow, lingering, sweet. She was so very lucky.

Jade followed Nico out of the room, down the stairs leading to the villa's huge open-plan internal courtyard. Complete with a large marble swimming pool and furnished with huge green plants, it was a space that managed to feel both relaxing yet decadent and even after three months, Jade couldn't believe she was staying somewhere so utterly blissful.

When she'd accepted Nico's invitation to return home with him, she'd expected to spend the summer in his small apartment in Naxos, working in a bar or restaurant, not living in his cousin's luxurious villa on a small island, helping to launch a new five-star resort. For days at a time, it had just been she and Nico living here, with a handful of staff, the builders and decorators heading home at the end of the day, and hard as she and Nico had worked, they managed to play just as hard. She'd never been happier. Even with trying to impress Mikhos by working long days, seven days a week.

'Jade, Nico.'

Think of the devil.

'Hi, Mikhos, we were just heading over to meet the boat. Thank you again for letting my sister stay here, I really appreciate it.'

He waved her thanks away. No wonder, she must have said those words at least one hundred times over the last week.

'It's not a problem, I have the room. Did you finish the guest villa check?'

'Each and every one,' she assured him. 'Everything looks great. I need to spend some time double-checking the bar and restaurant over the coming week, but everything is on track for next Monday.

'Good. This is an important week, Aurelia is counting on your help, as am I. Your sister won't be a distraction, I hope.' It wasn't a question.

'Not at all. If anything, she'll be a help, she's the most organised person I've ever met.'

A nod was her only response and, with a relieved smile, Jade and Nico escaped out into the sun.

Although it was late afternoon, the early June air was hot rather than warm, the sun beating down with summer intensity. She and Nico walked slowly, hand in hand, through the olive groves, the sea both beside and ahead of them. How she loved hearing the roar of the waves wherever she stood, catching flashes of blue in her eyeline, the smell of salt on the breeze.

They reached one of the island's many small beaches and Jade kicked off her flip-flops, wincing as her feet touched hot sand before sitting down, digging her fingers and toes deep into the soft grains, through the searing heat to the coolness below. The sea was quiet, almost still, tiny wavelets darting onto the shore, the sun hanging low, pink and purple streaks painting the horizon.

'I do love it here. In a way, I wish Mikhos hadn't built the resort, it's so peaceful. I hate the thought of other people walking on our beaches and swimming in our sea.' She laughed at her own words. 'How spoilt am I! If it wasn't for the resort, I wouldn't even be here and now I want to keep all this luxury for myself.'

Jade knew how lucky she was, many people dreamed of running away to the Greek islands while on holiday, but staying put after the tourists left simply wasn't an option when there were few enough year-round jobs for locals, let alone backpackers who didn't want to leave. She liked what she had seen of Naxos and was happy to start married life there, but she had to admit she didn't want to leave this tiny, peaceful place, the place where she and Nico had gone from toe-curlingly in lust to really truly in love.

'I hope you'll be happy in my apartment.' Nico sat next to her and she leaned against him, still unable to believe that this bronzed, toned Adonis was hers. 'It's not exactly like Mikhos' villa . . .'

'If I wanted to live somewhere like the villa, then I would have gone husband hunting on Mykonos or stayed in the Caribbean and flirted with millionaires old enough to be my father,' Jade teased him. 'I will love your apartment because I will be with you. You are all I need, Nico.'

She turned to him, pulling his head to hers, losing herself in his sure, searing kiss. As always, heat engulfed her, desire sweet and addictive shooting through her. The kiss deepened, intensified as she pushed him down, sliding her hands under his shirt, and in the addictive moment, she forgot about boats, sisters and any worries about the future.

Chapter Eight

Indi

Sunday 4 June

'So you're telling me you don't know where my bag is, let alone when it will show up?'

Indi took a deep breath, counting to ten to stop herself from snapping at the apologetic woman on the other end of the phone.

'No, I'm not in Athens. I took a ferry to Naxos and I have another boat ride ahead of me. How are you even going to get my bag to me?'

It had been a long day. First, she had flown to Athens, before travelling to a port to board a ferry to Naxos, where she had taken a taxi to a small quay on the other side of the island to await yet another boat. Indi was hot, she was disgustingly sticky, she was both hungry and nauseous after the ferry ride, and she had been awake for what felt like a week.

And all she had were the clothes she stood up in. She had hoped to grab a few essentials on Naxos to tide her over, but the car that had met her at the ferry had brought her straight to this tiny harbour village, where the only signs of commerce were a taverna and a supermarket. A supermarket that didn't sell as much as a pair of socks. She'd checked. Twice.

How she wished she'd at least packed her trusty Spice Girls T-shirt in her hand luggage. That was it, she was never venturing anywhere without a full extra outfit or three ever again.

'Fine. Please do keep me informed.' She finished the call and sighed. The chances of her bag getting here in the foreseeable future seemed few and far between. What a start to what was supposed to be a relaxing few weeks.

And her journey wasn't over yet.

Indi looked doubtfully at the white crests of the waves and then over at the sleek boat waiting to transport her to the island where her sister was working. Another boat! Her stomach was still queasy from the ferry.

Maybe she should have stayed at home. At least this proved, if she had any lingering doubts – which she didn't – that backpacking wasn't for her.

Indi leaned against the harbour railing and took a deep breath, the freshness of the air a tonic, and she started to feel a little better. It *was* very beautiful, she conceded. And if she was being honest, she was behaving a little like the big city girl at the beginning of one of those Christmas movies, the kind who by the end of the film had thrown away her stilettos and career to marry a farmer and manage a hot chocolate shop.

She took a second deep breath. The tang of salt, of pine, of heat filled her lungs, fragrant and fresh, and as she tilted her face, she felt sun-kissed warmth envelop her.

With no little relief, she saw a middle-aged man dressed in a smart navy and white uniform, the initials ACR picked out in gold thread on his shirt, step onto the jetty.

'Miss Drewe? I'm Antinous. On behalf of Angelos Cycladic Resorts, I am delighted to welcome you to our beautiful part of the world. Please do come aboard. We have a short voyage of around forty minutes before we reach Agios Iohannis.'

'Indi, please.' She held out her hand and he shook it, then looked around.

'Where is your luggage?'

'Hopefully in Athens, possibly in Abu Dhabi or Anchorage. The airline didn't seem too sure.'

'Ah.' His smile was sympathetic. 'Let me radio the office, we can chase it up for you.'

Indi was so used to doing things for herself, she nearly declined the offer, but managed to stop herself. It would be nice to let someone else take care of it, just as it was nice to let Antinous help her onto the boat and settle her on the comfortable cushioned seat with an iced glass of juice before he untied various ropes and started the engine.

She knew the resort Jade was working at was five star but hadn't really appreciated just what that meant, this degree of care and personal service. As she leaned against the cushioned back of her chair and sipped her drink, she realised that despite everything, she was looking forward to her break.

Within a few moments the boat left the jetty, soon leaving Naxos far behind. There was no sign of their destination ahead, all she could see were a few tiny uninhabited islands, the odd sail to distinguish another boat. The breeze felt good on her face, in her lungs, the late afternoon sun warm despite the wind chill as she wandered to the back of the boat and watched the waves dance behind her. Her breath caught as she saw a fin, then another, then two bodies arching through the air in perfect unison before plunging back into the depths.

'Dolphins!' She hung over the side of the boat to see them better, all her anxieties ebbing away as she watched the dolphins playing around the boat, delighting in their leaps, twists and turns, the graceful animals seemingly enjoying showing off before they swam off towards the horizon, complete together. 'Maybe it's an omen,' she half whispered as she watched them swim away.

'There she is. Agios Iohannis!' Finally, Antinous indicated that their destination was in sight.

Indi squinted at the jetty and beach, her heart hammering with anticipation. In just a few moments' time, she would see Jade and it was only now that she realised just how much she had missed her little sister.

Indi had rarely spent as much as a night away from Jade until she moved in with Will, and even then, she had spoken to her every day, made time in her packed schedule to have breakfast with her weekly, dinner every weekend, to call her every day. Time to check in on assignments and applications, to make sure she was eating properly. Their mother laughed and called Indi a mother hen, but better a mother hen than one who had no idea where her daughters were and if there was any food for dinner beyond bread and cheese.

But there was no sign of anyone at the shore, no one to catch the rope Antinous was waiting to throw and in the end he jumped ashore himself to moor the boat and help Indi disembark.

She surveyed her surroundings critically. The jetty crossed a small but perfect half-moon of sand to join a carefully laid path through olive groves. Otherwise, there was no sign of any human or habitation. She stood uncertainly, aware of how far she was from civilisation, surrounded by endless sea. There was as likely to be a cyclops or a witch ready to turn her into an animal on the other side of those groves as any kind of resort.

'Do you want me to call your sister?' Antinous asked.

'I'm sure she's on her way.' Indi looked around her at the olive groves clustering up a small hill, for a glimpse of her sister. 'Maybe she got caught up in something, I know she's really busy ahead of the opening. How far is the villa?'

'About a twenty-minute walk. Just follow the path up the hill, then turn left. You can't miss it.'

'Great, I could do with stretching my legs.'

She pulled out her phone. No message from Jade, not since the one letting her know the name of the driver who had met her in Naxos.

She quickly tapped out a message of her own. *I'm here. Walking to the villa, see you there xxx*

'Thanks so much for collecting me,' she said, waving at Antinous before setting off resolutely.

India Drewe did not rely on anyone. She'd learned that lesson young.

Despite her disappointment at Jade's absence, the constant ache of anxiety that accompanied her everywhere, even in dreams, since Will had issued what she had come to think of as The Ultimation, Indi quite enjoyed the short walk to the villa. Dusk was closing in, but small lights were discreetly placed among the trees to guide nocturnal travellers on their way. The island felt wild, utterly natural, but it was clear human – or dryad – hands had been at work; the olive groves were contained, the vines in the distance well tended, the path clear as it took her up a small but surprisingly steep hill. A spring bubbled up at her side and ran down the hill to gather in a natural pond before running on to the sea. She bent and dipped a finger in it, touching it to her lips and finding it sweet. A fresh water source on an island was a huge asset. At least if she was marooned here, she wouldn't die of thirst. Could one survive on olives?

At the bottom of the hill, the path branched, and she remembered Antinous' instruction to head left, towards the villa. The dusk was gathering apace now, and Indi was glad of the small solar lights guiding her way. But there was no missing it, just one square whitewashed building sat dramatically on the headland, solid and graceful – and huge. Villa seemed like too small a word for such a very imposing building.

There were no gates guarding the villa, instead the path led straight into a recognisable if informal garden, clearly designed to blend into the landscape. The front door was set into an arch, up three flat stone steps, double-fronted and as imposing as the villa.

Indi looked around for Jade one last time, checking her phone to find her message read but not replied to.

She squared her shoulders. It was a door and she was expected, she didn't need a formal introduction, she *was* an independent woman after all. Time to channel Beyoncé and act like one. Act like India Drewe. It was most unlike her to be so diffident.

It seemed almost incongruous to see a very ordinary doorbell set in the stonework, it wasn't as if whoever owned the villa could receive many unexpected guests, but after giving the door an experimental nudge and finding it firmly locked, Indi pressed the bell. It was unexpectedly loud and reverberated through the air, making Indi jump. She waited, shifting from foot to foot, realising just how hungry, tired and disgustingly sticky she was. She needed food, sleep and a shower and she didn't care which order they came in.

A minute went by, the air once again still, and the door remained firmly closed. Indi huffed out an exasperated sigh and reached out to press the bell again, but as she did so, the door finally and silently swung open.

'Jade?' The eager word died on her lips as, instead of her sister, a man came into view.

Correction: a shirtless man.

In fact, he wasn't wearing a great deal at all. A small – correction, minuscule, so minuscule it was a miracle it stayed on – towel was slung around lean hips, and there didn't seem to be any proof he was wearing anything else underneath.

Indi swallowed, mesmerised by his flat, muscled abdomen, the dimple either side of his hips, conscious of a physical awareness filling her, something almost primal. She couldn't help continuing to follow the lines of his body down past tanned, muscled legs before snapping her gaze back up to meet his own sardonic, mocking expression.

Oh God. He knew that she had been checking him out, and she also instinctively knew that he had checked her out in turn. How she wished she was wearing something other than travel-stained and creased clothes, that her chestnut curls hadn't frizzed up in the heat and that she had at least powdered her nose at some point in the last twelve hours.

Indi squared her shoulders and summoned up a smile. 'Hi, I'm looking for Jade. I'm Indi, her sister.'

A shocking thought hit her. This wasn't *Nico*, was it? She'd had the impression that Nico was more boyish, less . . . virile, masculine. How could she compete with *this* for her sister's future?

No, she admonished herself, of course he wasn't Nico! She'd seen him on calls plenty of times. True, there was a clear resemblance, but that was all.

'Jade's not here.' For one long moment, Indi thought that that was the end of the conversation, that she would have to make her way back through the olive groves, back across the sea to try to find a bed in Naxos, but instead the door swung open to reveal a wide, tiled hallway 'Come in, she shouldn't be long. I'm Mikhos,' he added over his shoulder. 'Nico's cousin.'

Ah! Mikhos. Jade's boss, Indi's host, self-made squillionaire and tycoon, a bona fide success story. From Jade's descriptions, she'd expected someone older, someone driven, serious, dour, not, not . . . not *naked and amused*.

Indi shouldered her rucksack and stepped over the threshold feeling a little as if she were entering Bluebeard's castle. 'Thank you.'

The hallway led to a corridor, closed doors on one side at intervals, glass sliding doors on the other open to an internal courtyard. The villa was built around the courtyard, she realised with a gasp of delight, an oasis of green and water, potted plants carefully placed to create a natural effect, the central fountain and small pebbled pools a contrast.

Indi followed Mikhos into the courtyard, tracing a winding gravelled path flanked by high palms, only to stop, amazed and slightly awed, as a marble swimming pool came into sight, a built-in hot tub bubbling away at one end. Tables, chairs and loungers were spaced around the pool and across a terrace and, to her relief, Mikhos gestured for her to take a seat on a comfortable-looking sofa. Too tired to demur or to ask any more questions, Indi did as he bade, half closing her eyes as he pulled out his phone and had a quick conversation in rapid Greek.

'I've ordered you some refreshments,' he said as he ended the call.

'Thank you. And thank you for hosting me. Hopefully, Jade won't be long, but I really appreciate you taking the time out of your . . . ah . . . busy schedule.' She couldn't help but drop her gaze back to the towel before snapping it back up to focus on the nearest plant, cheeks burning. Mikhos might at least have grabbed one of the robes lying on the loungers. Now she was sitting down, his towel was practically in her direct eyeline, it was most discombobulating.

'Anyway, thank you for letting me stay.' Indi hadn't realised she'd decided to try to break the world record for saying *thank you* as many times as possible in a minute. She tried for different words. 'It's very kind of you. Especially when it was all so last minute. I don't usually work that way. Usually, I am very organised, but it's been a difficult few weeks. Not that you need to hear about that.' *Lord above, stop babbling, Indi!*

The mocking look softened into something approaching sympathy and Indi looked away, aware her cheeks were going from flame to inferno. She didn't want sympathy from anyone. That wasn't how she operated.

'Kind? Strategic maybe. I have the feeling you and I may be of one mind where this engagement is concerned.'

Embarrassment forgotten, Indi looked up sharply, but before she could formulate a reply, a splash from the pool snagged her attention. Blinking, she watched as a gorgeous young woman, in a bikini made solely of pieces of yellow string, stepped out, just as Aphrodite must have stepped from the waves, long, dark, wet hair pushed back from a perfect oval face.

'Mikhos, *meli mou,*' she said, sliding damp arms around his neck, and murmured something in a husky voice that made Mikhos laugh. She smiled over his shoulder at Indi, a smile that was like being bathed in golden sunlight. 'Hello, you must be Indi. Welcome to Agios Iohannis. I hope you will soon feel just as at home here as your sister does.'

'Thank you.' No wonder Jade wanted to stay here in this beautiful place with these beautiful people. Indi had never felt quite so ungainly and as unkempt as she did right now, or as overdressed!

But this wasn't Jade's home and yellow string bikinis would look very out of place in Stoke Newington. Indi just needed to remember why she was here, give herself time to regroup, to sort out this little romance of Jade's and to lick her wounds privately. As long as she kept focused, all would be fine.

It had to be. She refused to let it be any other way.

Chapter Nine

Jade

Jade completely lost track of time, aware only of Nico, his mouth on hers, his hands on her body, the way he always made her feel so wanted, the way she hungered for him in return. It wasn't until his radio beeped that she came to, Nico sitting up, brushing sand off her back and out of her hair.

'The boat must be near.' Now he seemed nervous, the near-constant smile missing from his eyes, the mischievous dimple she adored hidden. 'It's nearly time to meet the family.'

He got to his feet in one graceful movement, youth and vitality inherent in every muscle and sinew as he held a hand out to her. She took it and allowed him to pull her to her feet. Jade brushed the rest of the sand off her ankle-length skirt and vest top, running her fingers through the ends of her hair. Nico watched her, still serious.

'You're beautiful.' His voice was low and reverberated through her. They didn't feel like words but like truth. The best thing was that he made her feel that way, made her forget the scar bisecting her left thigh, the one high on her shoulder, the criss-crosses of raised and puckered skin on her lower back. He touched them with care, with love, turned them from ugly reminders to a cherished part of the map of her body.

Jade tugged at her hair. 'But am I tidy?'

'Tidy?'

'I just want Indi to see me as a grown woman with a role here, not a daydreaming girl who needs to wake up,' she explained as they left the beach and took the path that would lead them directly to the jetty. 'I definitely don't want her to think I spend most of my time making out on a beach with you.' Some of her time, true, but not most of it.

'Your sister's approval means that much to you?'

'Yes, she's more than my sister, my best friend, even though she is eight years older than I am. I wanted to be just like her when I was younger. Sometimes I still do. I envy the way she knows what she wants out of life and just goes and gets it rather than drifting. She and Will have been split up for barely a fortnight and here she is, moving on. She's amazing.' And a little intimidating when she wanted to be.

'Like Mikhos. I hero-worshipped him when I was a boy, a young man. By my age, he already owned two hotels, I have yet to buy my boat. Maybe you have chosen the wrong Angelos.' He laughed, but there was an edge to his tone, and she cupped his face and looked into his eyes.

'I have chosen the perfect Angelos for me. You'll get the boat and then another and before you know it we'll have a whole fleet.'

'And enough children to crew them.'

'I'm not sure about that, let's start with one and see.' She sighed. 'I just don't want Indi to be disappointed in me. You know, she was barely sixteen when Daddy died, and obviously she was devastated – she had always been our dad's golden girl – but she pushed her feelings aside to make sure I was well taken care of. She even lived at home when she went to university, gave up so many experiences for me. I owe her everything.' Her hand reached down to brush the worst of her scars, hidden as always. A constant reminder of all Indi had done for her.

'But that doesn't mean you owe her your future,' Nico said softly.

'No,' she agreed. 'It doesn't, and she would be horrified at the idea that I thought I did. Emotional blackmail is really not her line. She just wants me to be safe.'

'And happy.'

'Happiness is an optional extra, I think.' She tried to smile, but the reality of that statement struck her. Jade hadn't realised how much happiness was missing from her life until her first morning on a yacht in the Caribbean. Every bone had ached with tiredness after a gruelling sixteen-hour day, a late night and obscenely early start, but she had watched the sun rise and a wild, unexpected joy had filled her. Part of that happiness had been that she knew she was free – free from the path Indi had laid out for her, free from expectations. That she was choosing her own destiny. Part of it had been the location, the beauty.

And that happiness had just intensified since moving to Greece. It felt like coming home.

Nico looked thoughtful. 'I guess she doesn't think moving to Greece and marrying me is particularly safe, does she?'

'Not anything like.' Now Indi was here, there was no hiding from the reality that she was bound to be unhappy with Jade's choice. 'She tried to hide it, but it was clear that she hated me going yachting, it was so far away and to her it seemed directionless. Her way of coping was to keep reminding me that it was short-term and I needed to think about what came next, persuading me to apply for a course in September so that I was coming back to something tangible. And that was just me leaving her for a few months, not forever. Choosing to stay in Greece is going to really hurt her and that's the last thing I want to do.'

It wasn't just Indi who was going to hurt. The one dark cloud for Jade when she looked into her future was the thought of being permanently separated from her sister.

'I can't imagine you wanting to hurt anyone. You were the peacemaker on the yacht. It was one of the many things about you I fell in love with.'

'All that drama!' Jade shook her head. It had never failed to amaze her how some of her colleagues had seemed to get off on causing the maximum amount of conflict and stress in a very confined space. 'And I don't want any drama while she's here either. But at the end of the day, this is *my* life, my choice and I choose you.'

Her hand dropped to her stomach. *I choose you as well,* she thought. She allowed her hand to linger for a few seconds, then dropped it to her side. She needed to be careful, if she did that in front of her sister, Indi would have the truth out of her in seconds and Jade wasn't ready to tell her. Not yet.

Nico stopped and turned her to face him. 'That's all I want. For you to freely choose me. If so, your sister will have no choice but to accept that.'

'I hope so. I want her to love you as much as I do.'

'Maybe not quite as much. That could be awkward.'

'Silly.' She reached up to touch his face, grounding herself in his gaze and touch. 'Come on, let's go.'

As Jade and Nico wandered around the curve into the path. Jade expected to see the boat heading towards them, but to her confusion it was moored up, Antinous wiping down the deck, no sign of any passengers.

'Oh no, Indi! I was supposed to be there on time to greet her.' Jade looked around wildly as if she expected her sister to emerge from the sea. 'Where is she?'

'She probably went on to the villa,' Nico said soothingly, slipping an arm around her waist. 'It's not like she can get lost, is it?'

'But why didn't she wait?' Jade pulled out her phone and stared in dismay at the brief message Indi had left. 'Oh! She got in ten minutes ago. I knew we shouldn't have dawdled. Come on, let's catch her up!'

Jade didn't look to see if Nico was with her as she broke into a fast trot, following the path that led up the hill and across the island to the villa, Nico laughing at her heels, exhorting her to slow down.

'This wasn't the plan,' Jade panted as she reached the top of the hill, holding her side as she stopped to catch her breath. 'I'm supposed to be welcoming her to my life, showing her that I am an adult making responsible decisions, not necking with my boyfriend in a dark corner like the hormonal teenager she thinks I am.'

'The necking bit was fun, though.' Nico's grin was unrepentant, and Jade couldn't resist pulling him to her for a long lingering kiss.

'Best behaviour from now on,' she warned him. 'Husband material, remember.'

'Don't worry, I told you, your sister will love me.'

Jade just wished she shared Nico's confidence. 'Of course she will. It's me that needs to grovel for forgiveness. Poor Indi, arriving after that long journey to a strange place with no one to welcome her.'

'If she went straight to the villa, then Mikhos is there, he'll take care of her.'

Jade shivered. 'Like the immovable object with the unstoppable force.'

'What do you mean?'

'I mean people as determined as Mikhos and Indi will either take to each other at first sight or dislike each other immensely. Either way, it's not going to be peaceful or pretty. Come on, the sooner we get there to run interference the better. If we want our engagement and our future baby announcement to go smoothly, then I vote we keep the pair of them apart as much as possible.'

She'd hoped to be able to catch up with Indi as she hurried down the path, but her sister was clearly far in front of them, the villa coming into sight without a glimpse of her and Jade felt her anxiety intensify. 'Indi would never have been late if it was the other way round. She would have been at the jetty ten minutes early, cocktails in hand with a folder detailing every minute of the stay and an entire history of the island.' Jade wailed as she stopped at the front door, 'Why didn't *I* put a folder together? I haven't made a single plan for her, not even for her birthday.'

'She didn't give you much notice and you've been busy working,' Nico pointed out.

'And swimming and sunbathing and spending time with you.' She sighed. 'Oh well, it's done now and it's not like we haven't got lots of time together ahead of us. I'll make it up to her.'

But somehow, she couldn't bring herself to move, a sense of inevitable change keeping her rooted to the spot. Real life was intruding on her idyll, and she was powerless to stop it.

'Jade? I thought we were in a hurry.'

She looked up at Nico. 'Do you think we will always be this happy? Are we idiots to think we can do this?'.

'There are no guarantees, but I give you my solemn promise that I will try.' Nico's expression was unusually serious, his eyes dark with sincerity. 'Jade, of course I want your family's blessing, because I know it matters to you that they approve of me, of us. But I don't *need* it, just like I don't need Mikhos' approval *or* his job. All I need is for you to believe in me, in us.'

'But it's not *just* us, not anymore. If we mess up, then that impacts on the baby.' It was so much responsibility and Jade had only just started to manage her own life.

'Even more reason for me to get it right.'

'But how do we *know* what's right? How can we make sure our decisions are good ones? Indi is always the one who knows what to do and when to do it, I've let her be the grown-up for so long. I can't bear the thought of our relationship changing, but things won't be the same after this, they can't be.'

'Change is an inevitable part of growing up.' Nico's voice was soothing as he pulled her close. 'You have new priorities in your life, that's natural. But that doesn't mean your relationship with your sister will be worse. She hasn't told you she disapproves of our engagement, has she?'

'Not yet.' But Jade knew that was a conversation in waiting.

'So you might be worrying about nothing,' Nico pointed out. 'Why worry about what might not happen? Right now, your sister has come all this way to visit you, that's a good thing. She's had a tough time, which means *she* needs *you* now. And in a couple of weeks it's her birthday, so let's make sure she has a wonderful holiday and goes home knowing you are in a good place with people who love you.'

He was right. Of course he was right.

Jade kissed him. 'Thank you.'

'What for?'

'For always knowing the right thing to say.' Jade took a deep breath. 'OK, I'm ready. Let's do this.'

The hallway was quiet, but Jade could hear the hum of voices and followed the sound through the courtyard until she reached the paved area around the pool, winding her way through the plants until she finally saw her sister sitting on one of the poolside sofas, a glass of wine before her, as Demeter unloaded a tray filled with a tempting-looking mezze of treats, while Mikhos . . .

'Oh no.' Jade closed her eyes, but when she opened them again, the scene was no better. Mikhos seemed to have *mislaid his clothes*. Aurelia was no more respectable, lounging on the side of the pool in a costume designed to show off her admittedly magnificent body and gravity-defying boobs as she chatted to Indi. 'Nico,' she hissed. 'Why is your cousin only wearing a towel?'

'I'm sure he's wearing something underneath.' But Nico didn't sound as sure as she would like.

'Indi is going to think she's ended up in some kind of frat orgy house!'

'It's summer, it's Greece, he's wearing more than half the tourists wear at the beach.'

'I know, but this isn't a beach.'

Nico nudged her affectionately. 'It's a poolside. Relax, Jade, come on and introduce me to your sister.'

'OK.' But really, could Mikhos be giving off any more alpha male vibes? 'Indi! You're here! I am so sorry I missed meeting you. I am so happy to see you!'

'Jade!' Indi was on her feet and Jade forgot all her worries, Mikhos' lack of clothes, the future in her joy at being reunited with her sister. She rushed to fling her arms around Indi and for a moment she was a little girl again, knowing she was safe because Indi was here. She always felt like a child next to her, the four-inch difference in their height emphasising the difference in age and roles.

The two shared similar features, although Jade had inherited their mother's Irish colouring, whereas Indi shared their father's autumnal tones, with her dark brown hair with warm red glints and grey eyes. And, of course, she had inherited his brain and drive as well.

Jade introduced Nico to Indi and then stepped back and scrutinised her sister anxiously. 'You look tired.' Indi looked washed out, deep shadows under her eyes, her hair lifeless, her skin pallid as if she hadn't seen the sun for months. 'You must have a good rest while you are here.'

'I'm fine.' As if Indi would say anything else, would let anyone try to look after her. 'It's been a long day and at least one boat too many. The ferry was bumpier than I anticipated.'

'In that case, are you up for a tour before dinner or would you rather just finish your wine and relax? I could bring dinner to your room if you're tired. Save looking around until the morning?'

It was peculiar being the one offering hospitality, choices, doing the nurturing, all usually Indi's roles. But a good thing too. This was Jade's home, her place of work, and she needed to show Indi that she had authority and a role here.

'I'm not sure I'm up for a full tour, but it would be good to freshen up.'

'OK. I'll take you to your room. I think you are going to love it! Your bags should already have been brought up.'

'Actually, about that, my bag has gone missing.' Indi sounded calm enough, but her eyes were over-bright and her lips tight, a sure sign she was stressed. 'I don't suppose you could lend me a couple of things?'

'You poor thing, of course I will!' Indi usually packed with military precision and neatness; the loss of her luggage would have completely thrown her. Jade mentally scanned through her wardrobe, trying to think of things Indi would like – and crucially things that would fit. Not only was her sister taller, but Indi was also much better endowed in the chest area, with a naturally hourglass figure Jade envied. 'Luckily, we have all the cosmetics you could need. We're in final pre-phase for opening and as we are so far from the mainland and guests can't just pop to a shop, we need to be able to handle any kind of request. I'll grab you a few things. Same with underwear, so you're sorted there. I'll pull out a couple of dresses for you to keep you going.'

'Your sister is far more my height,' Aurelia offered, looking up from her phone. 'I am sure I can find you some clothes too.'

'Thank you.' Indi sounded more than a little unsure and Jade bit her lip to stop herself grinning; Indi was more of a sensible one-piece swimming costume girl, the thought of her trussed up in one of Aurelia's tiny scraps of material was all too delicious. Part of Jade couldn't help but hope that it was several days until Indi's suitcase turned up. The results could be interesting!

'No problem, I have plenty to spare.' Aurelia waved off the thanks.

'Thanks, Aurelia, I'll pop by your room after I have taken Indi to hers and seen what I have. OK, it's this way.'

Jade caught Nico's eye as she led Indi out of the courtyard and he gave her a quick thumbs up.

'I didn't expect the villa to be so big,' Indi said as they stepped into the corridor. 'It's more mansion than holiday home.'

'Mikhos built it for himself a few years ago. There was a summer house on this spot before, but he always intended to turn the island into something more than a personal retreat. Now he's built the guest accommodation and facilities on the other side of the island the villa will house some of the permanent staff and the resort office. Nico and I have been based here for a couple of months now, which has been amazing.'

'And you're working in guest services you said? But there *are* no guests yet.' Indi looked confused.

'Not yet, but that's about to change! Up to now, I've been getting the villas and common areas ready, dealing with reservations, that kind of thing, helping Mikhos and Aurelia with anything they need on site, especially when they are away. But our first guests will arrive for three nights a week tomorrow. The first tranche are hand-picked travel influencers and bloggers and they will be followed by luxury travel consultants and journalists, before the first paying guests arrive in a little over two weeks' time. So your mission, if you choose to accept it, is to test out as much as you can over the next week or so. If there are any issues, we can fix them before anyone arrives.'

'Oh I choose to accept it. Anything to help. It sounds like you've been pretty indispensable.' Was Jade imagining it or did Indi actually sound impressed? 'I had no idea your job was so varied. I thought you were doing similar things to when you were a steward.'

'There has been a fair amount of ironing and counting linen,' she confessed. 'But the role has really developed over time as I have taken on more and more responsibility. Sometimes I'm the only non-contractor here on the island. Nico will be running all the boat trips, but until we have guests, he still works from Naxos, so he is often gone all day and, of course, Aurelia and Mikhos travel around a great deal.'

'Good for you.'

Indi obviously meant to be encouraging, to offer praise, but Jade could feel her teeth clench somewhat. Did her sister have to be quite so patronising? She wasn't playing at working here.

'And what about when the guests are here? It won't be just you living here then, surely?'

'Hardly, with forty guests at a time! Mikhos is bringing over his top team from Naxos, but the plan is that I'll stay on to help with reception and reservations for the rest of the summer at least, arrange trips, make sure the guests have everything they need, organising parties or special occasions, that kind of thing. A bit like being a steward on the yacht, but for twenty groups, not just one. I'm also assisting Aurelia over the launch period.'

'What does she do?'

'PR. She's a bit of a guru, especially where social media is concerned. She hand-picked each of the influencers and bloggers herself.'

'And are she and Mikhos together?' Indi asked. 'They seem very close.'

Jade laughed. 'You'd think so, wouldn't you? They *are* very close, they've known each other all their lives, but there's nothing romantic going on at all. Aurelia really is amazing, she's so clever, I'm learning loads from her and she's been very kind. It's nice to know someone who isn't part of Nico's family!' They reached the staircase leading to Indi's room. 'OK, so this is the guest wing. The staff wing is on your right, the office wing where I sleep is on your left. Opposite are Mikhos' own private rooms. I've put you in the corner suite as it has sea views on both sides. It's yours for as long as you need it. Use it as a base and explore the area, stay here and do nothing, whatever you want.'

Jade couldn't imagine her sister doing nothing, she wasn't sure it was even a possibility without breaking some obscure rule of physics, the kind that kept the planets spinning.

But, then again, neither could she imagine her sister being so quiet, or turning up without a fully researched itinerary, with every second meticulously accounted for, and she had been sent nothing to indicate that Indi had any plans for her stay at all, including on her birthday. The break-up had clearly hit Indi harder than she was letting on.

'This is you.' She quickly showed Indi around the room, delighted as Indi exclaimed over all the small touches Jade had put in place for her. 'Shower, rest, enjoy. I'll be back with some essentials soon. Let me know if you need anything.'

'I will, thank you.'

Jade stood at the door. 'I'm so glad you're here. We are going to have an amazing time and you are going to head back to London a relaxed, bronzed goddess and Will is going to spend every night of his early-midlife-crisis tour kicking himself for being such an idiot.'

Indi's smile was a little tremulous. 'Promise?'

'Guaranteed.' Jade crossed her fingers.

They *would* have an amazing time. She just needed to help her sister somehow accept her engagement and, even more unlikely, be pleased about the baby when Jade finally told her. Agios Iohannis was an island that worked miracles. She was counting on it working one on Indi.

Chapter Ten

Indi

Monday 5 June

For once, Indi woke up with no idea what time it was, and no idea what she was going to do with her day. All she did know was that she felt unusually at peace. The air was pleasantly warm, fresher than she knew air could be, her body utterly sated with sleep. She indulged in a blissful half-awake state for a while, teetering on the edge of snoozing a little more until the sounds started to become more discernible: the crashing of waves upon rocks, the squawks of the seabirds, and slowly, reluctantly, she opened her eyes.

She was greeted not by the fashionable if industrial grey that adorned every wall of her flat, but by walls painted a white so fresh it might have hurt her eyes if it wasn't so perfectly chalky matt. The sunlight that streamed in through the chink in the curtains wasn't the pale primrose of early morning light but the riper amber of later in the day. Indi sat up, stretching cramped limbs as she did so.

She fumbled for her phone, squinting as she made out the time, nearly dropping it again when she realised how late it was. Yes, there was a time difference, and yes, she had been exhausted, but Indi didn't think she had ever slept as late as eleven in her entire life.

Propping herself up on one arm, she went through the morning message ritual. A flood of marketing emails to be deleted, a dental reminder snoozed for when she returned. A formal acceptance of their three months' notice on the flat. She stared at it, tension edging at her peaceful mood. *He'd done it then.*

It wasn't unexpected, not at all, but seeing the words in black and white made the whole situation seem real. Will was leaving the UK and he was leaving her. She was nearly thirty and single and had just three months to find a new home in the high-pressure game that was the London property market. She couldn't afford to rent a Zone 2 flat single-handedly; she wasn't sure what she *could* afford if she didn't want to share, and she really *really* didn't.

But that worry, too, had to be postponed for when she returned.

When you feel overwhelmed by problems, her father said, *take them one step at a time.*

And right now, she was focusing on Jade.

Resisting the urge to check her work emails – Priya was right, she should at least hide the app, if not delete it outright – Indi moved onto her messages. The first was a picture of the cat from her mother, asleep in an elongated position, creamy belly on show. No words. Her mother could manage a photo or write a message, not both.

Indi smiled as she read a message from Jade.

I didn't want to wake you, you looked so peaceful. Had to head over to Naxos for a bit. Help yourself to anything, do NOTHING. Love you xxxx

OK, she sent back, followed by some heart emojis to her mother.

Her phone flashed with another message, this time from Priya.

So . . . how is Paradise 😎 🏝 ?

So far, an island miles away from anywhere, a half-naked host and my clothes have gone missing.

Oooh! Are the missing clothes anything to do with the half-naked host?

Will, remember?! He's not gone yet. He might change his mind. Besides. Too soon and not my type.

Ugh! Why is it that the fewer clothes a man wears, the less attractive they are?

I didn't say he wasn't attractive, but rich, arrogant, bronzed gods are a real turn-off in my eyes.

You keep telling yourself that. I want pics.

Give my love to Dev.

PICS. PS It is Not Too Soon, who cares if Will changes his mind, you deserve better and a holiday romance is exactly what you need. I will not be answering questions at this time.

Indi couldn't help laughing as she put her phone back down on the bedside table. Typical Priya not to sugar-coat the truth. But then again, she was right. Will wasn't going to change his mind, and even if he did, it was too late for them. The trust was gone and Indi didn't think it could ever be recovered. She lingered on that thought, waiting for the stab of heartbreak, but instead felt more of a dull ache.

But Priya was *definitely* wrong about the holiday romance part, that was the last thing she needed. No, Indi was going to concentrate on herself for a while, figure out what was next, what she wanted – after she had sorted Jade out, of course.

She indulged in a long shower before heading over to contemplate the clothes Jade had brought over the evening before, thankful for the unopened cosmetics and underwear her sister had also provided.

95

'Note to self, phone the airline and threaten them with retribution if my case isn't here today,' she muttered as she flicked through the offerings. Her choice was either a couple of the long, wafty dresses Jade favoured, both a size too small and horribly unflattering in cut, if, like Indi, you were well endowed, or the much skimpier clothes Aurelia had offered, which were also a size too small.

Indi hesitated, wondering for one moment if she could manage to create something fetching with a sheet before opting for a pair of shorts, which turned out to be more like hot pants, and a cropped yoga top, which at least contained her boobs, throwing a long see-through shirt over the whole. With her hair washed and combed back ruthlessly into a long, damp ponytail, she was at least respectable. Just.

As she descended the stairs, Indi tried to remember Jade's quick tour from the night before. The villa felt eerily deserted, her own footsteps the only sound, echoing on the marble floors, until she reached the glass doors which led into the now sunlit courtyard and surveyed the other wings of the villa: staff, office and Mikhos' private rooms. If only she could remember which was which, she didn't want to end up straying into Mikhos' lair by accident.

At that thought, every hair on her body seemed to stand on end, a frisson of something primal shivering through her, and she wasn't surprised when Mikhos himself sauntered into her view, coming to an almost preternatural stillness when he saw her.

Indi tried for a smile, determined not to let his almost overwhelming presence disconcert her any more than it had already done.

'Good morning!' she said brightly. 'Only, it's actually almost afternoon. I didn't mean to sleep so long.'

This morning, *thank goodness*, Mikhos was fully clothed, although his practically translucent white linen shirt suggested the lines of his body in a way that felt almost more indecent than his more overt semi-nudity. His dark hair was swept away from a strong brow, his gaze intent.

'That's good, you are on holiday after all.'

'True! I obviously needed it. Well, I'm sure you have plenty to do, so I'll just . . .' Indi tried to think of something she could plausibly just be doing on a small, strange island. 'If you could just point me in the direction of coffee,' she tried again.

'I have coffee. Come with me.'

It felt more an order than an invitation. 'Yes, sir!' Indi mouthed as she followed her host across the courtyard into a huge, long room that took up the entire ground floor, broken up into clear working, dining and sitting spaces, decorated in muted tones with surprising bursts of colour. Her mother would have approved of the very modern art on the walls and displayed on smooth wooden plinths. Indi stopped to look at a beautifully carved piece of driftwood, in one light totally abstract, in another resembling antlers, the whole almost pagan. A second plinth held a pot, tendrils snaking out, the outline of a face lightly etched into the clay. 'Medusa?'

'You know your myths.' Was that approval in his voice?

'Medusa is one of my mother's favourite themes. Her most famous piece is called *The End of Innocence*. Medusa as a metaphor for the end of childhood and the start of responsibilities.'

'Yes, Jade mentioned your mother was a sculptor and artist.'

'She's really well thought of.' Indi didn't hide her pride. Her mother might – and did – exasperate her with her ability to ignore the pressures of real life, but that didn't mean Indi wasn't immensely proud of her mother's reputation. 'She's inspired by myths in a modern context. Jade and I have posed as countless goddesses, nymphs and besieged women. I've been Medusa myself more than once.'

His eyes flicked to her currently contained curls and she laughed.

'Don't worry, I only turn men to stone on a weekend, unless they really irritate me.'

'Thank you for the warning. Coffee is this way.' Mikhos led her to the far end of the room, which was done out as a comfortable mixture of office and den. A huge desk complete with three monitors and a separate laptop dominated one side, a leather sofa and two comfortable chairs the other. Coffee and small nut and honey pastries sat on a high round table by the window, accompanied by a bowl of mouthwateringly fresh fruit. Mikhos nodded towards a clean cup and plate. 'Help yourself.'

Indi didn't need asking twice. She had been too tired to eat much last night, too stressed by the lack of her luggage to eat on the ferry. The coffee was the jolt of reality she needed, the pastries and fruit elevating her sugar levels, and by the time she finished, Indi felt much more herself. The villa no longer felt under an enchantment and Mikhos was nothing but a man. A handsome, virile, imposing man, but just flesh and blood.

'I was so tired yesterday, I don't remember if I thanked you,' Indi said. 'It is very kind of you to host me.' She paused, suddenly feeling gauche. 'I wish you would let me pay . . .'

'Your manners were perfect and as you can see, I can spare the room,' he replied, a glint of humour warming up his face, turning it from something remotely, austerely handsome to something infinitely more dangerous and, to her horror, the same pull of attraction that had ambushed her yesterday tugged low in Indi's belly. 'And if you really want to pay your way, then it would be helpful to have a soft launch before the reviewers arrive. Would you be able to help?'

'Of course, Jade mentioned something similar. What do you need me to do?' Indi was always glad of a task. Sitting around contemplating all the unwanted change in her life sounded far less appealing than being useful.

'See how the space works. Spend some time on the beach and order food and drink, test the restaurant and the bar, check out the spa, take out a paddleboard or a jet ski. Behave like a customer. I'll get Nico to take you on a couple of organised trips as well. Enjoy all we have to offer.'

'Sounds onerous, but I'll do my best.' They weren't exactly the tasks she had had in mind. Indi had never been on a beach holiday before. Maybe it was what she needed, although she felt a little daunted by the thought of so many days to fill with relaxation. 'I'll start with having a look round. Jade was planning to give me the tour, but I guess I won't exactly get lost on my own.' It was usually Jade waiting for Indi to finish work, not the other way round. It felt a little disorientating to be at leisure while her sister was busy.

'If you've had enough coffee, why don't I show you around?' He looked at her critically and Indi felt herself colour under his gaze, exposed in her borrowed garb. 'You need a hat. And sun cream. I'll ask Demeter, she knows where the spares are.'

Armed with said hat, a ginormous contraption which kept trying to flap away in the breeze and the highest-factor sun cream she could find, Indi meekly followed Mikhos out of the villa and through the pretty olive groves back the way she had come the evening before and up the deceptively steep hill. Today, in the bright midday sun, she could see all around her. Agios Iohannis wasn't a big island, possibly a couple of miles from end to end, populated with many small sandy coves and a few rockier ones. The sea lapped gently at the shore rather than crashing possessively, and the graduated colours showed shallows surrounding the island before darkening to depths. On her right, white buildings fanned out along the headland, far enough from each other to give the illusion of privacy. On her left, there was just one building, the large, luxurious-looking villa where she was staying, situated on the headland in the far corner. It was all very impressive.

'So that's the new resort?' Indi was relieved when they finally stopped and she could catch her breath. She looked around, sea in every direction, not another bit of land in sight.

'That's right. Welcome to *To nisi* – The Island.'

'The one and only?'

'As far as my target market are concerned, yes. At least I hope so anyway.' His smile was a little self-mocking and she liked him better for it. Maybe he didn't take himself as seriously as she had assumed.

'It's definitely got a get-away-from-it-all vibe.' She breathed in the achingly clean air and tried to imagine the tranquil space populated with holidaymakers and all the attendant staff needed to create the luxury experience she knew Mikhos had in mind. 'You don't mind strangers coming here in their hordes?'

Mikhos laughed. 'Hardly hordes. There are just twenty villas, excepting mine, and although each sleeps four, we are expecting mostly couples. They have been designed to attract the honeymoon and anniversary market, romantic getaways for those who want all the joys of isolation teamed with the service and convenience of a resort.'

'I get that, but if all this was mine, I'm not sure I'd want to share it.' Right now a room of her own was a far-fetched dream let alone an idyllic island!

'I'm in the holiday business, that means using every asset I have. Originally, I was going to just hire the villa out to family groups, for weddings, that kind of thing, but we're so far from the mainland, it didn't make economic sense, even at an ultimate premium price. But the whole island is still available for private hire for those that can afford it – there's a hefty price tag attached though.'

'I can imagine. Anyone taking you up on that?'

'I have two wedding parties with exclusive use of the island next year. But everyone involved has had to sign NDAs, I'm afraid, including me.'

Intriguing. 'Gangsters, tech billionaires or film stars?'

'Maybe all three. I would tell you, but—'

'You'd have to kill me. I am now definitely thinking gangsters.' Speaking of weddings . . . 'That reminds me. I've been meaning to ask. What did you mean yesterday?'

'Mean?'

Had he really raised just one eyebrow? Indi didn't know that anyone could actually do that in real life. She stared at him, fascinated, for a moment, then realised he was watching her in turn, clearly amused.

'About being on the same side as far as this engagement between Jade and Nico is concerned. I'm sure Nico is very nice,' she said hurriedly. 'But it all seems very sudden. Jade is very young and in many ways very inexperienced, especially when it comes to dating. Nico is her first serious boyfriend.'

'I agree, it's far too sudden.' Mikhos' short statement was balm to her worry, he had been around Jade and Nico over the last few months after all. He knew them as a couple.

'You think so?'

'Of course, Nico is a young man with a career to build. He is far too young to tie himself down to any girl, let alone an English girl he's known for five minutes.'

For a moment, Indi felt a spark of irritation at the casual dismissal of her sister before reminding herself that they were on the same side.

'Right.'

'Work, family, these things are important, but at Nico's age, women come and go. That's the natural order of things.'

The spark heated up. 'And up to now, has Nico shared your casual attitude to relationships?'

Mikhos slanted a glance at her. 'I didn't say *I* was casual. But Nico falls in love very easily. Last year, he fell for one girl, then she left and within weeks there was another. I have no doubt that next year he will fall just as easily again.'

Indi's heart sank. 'So he's, what? A playboy? Trying it on with any pretty tourist?'

'No, no, nothing so calculated, more of an incurable romantic. Look, I like your sister, she is hard-working, intelligent, but as you say, she's young. Life here is hard for outsiders, for couples starting out, even if I believed that this time Nico's feelings were deeper, even if they were more established, they would find life difficult. The truth is, with his history, Jade's youth, the shortness of the relationship, it would be madness to get married right now.'

'That's what I think.' It was a relief to hear that Nico wasn't a player but everything else Mikhos had said just confirmed Indi's worries. 'Jade doesn't fall in love easily, doesn't trust easily and clearly your cousin has swept her off her feet, so she can't see this for what it is. A holiday romance.'

'So we are agreed?'

'Absolutely,' she said, more resolute than ever after Mikhos' revelations. 'This engagement is a disaster. The sooner I can get Jade to see that and come home, the better.'

Chapter Eleven

Jade

Jade had initially been annoyed by Mikhos' last-minute request-but-really-a-command that she head over to Naxos to brief the booking staff based there on everything to do with The Island. After all, communication was already extensive, with shared files and up-to-date briefing documents, not to mention that she spoke to someone in the booking office several times a day. She suspected he was making a point. *Look how busy life is here, you can't even snatch an opportunity to have coffee with your sister.*

But, on the other hand, she always enjoyed a trip over to the larger island. The office staff there were nice enough and there were even a couple of girls around her own age who might become real friends in time. Nico had been tasked with taking her and she loved watching him sail. He was so at one with the sea, calm, sure-footed and graceful.

Nico was scheduled to lead a morning trip for guests staying at the Naxos Town hotel around some of Naxos' more hidden beaches and so they set off early, Jade reaching the office before 8 a.m. In the end, her briefing took much longer than anticipated, she lived and breathed The Island, so it was easy to forget that other people didn't know each villa individually, hadn't walked the path from the jetty to the restaurant hundreds of times, hadn't sampled the

103

taster menus. After dozens of questions, it seemed simpler to organise two trips there, one for the next morning and one for the morning after that, so that her colleagues could see the layout for themselves.

Jade had never realised she could be this confident, that she could speak up in a room full of co-workers, make unilateral decisions, enjoy a job and feel fulfilled by it. Be good at it. She'd never felt like this at the co-ordinator job Indi had found her at the university, the receptionist job Will had organised for her at his firm, the shops and cafes she'd worked in near her home. The teaching assistant role had been the best of the bunch, but she'd never been able to imagine doing it for the rest of her life, nor had she really wanted to train as a teacher, even though Indi was sure it was right for her.

But she *could* imagine her life here. No matter what Mikhos thought, she wasn't a starry-eyed, infatuated girl who expected a life full of moonlit beach walks. No, that wasn't true. She hoped she and Nico *did* enjoy a long lifetime of moonlit beach walks, but she knew there would be long, tiring days in between. Days like today with early starts and multiple tasks. But she wasn't complaining, it was all worth it to be here with Nico, and to be thriving in a job she loved.

It was after two when Nico picked her up for the late lunch they had planned to have together. Jade had expected they would go to one of the many cafes along the seafront or in the picturesque old town, but to her surprise he was waiting for her in his small jeep.

'I thought we'd have lunch in the apartment,' he said, greeting her with a kiss as she clambered up into the vehicle. 'There are a few jobs I need to do there and it's between lettings right now.'

Nico had spent six winters now in the Caribbean as a deckhand in the lucrative charter yacht business, where a six-month stint could net sixty thousand dollars in tips, with wages on top and few expenses. He'd used his savings from his first two years' yachting to buy an apartment in a complex overlooking the town. He usually rented it out as a long-term let when he was away over the winter and as a holiday rental in summer, living with his parents when working on Naxos. Every cent then went into his savings for a boat of his own. Nico wasn't interested in buying just any boat, he wanted the best fifty-foot yacht he could manage in order to offer bespoke luxury day trips or multi-island trips to couples or small groups. He might not want to conquer the world like Mikhos, but he had plenty of ambition and drive.

Jade was full of anticipation as the jeep climbed the curving hills out of Naxos Town. They had stayed in the apartment when she had first arrived on Naxos at the beginning of March – the first and only time they had been fully alone. She had many fond memories of it.

And it was their future home.

The apartment was one of twelve in an attractive three-storey block built overlooking the sea. Landscaped gardens and a seasonal pool made it an appealing holiday destination, even though it was a little out of town. The last time Jade had been here, it had been early March and quiet, but now they were into June, every apartment seemed busy; there were people lying on sun loungers around the now-open pool and towels flapped on every balcony and terrace.

Her anticipation faded, replaced by a hint of anxiety. Nico had bought the apartment as an investment and a bolthole, a backup before sinking all his money and dreams into a boat, he had never intended to live here as a permanent home and nor, she suspected, did any other owners.

'Does anyone actually live here all year round?' she asked as they walked through the tiled hallway. 'Or are they all lets?'

Tourism was the island business, it was *her* business, but she wanted neighbours and a community, not an ever-changing roster of people who were here to have a good time, especially in the place where they would be raising their baby.

'There's an English couple in 5b who are here most of the time, but otherwise, no.' She could see him coming to the same conclusion as she just had. 'But it's mostly couples or families who choose to stay here, so it's reasonably peaceful.'

'Good, that's good.'

Don't be spoilt, she told herself. They had a place to start their life together, that was more than many people had. They would get something less touristy one day.

Nico unlocked the door and ushered her in and Jade looked around the apartment with fresh eyes. She'd been charmed the first time she had seen the two-bedroom, open-plan space with its generous balcony, but now the balcony screamed death trap, the tiny kitchenette looked inadequate for family meals, the one main room narrow. Where would they dry clothes? Put things? There was no storage at all. The main bedroom only just fit a bed, there was certainly no room for a cot. The second bedroom was so small she couldn't imagine bookshelves, toys, anything in there apart from the essentials. It was a lot less than ideal as a home for a family. And she couldn't help but see the space through Indi's eyes. It screamed *Too Young*. It screamed *Impulsive*. It screamed *Careless*.

But it was all they had and she needed to make the best of it.

Jade pasted on a smile. 'I forgot how lovely the views are.'

But Nico wasn't fooled. 'Views are one thing, but this is no place for us to start a family in.'

'Of course it is. It has four walls, plumbing, electricity. Two bedrooms even. We are so lucky.' But as she spoke, the sound of some kind of cartoon blared in from next door and two seconds later a child started to screech outside on the landing.

'I don't remember it being so noisy,' Nico said, his eyes anxious, mouth compressed tight. 'This would drive you mad.'

'It's toddler season, remember? This is when young families come away, you know, before the school holidays, when flights are cheap. You said yourself, it's mostly couples here usually. And the winter will be really peaceful.' Maybe too peaceful if they were alone in a huge empty building.

'I should have bought something bigger.'

'Are you kidding? You are twenty-four and you own this place outright. That's amazing.'

But he clearly wasn't listening. 'We should buy something more appropriate.'

'Nico, there's no need. If we live here, it's just bills and food we need to worry about. We can manage that while you establish your business, even if Mikhos doesn't offer me a job. We're so used to the space and peace of Agios Iohannis, it's no wonder we're hyperaware of every sound, but we'll soon adapt. Why get into debt when we have everything we need right here?'

'We don't need to get into debt. I have my savings. I can easily afford to buy somewhere bigger, somewhere suitable for a family. For *my* family.'

Jade stared at him, his face pale but his jaw resolute. 'But your savings are for you, to start your own business. I can't ask you to use them. I won't.'

'You're not asking. I'm deciding.'

'But without a boat of your own, how will you get started? That is all you ever wanted.' Jade felt sick in a way that had nothing to do with her pregnancy. The first time she had gone on a date with Nico, he had told her that his dream was to own his own boating company, that he spent six months of every year working away from home in order to make that happen. And now he was going to walk away from that? 'What will you do instead?'

'I'm going to take the job as a trainee manager Mikhos keeps offering me.'

Jade half closed her eyes as his words sunk in. Nico behind a desk, not out on deck? 'No, Nico! No, I won't let you. Yes, I agree this apartment is less than ideal, but let's be honest, this whole situation is less than ideal. We didn't plan to start a family now, and nothing is in place, but that doesn't mean you give up on your dream. There has to be another way.'

'Like what? You go back to London to have the baby and I head back out to the Caribbean for the winter?' It wasn't like Nico to sound so frustrated, and her heart twinged with compassion. In his own way he was as proud as his cousin.

'A way we can do this together, I mean. And we can. Right here. Yes, it's small, but it wouldn't be forever. Your business is going to be a huge success, I just know it.'

'Jade, I've been thinking about this ever since you told me you were pregnant.' His expression was resolute. 'I hoped I'd walk in here today and realise that it was big enough, soundproofed enough, that we could begin to raise a family here, but it's clear that it would be too hard.'

At that moment, a baby started crying outside, adding to the wails still going on in the hallway and the high-pitched cartoon sounds from the neighbouring apartment. Jade blinked hard. 'This isn't what I want. I don't want you to give up your dreams. If Mikhos gives me a full-time job, then—'

'Then you'll still need to take maternity leave and we still need somewhere to live.'

'We'll cope. This is Naxos! We have beaches and the sea and the hills, the baby will have a whole world to explore beyond these walls.'

But Nico was shaking his head. 'The baby will soon turn one, then two, then three. Maybe one day we'll have another, how will we manage then?'

'By then, your company will be an amazing success and we'll be living in a mansion.'

'Or maybe we'll be tired and broke and you'll wish you had never married me.'

Jade walked across the small living room and slipped her arms around his waist. 'That will never happen,' she said softly. 'You are a good man, Nico Angelos. The fact you are even considering giving up your dream shows that.'

He pulled her close. 'I'm not giving up my dream, I'm changing it, and that is fine. That's being an adult. I don't have to compete with Mikhos, show the world that I am an entrepreneur too, work eighteen-hour days. Where would you and the baby fit into that? Look, Jade, I always knew I could prop up the boat business with crewing over the winter if needed, that's no longer on the table. I see too many families split by seasonal work. I don't want that for us. Besides, I'm not giving up on my dream, I'm postponing it. Maybe my son and I can start a business together.' He laid a hand on her stomach and she covered it with hers, overwhelmed with love for him.

'Or daughter.'

'My fierce pirate daughter,' he agreed. 'Come on, let me show you something I've been considering. I can come back and do the jobs here tomorrow.'

A few minutes later, they were back in the jeep heading inland until Nico turned off a track and pulled into an olive grove with a cleared field beside it. The views were breathtaking, the air achingly fresh.

'We're less than five kilometres from the town,' he said. 'And there's a small village less than 250 metres down the road, with a taverna, little shop, all the essentials. It feels isolated here, but it's not.'

'It's beautiful, just look at those views with the hills behind and the sea so clear in the distance.' Jade turned around slowly, taking it all in.

'The field is for sale as a building plot, the olive grove an optional extra. If I use my savings and sell the apartment, I can afford to buy both and build a villa here. Nothing fancy, but a home. For you, me and the baby.'

Jade looked around, at the flowers and olive trees, the blue sky a close match for the distant sea, then closed her eyes and listened to the birds. It was so peaceful, almost alarmingly so for a girl born and brought up in London. Any child living here would have a freedom she would never have been able to imagine, land to play on, the beaches and seas within a short drive, sun most of the year. Nico's parents and sister close by, Nico not out at sea from dawn till long past dusk but around.

The only downside was that her family would be so far away, but if they had a proper home they could come and stay whenever they wanted. That wouldn't be possible in the apartment. Maybe they could build a small guest annexe?

'You'd do this for me?'

'I'd do anything for you. I love you, Jade. I love that you are going to be my wife, that we are going to have a child. I meant what I said, this is my dream now. The boat can wait. What do you say?'

What *could* she say? 'If you're sure, then yes, this would be amazing, but—'

'No buts. This is our future and it's time I grew up.' He pulled her close and kissed her, but Jade couldn't relax into the embrace. How many times were people going to have to give up their dreams for her? Indi giving up Oxford, her teenage years, now Nico his boat. She wasn't worth this kind of sacrifice. No one was.

Chapter Twelve

Indi

'It's very kind of you to show me around, but I'm sure you have more important things to do.' Indi was uneasily aware that she was taking up a lot of Mikhos' time.

And uneasily aware of him as well. The sheer physicality of him, his energy, his presence.

'Not at all. I was planning a walk round and snagging check today anyway and it will be helpful to hear what you think of it all. To see the resort through fresh eyes.'

A task. That was something she could get on board with. And she did want to see the rest of the island. Besides, what excuse could she make? The very ground she was walking on belonged to him, there was nowhere really to go. 'In that case, thank you.'

They carried on in silence, but somehow it didn't feel awkward. There was something cathartic in having laid their cards on the table. They both wanted the best for the people they loved, they were both protective, although she couldn't help thinking that actually Mikhos was a little *over*protective, after all Nico was in his mid-twenties, well travelled, experienced.

Finally, they reached the jetty where Indi had arrived yesterday. She slipped off her trainers and padded onto the hot sand, enjoying the feel of it under her toes. 'How big is the island? About a couple of miles?'

Mikhos nodded. 'It's roughly a triangular shape. Less than a mile wide at the narrowest point, three miles at the widest and about two miles end to end. Hence the golf buggies. It's beautiful to walk around, but a four-mile round trip several times a day is hard on the staff.'

Indi looked around, taking it all in: the interior a tamed wilderness of groves, paths winding as if random through the trees and up the hill; the main path, wide and smooth enough for the golf buggy, bisecting and dissecting the island before curving around the lower coastline in order to deliver luggage, clean linen and room service to the guests; the sea almost always there, glimmering in almost every viewpoint; and nestled into the scenery, in coves, in groves, the twenty villas waiting for their first guests.

'I always think of a resort as something bigger,' Indi said. 'Several swimming pools, hotels, lots of facilities, that kind of thing, but once you're in one of those villas, you must feel like you're totally alone.'

'I own other hotels that are more like what you have in mind, but I didn't want anything too obtrusive here. The idea is to keep that feeling of peace, although there is a bar and restaurant, communal areas for guests who don't want complete isolation. But the selling point is that it's a bespoke, boutique resort, run as much as possible on eco lines – solar power where possible, for instance. We have the natural resources, so why not use them?'

'With the price tag to match? I mean, everything has to be brought over, right?'

'Absolutely, all food, all linen, all staff, although we are stocked for all emergencies. There are storms even in paradise, after all, and we don't want the guests to recreate *Lord of the Flies*.'

'It might ruin your reviews. What about non-going-feral

activities? There's only so much gazing into each other's eyes a couple can do, after all.' Ouch, she could feel the bitterness of that statement coating her tongue. Try as she might to focus on looking forward, not worrying away at what had happened with Will, she clearly had some anger to work through.

Mikhos slanted her a quick glance. Was that pity in his eyes? Of course Jade would have mentioned her break-up. In some ways, Indi wished she hadn't. She didn't want anyone feeling sorry for her, seeing her as vulnerable. 'The spa provides yoga, Pilates and other classes, as well as treatments. There's swimming obviously – every villa has its own pool in case guests aren't confident to swim in the sea, or it's too rough. We also have boats they can take out, kayaks, jet skis, and scuba diving, plus Nico runs boat trips either for couples or groups. There will be daily drop-off and pick-ups at Naxos too, or we can take people further afield, to Santorini or Mykonos, for a price of course.'

Indi blinked. 'Very comprehensive. And you want me to sample all of this?'

'As much as you can.'

'I'll do my best. Thank you.' Indi tried to sound enthusiastic, but she couldn't help but feel a little deflated. On the one hand, it sounded like an amazing opportunity to try lots of new things, but on the other, it sounded rather lonely. A sole paddleboard, the only person on a trip designed for two. Nothing was more designed to remind her of her newly single status.

Was that pang because she was missing Will, or because she was missing being part of a couple? It should be the first, obviously, but she couldn't, hand on heart, claim that it was.

Something else to add to her *work this through later* list.

'You're welcome. OK, this way. This is the first villa.'

*

Over the next hour, Indi found herself dazzled by the sheer luxe laid on for the lucky guests. Each of the twenty villas was a similar style and size, but they weren't exactly identical; one had a huge sunken bathtub looking out to sea, another a tiny completely private beach perfect for an all-over tan, a third a cosy reading corner, another a cinema room. Colour palates varied from creams and golds to rich turquoises to soothing greys, textures from natural linens to decadent velvets.

By the time they reached the last villa, Indi had run out of superlatives and adjectives, her mind whirling with all she had seen. 'This might be my favourite yet,' she breathed as she looked out at the sea surrounding the villa on three sides, located as it was on a small promontory.

The whole had a sea glass and driftwood theme, light natural tones contrasting with a deep marine emerald. Typically Greek on the outside, with thick walls painted white and deep-set shuttered windows, the interior was an airy, open-plan hideaway. Natural linen sofas heaped with green cushions were positioned to take advantage of the stunning views; the table was already set with locally sourced wooden dishes; the kitchen area, cleverly hidden behind shutters, contained a wine fridge as well as other essentials, vibrant plants adding colour and life to the whole. Open-tread stairs led to the first floor which housed the master suite, complete with a decadent en suite and a huge terrace furnished with loungers and umbrellas, as well as a table and chairs perfect for an intimate breakfast. A second staircase led to another en suite bedroom and the roof terrace, decked out with more greenery and fairy lights, a firepit and plenty of seating – a perfect evening hideaway. Downstairs, the main terrace contained a pool, sunken hot tub and a jetty over the sea so guests could easily access the water and the small motorboat which came as standard with this villa.

'Is it safe?' Indi asked as she walked out onto the jetty and looked down into the clear turquoise water.

Mikhos stood watching her. 'It's just been built.'

'Not the jetty, the water access. There's no lifeguard after all.'

He nodded. 'This side of the island has a high coastal shelf, it means you would need to swim a good twenty metres before getting out of your depth. All guests have to sign a waiver and conditions are sent to them every morning advising on suitability for swimming or other sea activities.'

'So how much would a stay here set me back?'

Mikhos told her and Indi whistled.

'Plus flights and food, I suppose – it's not all inclusive?'

'No.'

'It's a lot for a week, but—'

'Not a week, a night.'

'A *night*?' Indi thought of herself as cosmopolitan. She'd been raised in Stoke Newington, lived in Islington, went on city breaks and stayed in boutique hotels, had eaten in some of London's most acclaimed restaurants, but right now she felt utterly parochial. 'People *pay* that?'

Mikhos grinned. 'I hope so. In fact, we are booked out until the end of the season, with bookings coming in for the next two years, and we haven't had a single review yet.'

Indi sat down on the jetty and dangled her feet in the water. 'In that case, I will definitely get the most out of my stay. I can't imagine I'll ever be in a position to come here as a paying customer.'

'Not even on your honeymoon?'

'Right now, that feels like a long way away.'

'Ah, I forgot. I'm sorry, Jade mentioned you had split up with your boyfriend. Was it recent?'

'A couple of weeks ago.'

'Very recent then. It must be hard, especially with your sister engaged.'

Indi lifted her chin defiantly, she was not going to play the victim here. 'It's probably for the best, it turned out we wanted different things.'

To her surprise, he came and sat down beside her, tall and solid and almost unnervingly masculine. 'What did you want?'

Indi bit her lip. She wasn't really the confiding-in-strangers type, she was barely the confiding-in-people-she-really-loved type. But there was something freeing about letting some of her feelings out, especially to someone who, after her holiday, she was unlikely to ever see again.

'I suppose just the usual things that people who have been together for four years think they are moving towards. I'm thirty next week and I always kind of assumed I'd be engaged by then. Planning a wedding, starting to think about wanting children. But Will decided that he didn't want any of that – he wanted fewer ties not more. The thing is, I didn't even see it coming. I thought he was about to propose, instead he was breaking up with me.' She looked down at her hands. 'I can't help wondering if maybe it *was* obvious but I chose not to see. I keep going over and over it, trying to see just where it went wrong, if I could have changed things, to work out if I even would want to. But what's the point? It's over, done. Here I am, single, while my little sister is engaged. The world is topsy-turvy.' She bit her lip, the unexpected intimacy of the conversation making her feel exposed, vulnerable. 'I don't know why I'm telling you all this. Sorry.' What *must* he think of her spilling out all her emotions like this? It might be a small island but somehow she would have to spend the next fortnight avoiding him, although after this it was equally likely Mikhos would do his best to avoid *her*!

'I was engaged once.'

That was unexpected. She turned to look at him, intrigued. 'What happened?'

'Like you, we wanted different things. It's no great tragedy, we were young – too young.' Indi swore she could see a flicker of hurt in his eyes, but before she was sure, it had gone.

'Is that why you are so against Nico and Jade getting married?'

'Among other things. Life can be hard here, they haven't been tested yet. I just don't see the need to rush. What about you? I take it your opposition to the engagement isn't because you think it should be you not her?'

'No!' She should be insulted by the suggestion, but she could see why he might think it. She had even considered it herself. 'Not at all. I want her to be happy. I love how confident she seems here, how much she is enjoying her job, that she seems to have found someone who respects her.'

'But?'

'Like I said, Nico's her first boyfriend. She's naïve in many ways.' Indi sighed. 'I don't know if she mentioned that our father died when she was only eight?'

Mikhos nodded. 'It's been mentioned. How old were you?'

'Sixteen.'

'I'm sorry. I know a little how it feels. I was twenty-four when I lost my father. There's never a good time.'

'No,' she agreed. 'There really isn't.' She reached out and touched his arm. 'I'm sorry for your loss as well.'

He just nodded and she carried on.

'Jade was injured in the accident that killed our father.' Indi blinked hard, guilt as always swallowing her whole when she remembered Jade, so small, so helpless, lying in hospital, her life hanging in the balance. 'She missed a lot of school due to needing operations and recuperation. Each time, friends would move on without her. She was pretty lonely as a result. That's why I am so worried that she has fallen so hard for Nico so quickly. She missed out on so many rites of passage. Including falling in love.'

'It must have been very hard.'

'It really was.' Indi had also seen her own friends drop away over the years, her life had been so different to theirs. She hadn't had a proper sixth form or a proper university experience, always rushing off to take Jade somewhere, to cook, to sort laundry, to manage the household. 'Don't get me wrong, I wouldn't want her to marry *anyone* at twenty-two, especially someone she's known for so short a time, but for her to take such a huge step so far from home terrifies me. What you said just now about needing to test a relationship? That's exactly it. What happens when happy ever after hits real obstacles and she's here alone without me?'

Mikhos' expression was inscrutable. 'You can't be responsible for her forever. Maybe it's time she stood on her own two feet.'

'I thought you were as anti this engagement as I am?'

'I think it's a terrible idea.'

'So what can we do?'

'We can tell them our concerns, but in the end we have to let them make their own mistakes. That's how we learn after all.'

He was speaking nothing but the truth, but there was nothing more painful than learning that way, and all her life Indi had done her best to shelter Jade from pain, her little sister had experienced too much too young. Standing back and doing nothing felt wrong somehow.

'What did you learn from your engagement?' Indi asked.

Mikhos got to his feet in one lithe movement. 'That, at the end of the day, you can only rely on yourself.'

Ouch. Indi reluctantly pulled her feet out of the water and stood up to stand beside him. 'Was it a bad break-up?'

His expression clouded. 'It was a long time ago.' At that moment, his phone rang. 'Excuse me, I need to take this. Can you find your own way back?' And with that, he was gone.

Indi stared out at the sea, mind whirling. What had just happened? Had she really just asked a man she had met less than twenty-four hours ago intrusively personal questions *and* opened up to him? She must be feeling more vulnerable than she realised.

It would be safer – and sensible – to keep her distance from Mikhos in future. Life was already complicated enough without adding a handsome millionaire into the mix. But as she made her way through the villa, she could hear Priya in the back of her mind. *A holiday romance is exactly what you need.*

Indi looked around guiltily as if she had spoken the words aloud. Mikhos was being hospitable, not romantic and the *last* thing she was interested in was romance. As soon as she got back to the villa, she was going to text Priya and tell her so.

Chapter Thirteen

Jade

'How was your massage?'

Jade sat on the edge of Indi's bed and watched her sister frown into the mirror. The spa package Indi had tried out was supposed to offer ultimate relaxation, but judging by Indi's tense expression, it hadn't worked as planned.

But, then again, her case *still* hadn't shown up, although the customer liaison team over in Naxos had been doing their best to track it down.

'Massage, facial, hot tub, pedicure, manicure and head rub after a one-to-one yoga relaxation session. It took most of the day – turns out self-care is quite time-consuming.' Indi started to flick through the clothes Jade and Aurelia had donated, pulling out a bronze outfit that was one of Aurelia's more conservative offerings. 'It was lovely, but it did seem indulgent, all those people there just for me.'

Jade laughed. 'That's kind of the point, though. It's *supposed* to be indulgent.'

'I know. I just wish I'd postponed until you can join me. Don't get me wrong, I'm pleased you're happy and busy, but I would rather have done it with you.'

Jade hoped she wasn't looking too guilty. She had had a valid reason to get out of the spa day, thanks to the trips she had organised for the Naxos booking office team over to the island, but she had been relieved rather than disappointed, knowing that her pregnancy made some of the treatments unwise. 'Me too.'

Maybe she *should* tell Indi about the baby now, she was almost eleven weeks after all, and she was noticing changes, her breasts were larger, even though her stomach was still flat. The nausea had eased though, thank goodness, as had the tiredness, physically at least. Emotionally she was still all at sea. She desperately wanted to confide in her sister about Nico's determination to ask Mikhos for the job Mikhos had offered him, learning the ropes with the idea of taking on a senior management role one day, about the house he was determined to build, the guilt she felt for the sacrifices he was making. But for the first time ever, she didn't know what to say to her sister, how to broach the subject.

Indi wiggled painfully into the bronze outfit. 'Is this a bit much?'

'Not at all, that colour suits you!'

It really did. The dull bronze brought out the chestnut in her hair, the warmth in her skin, the style showed off her curves. In fact, her sister looked fantastic even though the playsuit was as unlike Indi's usual style as an outfit could be.

'Aren't I too old for playsuits? I look like an overgrown toddler who hacked at her princess dress with her scissors.'

'Not even slightly. Honestly.'

'You don't think I'm a bit . . . exposed?' Indi tugged at the silky material.

'I would kill for a cleavage like that. I can't believe you got the height *and* the boobs, so unfair.'

'You got the non-frizzy hair and the killer metabolism, so I think we are even.' Indi made one more fruitless attempt to hoick the neckline up. 'I'll try the airline one more time before we go down.'

'I think you might need to reconcile yourself to your case not showing up.'

'I can't carry on borrowing clothes.' Indi looked horrified at the thought.

'No, but you could head over to Naxos tomorrow or the day after. Then you can at least do some shopping for essentials.'

'That's a good plan.' Indi visibly relaxed. 'Yes, I'll do that. Thanks, Jade.'

'Talking of plans, it's a week until your birthday and it's a special one.' Jade knew that Indi had probably planned a very different birthday, had hoped for a surprise party to rival the one she had thrown Will last year. Had hoped for a proposal. It was up to Jade to make it up to her. The timing wasn't great, with Indi's birthday slap bang in the middle of the launch week, but she was sure she could manage something special. 'What do you want to do?'

'You know, I don't want to make a big deal of it.'

Jade narrowed her eyes and scrutinised her sister. Indi was the worst person to plan a surprise for because she had usually made her own plans long before any normal person got organised, and she loved birthdays. An occasion as important as her thirtieth should have its own Trello board with tasks assigned and colour-coded lists shared with her family and friends, not be dismissed as no big deal. Bloody Will. He was not ruining this.

'A Spice Girls' karaoke evening? Themed dinner – every dish a different spice?' Jade smiled hopefully at her sister, but Indi didn't reciprocate.

'Honestly, I just want to spend time with you, I've missed you, Jade-baba.'

'I've missed you too. I am so happy you are here.' It was true but Jade was starting to buckle under the guilt of keeping secrets from her sister. 'Come on, let's go down for dinner.' But as she followed her sister out of the room, Jade vowed that she would make up for all the secrecy, starting with making Indi's birthday special no matter what she said.

Jade and Indi were the last ones down and Jade cast an anxious glance at Nico. She had asked him to hold off talking to Mikhos about the job until they had had an opportunity to discuss it properly. It didn't help that there was still a coolness between the cousins, the argument they had had about the engagement still not resolved. That was down to her as well. Maybe she was as naïve as her sister and Mikhos thought, she hadn't expected falling in love and making a new life together to be so complicated.

She poured herself a glass of elderflower cordial and took a glass of wine over to her sister, who accepted it with a smile. Luckily, no one seemed to think it odd that Jade was sticking to soft drinks. She wasn't much of a drinker anyway and her excuse that she wanted to keep a clear head as she was so busy was plausible enough.

'The staff enjoyed their visit here today,' Mikhos said as he sauntered towards them. 'That was a good idea, thank you for thinking of it and organising it, Jade.'

'You're welcome.' She could feel her cheeks warming at the praise. 'I think they got a lot out of it.'

'Nico, are you going over to Naxos at any point tomorrow or Friday?' Indi asked. 'Can I get a lift if so? I think I need to accept that the chance of my suitcase turning up is low to zero and, kind as Aurelia and Jade have been, I can't keep borrowing their clothes.' She tugged at the playsuit, clearly self-conscious.

'But it is no problem, you are very welcome to use anything of mine,' Aurelia said warmly.

Jade suppressed a smile. The bronze playsuit was probably one of Aurelia's more conservative offerings, and on the shorter, slimmer woman, it had been a very different garment. Short, yes. But not *as* short as when it was stretched over Indi's longer torso, the low neckline revealing, but not *that* revealing. No wonder Mikhos was doing his best not to look at Indi.

Jade's eyes narrowed. He really *was* trying not to look at Indi, unnaturally trying even. She hadn't really seen Mikhos and Indi interact at all, but she knew they had spent a lot of Monday together.

'You look magnificent,' Mikhos said unexpectedly. Aha! Proof he *had* been looking!

Everyone went quiet and stared at a now fiery Indi, the silence stretching to the point of awkwardness. Indi's cheeks reddened even more.

'You do,' Jade said hurriedly, aware how embarrassed her sister was. She was equally intrigued by Mikhos' comment, she had never heard him compliment anyone on their looks before, certainly not with that degree of intensity. 'You have the height to pull anything off. You suit that style much better than your usual going-out clothes.' Jade would have said that Indi dressed like a fifty-something woman, only their mother fell into that category and she was infinitely more stylish than either of her daughters.

'I agree, you look beautiful,' Nico said with that good-humoured smile Jade loved more than his flirtatious one. Flirting was fun, but good humour infinitely more important in a husband. 'But, of course, I can take you to Naxos if you wish. I'm busy tomorrow morning but might be able to take you after lunch. If that doesn't work, then how about Friday?'

'I'm heading over to Naxos tomorrow morning,' Mikhos said. 'I need to go into the office. I'll take you if you want to spend some time there.'

'Thank you.' Indi couldn't have sounded more doubtful if she had tried. 'That's really kind.'

It *was* very kind of Mikhos. Suspiciously kind. What was going on?

'Nico, I do need you to head over later tomorrow, though. Aurelia needs dropping off in Naxos Town mid-afternoon and there's a pick-up to do just after,' Mikhos continued. 'I've hired a freelance publicist to help with the launch next week and they arrive tomorrow. It would be good for them to get the lie of the land over the weekend.'

Jade looked up in surprise. 'A publicist? But isn't that Aurelia's job?'

'I'm sorry, Jade, I have been meaning to let you know, but it all happened so fast and you have been busy today,' Aurelia said apologetically. 'I have to go to Athens and I don't know if I will make it back by Monday. I called in a favour and I have managed to find someone to help out, but I appreciate it's not ideal.'

'But all the influencers are *your* contacts, Aurelia. You have the schedule and you picked them. Can we manage without you, even with a temporary publicist?' Jade couldn't believe Mikhos looked so laid-back, Aurelia's expertise was a pivotal part of his launch plans.

Aurelia smiled. 'It's all in hand. I have worked with this publicist before and I have complete faith in her and, with your support, Jade, I know all will be fine. After all, you know the island better than almost anyone.'

'It just means shifting some responsibilities around,' Mikhos said. 'The main office can pick up any booking queries and I'll bring someone over from there to help in guest services to free you up. As Aurelia says, it's not ideal, but it can't be helped.'

Jade's pulse began to race. 'Free *me* up?'

'Yes. You'll need to manage the publicist and the influencers. Make sure everyone is in the right place at the right time, that kind of thing. That's not a problem, is it?'

Jade swallowed. On the one hand this was exactly the opportunity she had been waiting for. The two trips for the Naxos staff she had organised had been a huge success, now here she was, being given an enhanced role, more responsibility. But on the other hand, she liked being *behind* the scenes and Aurelia was very much up front and visible.

But she couldn't turn such an opportunity down. 'Of course not,' she said hurriedly. 'Obviously I will do whatever is needed, but I don't know anything about social media.' Jade worked hard to keep the panic out of her voice, to sound professional, but she was acutely aware of Indi's concerned gaze fixed on her. Frustration warred with anxiety. She didn't need Indi's concern, not here in her workplace. But then again, Indi knew Jade better than anyone in the world. Knew how she hated being the centre of attention. With Aurelia holding court, nobody would ever have noticed Jade at her side. But this was her chance to prove herself indispensable. Taking a deep breath, she picked up her glass. 'What will you need me to do?'

Influencing was far outside Jade's experience and understanding – she didn't even *have* social media, possibly the only twenty-two-year-old in the western world to not have even one account. But the bullying she had received in her early teens had shown her that spaces that relied on physical perfection and popularity were no place for her.

'My job is to be a mixture of confidante, counsellor and sergeant,' Aurelia said. 'But my replacement will be able to take on a lot of that, she's very experienced. You need to do two things: make sure the guests enjoy themselves and make sure they follow the itinerary. They are here to work after all, but some need cajoling into remembering that. You already helped me plan the activities and events, so you know those inside out. You'll be liaising with the event staff and the activity leads, the bar and restaurant, that kind of thing. You just concentrate on the schedule going to plan and let my replacement worry about the social media side.'

Jade nodded warily. That didn't sound *too* different from her work on the yacht, the work she expected to do as guest liaison lead once the resort opened properly.

'I was planning a welcome meeting the day they arrive, so you'll need to run that, make sure they know who you are, that the itinerary is clear, that kind of thing. Then, of course, you'll need to socialise with them, be at the Tuesday night party, the Wednesday dinner, join in on some of the activities. It should be a lot of fun.' Aurelia and Jade clearly had very different ideas of what constituted fun.

'How large a group?' Jade carefully put her glass down, proud that her voice didn't waver, that the only person with any idea how much she was freaking out inside was Indi.

'We're expecting six couples, who get a villa to themselves, and twenty-eight individuals, two to a villa. So that's forty in total. There should be a real buzz, they are a lively lot.'

Jade swallowed. That meant standing up before forty people, eighty eyes all fixed on her. Eighty eyes belonging to influencers. To the kind of people who spent their lives in front of the camera, not hiding from it. The kind of people who enjoyed the spotlight.

The kind of people who intimidated the hell out of her.

'We have a mix of Instagram stars, TikTok stars, reality TV stars and YouTubers, so a real mix,' Aurelia continued, reeling off a list of names that meant absolutely nothing to Jade but who were obviously a big deal.

'Great!' It sounded like utter hell.

'Call me any time if you need anything,' Aurelia told her and all Jade could do was nod.

Nico slipped an arm around her waist. 'You don't need to worry, Aurelia, Jade will be brilliant.'

Indi still looked troubled and Jade knew exactly what she was thinking. She was wondering how a girl who had deleted her Instagram at thirteen because she felt so inadequate, a girl who once got so anxious before a school presentation she had fainted, would be able to stand up in front of a gathering of social media stars and hold a briefing.

'I can help,' she said.

'Don't be silly, Indi, you're here on holiday.' Jade was aware of mixed emotions in her instant refusal. Of course she wanted her sister to have a complete break, but she also didn't want her sister taking over what was her job and she knew Indi too well to think there was any way that wouldn't happen. Trying out the spa and taking out a jet ski was one thing, getting involved in Jade's workplace was quite another. She liked that Agios Iohannis was hers, that her role here had been forged by her own hard work, not helped along by her sister. She didn't want any blurred lines even though – especially – Indi would undoubtedly excel at whatever role she was given.

'Yes, and I have done three whole days of relaxation and I am done. I am much happier being busy, honestly. I could pick up some of your work. Help with the influencers, whatever is needed.'

Take over because you are not capable, Jade mentally translated.

'You don't know the software or our systems, or the product. It's really nice of you, Indi, but you might end up causing more work than helping.' Jade tried to keep her voice light, not to show how irritated she was, to ignore the hurt in Indi's eyes.

'I work in project management, it's my job to pick things up quickly. Honestly, put me to work if you can use me.'

'That might be helpful,' Mikhos said, to Jade's frustration. 'Let's talk in Naxos tomorrow. It's going to be a busy week, if you do have skills we can use, it would be silly not to take advantage.'

'Great. Don't worry, Jade. I know you're in charge. I won't step on your toes, I promise!'

Jade tried to smile, but she was far from convinced. Indi might think she was capable of staying in the background, but the chances of her staying there were slim. Between her, the unknown publicist and the host of influencers, the next week was going to be quite the challenge. A challenge Jade had to smash to help build a future for her family. No pressure at all.

Chapter Fourteen

Indi

'Here she is, Naxos.'

Indi tried to imagine taking anyone – Mikhos – to Stoke Newington and replicating that centuries-old pride in her voice. It just went to show what a young upstart London was. A few fields, maybe a trading station, while this island had once been the home of a god and his wife.

She leaned on the boat's bow, looking around her. How could it be just four days since she'd last been in Naxos? It felt like weeks, months.

Mikhos had brought her across from the island on a smaller, speedier boat than the one in which she had arrived, which meant she couldn't hide down in a cabin or the other side of the deck but had had to remain by his side at the tiller, the sea breeze whipping her curls into a frenzy worthy of Medusa herself, the salt spraying her skin. He hadn't tried to make conversation on the journey, one hand on the tiller, often on the phone, barking out comments in imperious Greek, looking very much as his ancestors must have when they set sail across these seas. It was surprisingly – and alarmingly – sexy.

She did her best to tell herself she was impervious to Mikhos' charm, but she was always aware of him, every gesture, the twisted, impatient smile, the sudden, unexpected softening of tone which never failed to make the hairs at the back of her neck prickle, her body tighten.

'So? What do you think?'

'She's beautiful.' No lie needed. Naxos was a craggy island touched with green and blue, tamed but enhanced by the white square dwellings, roads twisting around its hills and mountains, not marching across. The sun bounced off the sea, the buildings, the cobbles, the air salt-fresh. No wonder Jade wanted to make her life here. It was idyllic. 'Why didn't I leave from here the other day?'

'Agios Iohannis is the other side of the island – depending on currents, it can be quicker to moor there and make the journey across by car. It can also be a lot choppier this side.'

Indi had a flashback to the sickbags handed out on the ferry and shuddered as Mikhos made a final adjustment to the rope and nodded at the jetty.

'Ready to shop?'

'Give me a couple of minutes? I just need to . . .' She gestured at her hair, quickly pulled back into a knot once she'd realised the strength of the wind, but too late to prevent the damage.

'Take as long as you need.'

That was unexpected, Will used to huff impatiently, then stride up and down making it clear she was holding them up, whereas if Mikhos was impatient, he didn't show it, instead walking around the boat tightening knots, rubbing down paintwork, tidying, every movement deliberate and measured and capable. He seemed more relaxed here than he did on the island, less formidable, humming under his breath, occasionally breaking out into a whistle. It was interesting to see him be so unguarded. Indi was almost sorry when she had tugged the knots out of her curls and repaired her make-up and the momentary lull ended. It was only as she pulled her hair back into a loose ponytail that she realised he was as aware of her as she was of him, his body angled towards her, stopping the instant she returned the borrowed cosmetics and comb to her (borrowed) bag.

Indi lifted a hand to an escaping curl. 'My hair is crazy, it has a mind of its own. No wonder Mum gets Jade to model as Helen and I get Medusa.'

'Medusa was famed for her beauty before Athene cursed her. And even then, it was only her hair that changed. Your hair is like autumn.'

He half lifted one hand as if he were going to touch her before dropping it. Indi realised she had stopped breathing, anticipation clenching her entire body.

When was the last time her whole body had hummed with awareness of another human being, of a man? When was the last time someone had commented that she was beautiful? She couldn't actually remember.

Maybe there had been more wrong in her relationship with Will than different goals and she had just never noticed. It was a lowering thought.

Quickly, she grabbed her bag and stepped off the boat. 'It's kind of you to bring me today. Let me know when you need me to be ready to return. It won't take me long to grab a few things.'

'Don't worry. I like to check in with my hotels here in person weekly and the main office more often if I can.'

'Are you usually based here?'

He nodded. 'Naxos is my home, but I've been away a lot recently, mainly getting Agios Iohannis ready for launch of course, but also the Santorini and Mykonos hotels are a lot newer and need more input.'

'It's hard work being a multi-island hotel tycoon then?'

Mikhos looked a little surprised by the description, then laughed. 'Owning six hotels is a lot, true, but owning them at four different locations separated by sea does add an extra complexity to logistics. Luckily, I have built a dedicated team. Anyway, if you're up for a trip around Naxos after lunch, then I plan to visit the other two hotels I own here. You'd be very welcome to join me.'

'I'd love that, thank you.' She fell into step beside him. 'Will you stay on Agios Iohannis once the resort is fully open?'

'Not full-time, I'll split my time between here, the island and Mykonos. It doesn't do to be too settled in my business. I need to talk to my customers, keep an eye on my competitors, plan for the future.'

She couldn't imagine him settled, with neighbours and friends and an ordinary office. He was suited to the island, lord of all he surveyed.

'Right,' he added. 'This way.'

Indi had been too tired to take in much of Naxos Town, or *Chora*, as Mikhos called it, when she'd arrived on the ferry, and she looked about now with interest. The town was a cluster of white buildings and winding streets climbing up the hills framing the harbour, a promontory leading out into the sea ending up at a ruin reminiscent of a doorway.

Indi accompanied Mikhos as he walked with the utter confidence of someone who had trodden these paths thousands of times before, along the jetty towards the main street that ran along the seafront. He was clearly well known here, holding up his hand in acknowledgement, shouting out greetings and ripostes.

The harbour was home to all manner of boats, from expensive-looking yachts to smaller fishing vessels. At one end, docked together, were three boats all painted in the navy, gold and white Angelos livery. A reminder that around here Mikhos was a big deal indeed.

Finally they reached the street. It was mid-morning but already busy, a ferry further along the harbour disgorging day trippers, backpackers and holidaymakers, the pavement cafes filled with people enjoying late breakfasts or coffee breaks. There were, Indi was relieved to see, plenty of shops, both here on the main street and in the cobbled alleyways enticingly leading up into the old town. She should be able to put a suitable wardrobe together pretty quickly. It would be a relief to wear clothes that actually fit. Today, she was wearing Aurelia's loosest-fitting outfit – a yellow maxi dress that still exposed more side boob than Indi was comfortable with anyone seeing. Although to be fair, as far as Indi was concerned any glimpse of side boob was too much. She'd put one of Jade's yoga bras under the dress, it looked a little odd, but at least it was better than flashing the whole island. Side boob was a very different thing when gravity and a DD size were involved. Something Aurelia didn't have to worry about.

Speaking of . . . 'When's Aurelia actually leaving?'

'She's booked on a ferry this evening. I wanted her to have the morning with your sister to hand over her notes and make sure she is ready to take on her extra responsibilities,' he added, steering her towards a small cafe filled with locals rather than tourists – always a good sign. 'This place does the best coffee on Naxos if you want refreshments before you shop.'

Conversation paused for a few moments as Mikhos exchanged greetings with the owner, a woman in her sixties who embraced him enthusiastically before seating them at a small, shaded table with a view of the harbour and the ruin sat in the middle of the sea, connected to the island by a causeway filled with tourists walking to and from the islet.

Mikhos followed her gaze. 'The Portara. It's worth a visit at sunset.' He paused. 'It's considered romantic.'

Indi could feel her cheeks start to burn and hastily searched for a way to turn the conversation away from romance. 'When was it built?'

'Sixth century BC. Some say the temple was for Apollo, others Dionysus.'

'It seems incredible that we are sitting here looking at something two and a half thousand years old. My mother would be all over this place.' Not just the island. One look at Mikhos and Tabita would be consulting her muse. Who would she want him to model for? Indi studied him discreetly, the strong jaw, broad shoulders, keen eyes. Paris? No, Achilles or Ares. Someone warrior-like anyway . . . She quickly pushed the thought away as the cafe owner returned bearing two small cups of thick dark coffee topped with foam, setting them down along with a bowl of sugar and a small jug of milk.

'Greek coffee is meant to be drunk black and sweetened to taste,' Mikhos said, watching her. 'But it can be a bit intense for foreigners.'

Indi wanted to retort that she could handle it, thank you very much, but a cautious sniff told her that she would be very glad of the milk and she added it almost defiantly, aware that somehow he knew exactly what she was thinking.

'It's beautiful here, just sitting and watching the world go by,' she said with a small sigh. 'I can see why Jade has fallen in love with it.' She looked across at Mikhos. 'Do you really think she's ready for the extra responsibility you've given her? In fact, I was wondering why, under the circumstances, you have given her a job at all? Without a job, a place to stay, surely she'd have to come home.'

His gaze sharpened. 'Is that what you would do?'

'I certainly wouldn't make it so easy for her and Nico to be together.'

Mikhos took a sip of his coffee. 'I think maybe you underestimate her. Your sister has a natural flair for customer service, she's a hard worker and has a genuine love for the island. It would be foolish of me to lose her because I disapprove of her relationship. And what would sacking her do to my relationship with Nico? I have six hotels now, I am actively looking for more, I want my cousin working *with* me, part of my business, not feeling that I have interfered in his life. No one wants starstruck lovers feeling hard done by, especially not when I have so much at stake. Much better to give them a dose of reality, a look at their future. Jade will be working every hour, Nico will barely be there, soon he'll be doing sunrise-to-sunset trips seven days a week. Let's see how romantic she finds the reality of life in Greece when she's had five hours' sleep and she has to be on her feet smiling all day and never has the same time off as her fiancé. If by the end of the summer they are still together, then maybe we need to consider they do know what they are doing.'

'Clever,' Indi acknowledged.

'Plus, with Aurelia not here, I need someone who knows the island intimately. Jade is that person. The consultant Aurelia has recommended won't be able to get the degree of knowledge needed in the time, I need both skill sets.'

'That makes sense. It's just . . .' Indi paused, biting her lip. She didn't want to be disloyal to her sister, but that old need to protect her was too strong. 'It's just she's shy, probably shyer than you know. Self-conscious. I don't know how she'll be, in a role where she is having to speak in front of a crowd, lead a group.'

Mikhos leaned back. 'Do you always do this?'

'Do what?'

'Put all your energies into worrying about your sister? I get it, I love Nico more like a brother than a cousin, would give anything for him to accept the role I have offered him in my company, want him to be happy, but he is his own man. What about you, India Drewe? Who worries about you?'

'I can take care of myself.' But she sounded less confident than usual. Clearly the events of the last few weeks had shaken her more than she liked.

'That's not what I asked.'

Indi could feel herself flush and she stared out of the window, not sure how to reply. 'No one, I suppose. It's been my role to take care of my family for the last fourteen years.'

'And you're fine with that?'

'I have to be.' There was no point wishing life was different, all she could do was deal with the cards she had been dealt.

'None of us *have* to be anything.' His gaze was keen, too keen – she felt like he could see right inside her, behind the confident screen she wore like armour. It was terrifying, like being undressed in front of strangers.

And that was a scenario she wished she hadn't thought of, not where Mikhos was concerned. She was far too aware of him as it was.

'Who worries about you, Mikhos Angelos?' she quickly countered and he laughed.

'My mother and my aunt, and that's quite enough for any man! Come on, let me show you where the office is before you go shopping. If you are going to help out over the next few days, then you will need a login and a bit of basic training on the database. But there's no pressure, you are at complete liberty to change your mind and spend the next week lying on a sunbed watching us run around.'

'Absolutely not.' This was much safer, work was comfortable, easy, something she could talk about for hours. But as they left the cafe, she couldn't help but think of the concern, the kindness in his eyes when he asked her *What about you, India Drewe? Who worries about you?* and part of her wished she had had an answer. That there was someone she could unload her worries on.

But there was only her, and that was the way it was, the way it had always been.

Chapter Fifteen

Jade

Thursday 8 June

'I can do this,' Jade told herself with as much confidence as she could muster. 'I can do anything I am needed to do.'

Say it until you mean it, Indi had always told her. It had never actually worked before, but this time Jade was determined it would. She was a different Jade Drewe to the quiet teen always on the periphery, the girl who couldn't find her place in life. She had a job she loved, a man she loved and soon she would be a mother. She couldn't allow fear to hold her back, not anymore.

She took a deep breath and smiled at Aurelia, who was sitting opposite her, a huge folder open on the table between them. She almost felt sorry for the incoming influencers. It was clear there was no such thing as a free holiday; the timetable Aurelia had put together would put a military bootcamp to shame. Jade just wished she wasn't the one enforcing it. Hopefully the publicist Aurelia had recommended would be up to speed quickly and Jade could return to her aide-de-camp duties and not stay as acting sergeant major!

It had already taken a couple of hours to go through all the details. 'Remember, everything you need to know is in here.' Aurelia tapped the folder. 'Don't lose it and don't let *anyone* else see it.' For once, the famously laid-back woman looked decidedly on edge. 'There are biographies of all forty influencers in here and I do not want to be sued for libel . . .'

Jade eyed the folder, her curiosity piqued. Sounded like there was some good stuff in it.

'Timetables for every day, emergency numbers, tips for how to get them to behave . . .' Aurelia looked at Jade. 'You will be absolutely fine, I have total faith in you. You were a teacher, weren't you?'

'Teaching assistant.' Jade could hear a quaver in her voice. 'For the nursery.'

'It's the same idea. Remember not to show fear.'

'Isn't that animals?'

But Aurelia had already moved onto the next item in her exhaustive briefing and Jade didn't have time to dwell on the potential consequences if she did end up showing fear. Forced hair extensions? A permanent pout? Cursed to hashtag her every move forever?

'You're not on social media?' Aurelia asked once they had come to the end of the biographies and Jade had been quizzed on every name. Twice.

'No,' Jade admitted humbly. 'It's not really my thing.'

Aurelia's cat-like eyes narrowed. 'It *needs* to be your thing. You need to know the difference between Instagram and TikTok, understand each influencer's platform, their style. And be prepared to be featured yourself.' She looked Jade over, not in judgement but still very thoroughly. 'You need to stand taller, shoulders back, chest out. What's your best angle?'

'My best *what*?'

'Your selfie side?'

'I . . .'

Aurelia's gaze softened. 'Jade, you are twenty-two. How do you not know your selfie side?'

'Because I'm not one for taking selfies. I'm a more live-in-the-moment girl.' It was an effort to stop herself from reaching down to touch the scar on her thigh but with a shiver of humiliation Jade saw Aurelia clock the instinctive movement and check whatever she was going to say.

'Come with me,' she said instead. 'We have time for a quick lesson. Then I want you to practise and send me your efforts, OK? You are going to be brilliant, just be your normal sweet self. They will love you.'

'Thank you.' But as Jade got up and followed Aurelia to the pool for her lesson, she couldn't help wishing that she had the same confidence in her abilities as Aurelia did. No matter, she vowed, whatever happened she was not going to let the older woman – or herself – down.

If Nico was the type to show impatience, he would have been pacing up and down the deck firing off a series of messages demanding to know where the hell they were when the two women finally turned up at the jetty. Aurelia's mountain of bags had already been delivered and stowed safely, although with characteristic thoughtfulness, she had pulled a few outfits out and put them aside for Indi. 'She is probably just covering the basics,' she explained as she handed them over to Jade. 'There are some more dressy things here in case she wants to go clubbing or to a party, some bikinis, things like that.'

Indi partying or wearing a teeny bikini sounded unlikely, but Jade thanked her and took them anyway.

'And these are for you.'

These was a bag filled with the shimmering highlighters, bronzers and several other powders and creams that were apparently essential for a successful candid shot around the pool. Also, to Jade's surprise, the bag included a couple of barely there bikinis, beach wraps with more holes than fabric, a shimmering silvery slip of material that was possibly a dress, the shortest shorts Jade had ever seen and some tiny tops.

'I love your unique style.' Aurelia nodded at the flowing maxi skirt, the vest top cut high on Jade's back and covering her midriff, every scar hidden. 'But you may find yourself wanting to . . .' she paused. 'To experiment. You're a beautiful girl, Jade. You don't need to hide away.'

Startled, Jade met her kind gaze. Of course, Aurelia knew exactly what Jade was hiding away. The swim shorts she preferred didn't completely cover her thigh, the matching top rode up to show the line that ran from her ribs to her stomach, the water would slick her hair back to reveal the scars on her forehead usually concealed by her fringe. After a month sharing the same villa, Aurelia had seen all that Jade tried to hide, although, with her usual kind tactfulness, she had never once asked her about them or allowed her gaze to linger with any curiosity.

'That's very kind, I—'

'You don't have to thank me or promise you'll wear them. They're there if you want them. You'll be fine, Jade. I have every confidence in you.'

'Thank you.' Jade hugged the older woman, her eyes filling as she did so. Aurelia's kindness was understated, almost offhand, but very real. 'Don't stay away too long.'

'Take care of yourself.' Aurelia paused. 'And believe in yourself, I do.'

Jade felt curiously bereft as she waved the boat off. She made friends slowly, painfully, awkward and tongue-tied at first. It wasn't until she saw Aurelia disappear over the horizon that she realised just how much she had grown to like her.

'OK,' she said out loud, needing to fill the silence. 'What now?' After a look at her list, Jade headed to the restaurant, to help the newly arrived barman with his final preparations.

She soon forget her worries about the days ahead as she helped place the bottles onto the shelves, laughing at the barman's attempts to teach her to flirt in Greek as she helped him stock the cupboards with the glasses.

'Try that one on Nico.' He grinned after saying something that sounded very suggestive and Jade felt herself blush.

'Not without running it through Google Translate first,' she retorted and he shook his head.

'Coward!'

The evening was drawing in by the time she'd finished and she stood back, full of pride as she took in the whole effect. The glade where the bar was situated was fairy-tale perfection, with its hidden nooks of cosy tables for two, private enough for the most romantic of honeymooners, while the sofas in the middle of the room invited more sociable types. The stage at one end was ready for a band or other entertainment, the lanterns and fairy lights providing the most Instagrammable of backdrops.

Talking of which. Was Aurelia right? Was it time to stop hiding and set up her own account?

She held her phone up, selected her camera and zoomed out as far as she could to get the full effect, but as she did so, Jade realised the sky had darkened, the glade only visible thanks to the newly hung lamps and lights.

It's only six, she realised, aware for the first time of the chill in the air, that outside her sheltered space, the wind was beginning to whistle through the trees and whip the waves up into a white-topped frenzy. *I think there's a storm coming and Mikhos and Nico aren't on the island. Nor is Aurelia. Which leaves me the most senior person here.*

For a moment, Jade was overwhelmed by sheer panic, standing still as the wind intensified, but she forced herself to move, pulling out her radio to send the alarm to the groundspeople and other staff. Every villa would need to be checked to ensure all windows were closed, outside cushions brought in, pools covered and furniture stored safely. Jade had experienced one storm since coming here and it had been intense.

In addition, all the water equipment had to be checked and the bar furniture put inside, the roof and doors closed. Luckily, some of the staff had already anticipated the commands and within minutes the island was a flurry of activity.

It didn't take long for the first spots of rain to start splashing down, the wind whipping up stronger than ever. Neither boat had returned and, pulling one of the restaurant throws around her to ward against the unaccustomed chill, Jade walked to the jetty and peered out at the blackened horizon, at the tossing waves, anxiety twisting her stomach – she'd expected both boats back long before now.

'I hope they're not out there,' she whispered, jumping as a flash of lightning snaked down from the sky to the sea, followed far too quickly by a roar of thunder.

Jade turned and fled up the hill, the rain stronger now, soaking through the throw to her dress, right through to her bra, her hair soaking, fumbling for her radio as she ran.

'Has anyone heard from Naxos?' she demanded as she pressed the call button with slippery fingers that didn't seem to want to co-operate, not sure whether the negative she'd received was reassuring or not. Surely if they were at sea and in trouble, they'd have radioed for help? She shivered, she couldn't think of Nico or Indi and Mikhos out there at the mercy of the storm-tossed sea.

It seemed to take forever to get back to the villa, the dark, wind and rain increasing with every step, the howl of the wind deafening her, its strength making her stagger with its force. Some island paradise right now. The part of her brain that wasn't filled with worry for her sister and for Nico couldn't help picturing the impending arrival of the influencers, their faces as they saw the sea of mud churning under her feet, the trees bent double, the sun blotted out by angry dark clouds. Hashtag Hades.

Finally she made it back. The villa felt preternaturally silent, even though the island now boasted a full complement of staff. She'd been dreading the day the luxurious villa she'd called home for the last few months became a bustling place of work, every room filled. Now she was glad she wasn't alone. When she reached the huge kitchen, it was filled with staff sat around the table, while Demeter, unflappable as ever, was cooking up the kind of hearty stew an evening like this demanded.

Jade spoke no Greek, but there was no mistaking the clucking sounds of concern as she dripped her way into the kitchen. A large towel was wrapped around her shoulders, while one of the maids mopped up the watery trail she had left behind her like a real-life Niobe, waving aside her apologies. The towel was replaced with a blanket and she was pushed into a comfortable chair, a hot tea by her side, a hunk of bread and a pot of a delicious garlicky yogurt dip set in front of her, although her stomach was tight with anxiety, her appetite killed by worry.

Her phone had no signal, not surprising, it could be temperamental in this corner of the island on the clearest of days, and she had no idea how to use the main radio, the one that connected back with Naxos. 'Nico? Mikhos?' she asked.

To her relief, Demeter smiled reassuringly. 'Naxos,' was all she said, but it was enough.

Jade checked her phone again and, despite the lack of signal, sent a message to both her sister and her fiancé, hoping that at some point they would be delivered. She picked up her tea and sat back, relief almost overwhelming her. Maybe this wasn't such a bad thing, overall. Hopefully Nico had met up with Indi and Mikhos and if they were marooned together, then this could be the perfect time for Indi and Nico to get to know each other. So far there had been little opportunity for her sister and her fiancé to spend any real time together. Who knew, they might return tomorrow the best of friends, with Indi blessing their engagement.

It wasn't until much later that Jade remembered the new publicist that Nico had been sent to pick up. It wasn't much of a welcome for them. Whoever they were.

Chapter Sixteen

Indi

Thursday 8 June

Indi checked her phone again, trying to dampen down her anxiety when she realised there was still no response to the several messages she had sent her sister. The island was so small and the storm so brutal and Jade would be in the heart of it, without Indi by her side.

Mikhos had fulfilled his promise to take Indi on a quick tour of Naxos as he checked in with his hotels in person. They had just reached the third, right on the other end of the island, when the storm warning had come in, an expected squall strengthening, causing the cancellation of ferry services and the early return to harbour of all the pleasure cruises and day trips catering to tourists, as well as those fishing boats still out at sea. It had still come as a shock, to see how quickly the blue sky had turned black, the intensity of the wind and rain. It had been a far worse shock to realise there was no way to return to Jade, that her only option was to wait out the storm at the hotel.

Mikhos returned to the table, two pints of the local beer in his hands, smiling reassuringly as he set one down before her. 'Agios Iohannis has withstood many storms, Indi. Don't worry. Jade will be quite safe. The phones are down, that's all.'

'I know.' And she did, intellectually. She just wouldn't feel it until she saw her sister with her own two eyes. 'I worry about her, that's all.'

Indi looked out at the swirling rain, the trees bent double by the wind, and shivered. Mikhos had told her that ninety-five per cent of the time the weather in these islands was glorious. But the other five per cent was dangerous in ways that felt alien to city-bred Indi: flash floods, wild fires, earthquakes. Storms like this could have tragic consequences to those that ignored them, far safer to stay put.

'Now, *that* we've established.' There was a teasing tone to Mikhos' voice, but he didn't sound sarcastic or annoyed, as Will increasingly had over the last year.

Indi stiffened. Where had *that* thought come from? Will had understood her unique circumstances, he hadn't begrudged all the time and energy she'd devoted to her sister, her mother, had he?

No, not at first, but now she was looking for it, there had been a pattern of snippy comments and frustration in recent months when she had cancelled plans or refused invitations. Not constant, not enough to warn her he was no longer happy, but there nonetheless.

'Honestly, she will be fine. The villa is built to withstand all weather and Demeter and Georgios are very experienced.'

'I know. Sorry.' Indi tried for a smile. 'I'm not being good company, am I? I will do better.'

'The storm won't last long,' Mikhos reassured. 'But I think we need to be prepared to stay here for the night. Will that be a problem?'

'No, of course not. I'm just grateful that we were already safely here and not sheltering in the car on the side of the road. Besides, most people pay a fortune to stay here. It would be silly of me to complain about an unexpected night in a five-star hotel.'

His mouth quirked into one of his disturbingly sexy smiles.

Sexy? She shouldn't be thinking such things, she shouldn't even be *noticing* them. She was in mourning for her relationship. For what might have been.

In mourning, not dead. She could hear Priya so clearly, it was like she was right there. *You know what they say about horses and getting back on, don't you?*

Shut up, Priya.

To her relief, Mikhos interrupted her imaginary conversation before it developed into a full-blown argument. 'I'm glad you approve, this is my favourite of all my hotels.'

'I can see why.' She seized the nice safe topic eagerly. 'Your other hotels here on Naxos are gorgeous, there's no denying that, but they are like really expensive chocolate or a really ripe cheese with truffle. Amazing in small doses, but maybe a little rich for every day, more of a special treat. Which is what they are, I suppose.' What on *earth* was she babbling on about? *Shut up, Indi!*

The amusement in his eyes deepened. 'Interesting analogy. No one has ever compared my hotels to cheese before. What kind is this hotel?'

Indi cringed. What had made her pull *that* simile out of her head and even worse share it? But she'd started and she couldn't see any way out of finishing.

'Well.' She considered the question. 'Actually, I would say it's more like a perfect loaf of bread. It's the kind of place you walk into and instantly feel like you're at home. Only a home that's better designed and infinitely more comfortable than anything you could actually own. The kind of place that makes you think you want to quit your job and run a taverna on a small island.'

Indi stopped, a little shocked by the words and sentiment. She'd *never* been the type to dream of leaving London for a simpler life in the sun, this was the kind of talk Tabitha indulged in, not Indi.

But then, neither had she walked into a place and so immediately felt like she belonged.

It was clear that Mikhos specialised in boutique indulgence. Obviously Agios Iohannis was the last word in luxury, but so were his other hotels here on Naxos. Take the first she had visited, home to his company offices, as well as a five-star resort, set in an idyllic spot on the edge of Naxos Town, right by the water. It was stunning, a complex of luxury apartments ranging from airy studios to two-storey two-bedroom apartments, all with swim-up access to the amazing feature pool at the heart of the resort. The bar area was as achingly cool as the clientele, the chef cutting-edge and the cocktails outrageously priced, even to her London eyes. The kind of place she would never consider staying in, not rich enough, not hip enough, far too diffident to treat herself to such luxury.

In contrast, the hotel they were stranded in felt more traditional, a stone-built construction at the far end of the island, almost on the beach. It wasn't as overtly luxurious as the villas on the island, nor as obviously destination holiday as its sister hotels here on Naxos, but there was something about the old-meets-new style, the loving craftsmanship that had clearly gone into every detail, the stunning views that spoke of love and care. Indi hadn't seen the bedrooms, but the public areas were well thought out, sumptuously comfortable and designed for privacy for those who preferred it. Even though she was sure the price tag was as outrageous as the other hotels, somehow here she felt comfortable, like she belonged.

Mikhos picked up his pint. 'This actually *was* once that taverna on a small island. It was my parents' bar.'

'It was?' She imagined Mikhos as a small boy, running around the room, all tousled dark curls and mischief.

'You can still see the original building. This part we are in was the main room. They had tables outside, a few bedrooms above the bar. It wasn't big, but they made a living, just, working eighteen-hour days from Easter to October.'

Indi twisted to look around at the room, with its stone walls, apart from one made of glass looking out over the sea. An arch opposite led into the large modern bar area, which would open out onto the extensive terrace and pool, although tonight the doors were firmly closed against the elements. The room was furnished with comfortable sofas, low tables, creating inviting spaces for people to sit and eat or read or drink or chat, the clever lighting inviting intimacy.

Intimacy. Like in this sheltered corner where they sat. Where she was preternaturally aware of his every movement, every shift in position, every flicker of the eyes, every half-smile. Of the way his voice was pitched low, warm, just for her.

It was easy to forget why they were here, that really they were two strangers forced into companionship by the storm, by their love for their linked families. Easy to allow herself to forget that she had so very recently been so very hurt, that maybe she was looking for validation, for someone to make her feel that she wasn't broken.

Priya thought she should have a holiday romance. Indi had no idea where to begin with that concept. Especially sitting opposite the kind of man who had 'satisfying fling' written all over him, from his intelligent gaze to his slightly twisted smile, a smile that did funny things to her insides.

She hastily looked down at the table, only for her gaze to snag on his wrists, strong, corded, a dark olive, capable.

She snatched her gaze away. What was she *doing* fixating on his *wrists*, for goodness' sake? What she needed was a long dose of solitude and reflection, not indulging suddenly rampant hormones. Maybe she should have booked into a nunnery for her holiday.

She had to think of a really unsexy subject to pursue instead.

'Can I ask you something?'

His eyes sharpened in interest. 'Of course.'

'How long have you been using that booking software?'

Mikhos could not have looked more startled. He stared at her for one long moment before laughing, a deep, proper belly laugh that warmed her through to her toes. 'Now that was not what I was expecting!'

'What were you expecting?'

'Anything from my star sign to how I got started in hotels to why am I still single. I did wonder if you would ask about my favourite cheese.'

Indi's cheeks warmed. 'I don't believe in star signs, although I bet you are a Taurus; I am fascinated by how you got started here obviously; I'm keen to move on from cheese as a topic; and your love life really is none of my business.' True, but it didn't stop her being intrigued. He'd been engaged once he'd told her, but Jade hadn't mentioned anyone current. He was successful, still young, drop-dead gorgeous. If she was in the market – which obviously she wasn't – she'd not turn down a coffee with him. 'But I do know a little about booking software and yours looked perfectly functional, but there are better models out there.'

'How do you know about booking software, India Drewe? I thought you worked in a university?'

'As a project manager, yes, which makes me something of a jack of all trades. Last summer, we did a huge project updating our booking system, we let the student halls out in university holidays, it's a really lucrative income source. Anyway, I was in charge of a scoping exercise before we went out to tender and then managed that process, so, as a result, there is little I *don't* know about booking software. What you have is functional, it's fine, but now you're getting so much bigger, you really want more of an integrated CRM system. I'd be happy to make some suggestions, set up some meetings if that would help?' She sat back, relieved by her successful diversion of the conversation. CRM software was a much safer topic than Mikhos' love life.

'Yes.' He sat back, a smile quirking his really rather mesmerising mouth. Indi realised she was staring and quickly focused on her drink. 'You're right, I have used that software since I opened this place. I know it's probably time for an update, but upgrading systems isn't as high up the improvements list as maybe it should be. I'd be interested in your recommendations.'

'Great!' Obviously Indi didn't *need* to feel useful to be happy, but she knew she was much more content with a task. 'I'll get on it tomorrow.'

'There's no hurry. You're on holiday.'

She narrowed her eyes. 'I bet you didn't build a hotel empire by taking your time.'

'I guess not. But I am in the business of leisure, and if you don't go home fully rested, I will have failed. I don't want that on my conscience.'

She stared at him, fascinated, aware of something that had been nagging at her since they met. 'Your English is completely fluent. I mean, I know pretty much everyone here is impressively multilingual, but yours is seamless. Sometimes there's not even the trace of an accent.'

'That's because I have a secret weapon.' He sat back and grinned at her.

'Do I have to guess?'

'Go on then!'

'You went to school in the UK? You grew up watching nothing but reruns of *Fawlty Towers*? You have a computer chip in your brain? You had one of those accidents where you wake up fluent in another language?'

He shook his head at each guess, his eyes alight with laughter. 'All very good guesses, but all wrong. My mother is English,' he explained. 'We spoke English at home.'

'Really? How long has she lived in Greece?'

'Since she was twenty-two.'

Just like Jade.

He nodded, obviously correctly reading her mind. 'She came over to the islands for the summer and fell in love with the sky and the sea and the man behind the bar who flirted with her. Next thing, she had given up her job and moved here to run the bar.'

'Was she happy?'

'You'll have to ask her that. But I know it wasn't easy. Her romantic dreams soon crumbled against the reality of the long hours, the financial uncertainty and my dad's ways, although he did love her and she him. She never considered going back to England, even after he died, is happily settled in Naxos Town and a key part of my company, but her life has not been the endless summer she had envisioned, far from it.'

The pieces had all fallen into place. 'Is that why you're so set against Jade marrying Nico?'

'Partly. And, like I said, I don't think Nico is mature enough. Oh, he tells me I am not the head of the family, that I can't tell him what to do, and he's right. But I *am* a decade older than him, I'm more like a big brother than a cousin. I taught him to swim, to ride a bike, to drive, to sail. I know him. He's kind, you don't need to worry about that, hard-working, but he's still a boy, even if he is nearly twenty-five. As for your sister, like I say, it's easy to fall in love when there are hours in the day to stroll hand in hand along the beach and enough work to mean you're not worrying about money, but sooner or later, you are going to find yourself working sixteen hours a day with barely enough to get by. That's the nature of what we do. Will that make your sister happy?'

'I don't know,' Indi admitted. 'Like you, I worry she doesn't see that far ahead, that she's caught up in the romance of it all. That she and Nico haven't been tested and have no idea what marriage really entails.'

She broke off as the waiter approached with a tray laden with plates of delicious-looking food, a traditional mezze of hummus and olives, feta and taramasalata, small perfectly cooked skewers, tiny fried fish and freshly baked bread, accompanied by a salad so fresh and inviting, it reinvented the word. By the time he had unloaded it and Indi had put at least a bit of everything on her plate, she was ready for a change of subject. Worry about Jade was a constant, but there was nothing she could do right at this moment. Instead, here she was, dining tête-à-tête with a handsome man, why not enjoy the experience?

'This is incredible,' she said after a while. 'Thank you.'

'This kind of meal has been served here for generations. It was really important to me to preserve the heart of the taverna in more ways than just by keeping a few walls.'

'I get that. So what prompted you to turn the family business into a hotel? Did you always want to work in tourism?'

He speared an olive. Indi found it hard to look away as he raised it to his mouth. *Drooling over an olive, Indi?*

That's a new low. 'Not at all. I couldn't wait to get out. When I left university, I went to work for Aurelia's father in Athens. He and my father were boyhood friends, despite their very different lives, and he offered me the opportunity to try something new. I didn't hesitate. It was everything I wanted. I wore a suit, had an office, dealt with huge sums of money every day – it was a long way from a boyhood of serving drinks and mopping floors.'

'How did your parents feel about that?'

His mouth twisted. 'Conflicted. My father's family have owned this land, a bar here, for generations. He was both glad I had broken away from the uncertainty of a small business reliant on tourism and heartbroken that I had rejected the family legacy. It was complicated. And then he died.'

'And you came back?'

'I couldn't leave Mum to struggle alone, I couldn't sell this place. I couldn't let things continue as they were. So I took my savings, wrote a business plan, persuaded Aurelia's father to invest and built this. Everyone thought I was mad,' he conceded as their plates were cleared, their beers replaced with a deep red wine and small honey and nut cakes set before them, alongside a cheese platter. 'The debt was mounting, I never slept, my mother was wringing her hands, metaphorically and literally. They said the same when I built the second hotel, the third, when I expanded across to Mykonos and then to Santorini . . .' He laughed. 'They'll be saying it now. The island is too isolated, I have invested too much. We'll see.' He didn't look as if he gave a toss about what anyone said. It was refreshing.

'Where did the engagement fit into this?' Oh lord, where had *that* question come from? So much for a resolution to steer the conversation away from his love life! She must be tipsy. But then again, she was on holiday, wasn't she?

He grinned. 'Just the star sign and my favourite cheese left.'

'Sorry?'

'Questions you are going to ask me. For the record, I am a Pisces, and when in Greece, of course it's feta, if I am vising my grandparents in England, I am partial to a really good stilton. Now you.'

'Gemini, the most ripe mature Cheddar, ideally with cheap pickle and thickly buttered fresh white bread.' She regarded him, she couldn't deny how curious she was, she just wasn't sure she wanted to investigate why she was so interested in Mikhos' past. 'How old are you now? Thirty-four?' He nodded, clearly amused. 'You're rich, successful, not too hideous to look at. Not so young that you aren't established, not too old to be set in your ways . . .'

'Still a full head of hair and all my own teeth?' He grinned at her, and she couldn't help smiling back at him.

'Your dating profile is writing itself.'

'I'm taking notes just in case it comes to that.' He picked up a small piece of baklava. 'Going back to your question, although I promise you, it's not that interesting. I was engaged to a friend of Aurelia's. Katerina.' He lingered slightly over the name and Indi was aware of a pang of something. Not jealousy, that would be absurd, but *something*. 'She was from another prominent shipping company and everyone said *hadn't I done well*. Including me, if I'm honest. I couldn't believe a woman who bought her clothes in Paris wanted to be with me.' He picked up his wine but didn't drink, staring into space. 'She was beautiful, confident, sophisticated, international, everything I aspired to be.'

'I think I'm in love with her myself.' And as intimidated as hell. If that was who Mikhos dated at the start of his adult life, what did the rest of his relationship CV look like? 'What happened?'

'She had no interest in leaving Athens, didn't want a fiancé who was pulling down walls or serving tables, or making drinks, wanted no part of island entrepreneur life, the unsteadiness of tourism. She wanted the suited young executive climbing his way up the company hierarchy. So she called it off.' He sounded surprisingly matter-of-fact.

'Oh, Mikhos. I'm sorry.'

'It's no great tragedy. I haven't spent the last decade mourning my lost love or anything. My pride was probably dented more than my heart, if I am being honest. And the truth is, building the business has taken all my time and energy, there hasn't been much space for relationships.'

'You've been single for the last decade?' She couldn't hide her surprise. Even if he did work all the time, it seemed impossible some woman hadn't snapped him up.

His smile was wicked and heated her right through. 'I didn't say that. But work comes first and that, in the end, has always been an issue. I'm in no hurry, although my mother has a very different perspective. What about you, India Drewe?'

'What about me?' Indi asked warily. She wasn't sure she wanted the spotlight to be turned onto her.

'I got it wrong with Katerina, we are both sure Jade and Nico are rushing into things. What did you get wrong with . . . Will, is it?'

'Nothing,' she said, startled, then stopped. 'Only that's obviously not true, is it? Because if I had got things right, then I would be with him now, not you.'

Mikhos' eyes gleamed. 'Sorry to disappoint.'

She held his gaze. 'I didn't say I'm disappointed.'

He leaned forward, his voice low, dark, and her insides squeezed. 'India Drewe, are you flirting with me?'

Chapter Seventeen

Indi

Are you flirting with me?
Was she?

Myriad answers flitted through Indi's brain, each one more inane than the last. She gestured, helplessly, knocking her still full wine glass over. By the time the waiter had cleared it up, poured her a new glass and brushed aside her apologies, the moment had gone.

Thank goodness, she told herself firmly and not completely truthfully.

Indi didn't know how to flirt, nor if she did manage it accidentally, how to progress from flirtation, how to enjoy something spontaneous and fun. But right now how she wished she was the kind of woman who could give a witty reply instead of spilling red wine all over the table.

'So,' Mikhos prompted. 'You were going to tell me about Will.'

'Was I?'

'I told you all about my disastrous past, remember?'

She had asked, she supposed he had the right to question her in return. 'That seems fair. But it's not particularly interesting.' In line with most of her life in fact. 'There was no catalyst for us, no obvious moment where it all went wrong. In fact, if you had asked me a month ago, I would have said everything was perfect. Will would have given you a different answer, though. He'd been unhappy for some time, I think, he just hadn't said and I hadn't noticed. Didn't want to notice.'

'Why was he unhappy? You are obviously a very caring woman, intelligent, you seem like good company.' His smile was wicked. 'Not too hideous to look at. Not so young that you aren't established, not too old to be set in your ways . . .'

Indi flushed as she heard her words quoted back to her. 'Thank you for the compliments. Truth is, he was bored. Wanted, I don't know, some adventure.'

'And you don't?'

'It terrifies me,' she admitted. 'I'm a planner. I like to know where things are going, what lies ahead, try to mitigate any problems before they occur, have contingencies in place for any disasters.' Was it the wine making her open up, or Mikhos himself? Either way it was surprisingly cathartic.

'They sound like excellent qualities for a project manager.'

'And in a girlfriend?' The moment she asked the question, Indi wished she hadn't, but somehow, she found herself nervously awaiting his answer.

Mikhos looked at her steadily, his eyes dark and unreadable. 'It depends on the girlfriend.'

'I knew what I wanted out of life. Nothing exciting, nothing ground-breaking, but safe, happy, you know? And so I put in targets, milestones, ways to measure if I was on track. Will came along at exactly the right time. He was a friend of a friend, we just clicked. There was none of the drama and angst so many of my friends seemed to experience and that was good, I didn't want that emotional rollercoaster, although many of them seemed to love it. We met, we dated, we moved in together, all right on schedule. I turn thirty next week and that felt, I don't know, like some kind of momentous milestone. I wanted to have achieved a level of seniority at work, I wanted to be engaged. The nearer my birthday got, the more it all seemed to be falling into place, only what I didn't see was that the more certain I was this was right for me, the more Will was pulling away.'

'And how do you feel now? Still certain that those are the things you want?'

Indi clasped her refilled wine. 'I should, shouldn't I? After all, it happened less than a month ago. If it was right then, it should still be right now. I should be back in London doing whatever it takes to save what we had, having deep intense conversations with him, not with you. I should at least have considered his need to go travelling, not just shut it down.' Although she had offered to meet him halfway, hadn't she? It had been a safe offer though; he was never going to accept, she'd known it at the time. She wasn't sure what that said about their relationship, about her feelings for Will.

Mikhos was leaning forward, all his focus on her. 'You didn't want to travel? You weren't even tempted?' he asked curiously.

'I've never allowed myself to be tempted,' she admitted. 'I didn't have the opportunity when I was younger. Jade needed me, Mum needed me. I didn't even move out of the family home until I was twenty-eight, until Jade was eighteen.'

'Why so late?'

'Jade was still having operations into her teens, I couldn't leave her. I think I told you that she was injured in the accident that killed our father. She was in the back of the car, on his side, she was crushed by the impact.' Her voice trailed off and she swallowed, hollow, sick, the adrenaline beginning to take over her body with the memories. 'I was completely unhurt. I walked away, she was cut out. It was touch-and-go, for a while. The head injury, the trauma. She was in hospital for weeks. And then several more operations as she grew. Her leg was crushed, her ribs broken, her arm. She was lucky, they said . . .'

'I see. Now it makes sense.'

'What does?'

'The way you watch her. Like she's a newly fledged chick.'

Indi managed a half-smile. 'I do fuss over her, I know that. It's hard to let her go, to let her make her own mistakes. Look at me right now, instead of trying to fix my life, I am here, trying to fix hers.' But right now, that didn't feel like any kind of hardship. With the wine, the music, Mikhos' attention all on her, she felt like she was exactly where she wanted to be. 'Dad and I were arguing that night.' The words spilled out before she could stop them. 'We never got the chance to make up. I never got the chance to tell him I was sorry. That I loved him.' She swallowed, her throat thick, painful as she said out loud words she had never said before.

Mikhos laid his hand over hers, firm, reassuring. 'Indi, he knew. Of course he knew. I argued with my father all the time. He told me I was turning into a city boy, forgetting my roots, but I knew he was proud of me, boasted to all his friends about his big-shot son.' His smile was full of memories. 'What was the argument about?'

'It was so silly. Just a teenage spat. I wanted to take art A level, he wanted me to concentrate on the sciences. I was sulking, like only a teenager can, but I knew even then he only wanted what was best for me.' Just like she wanted what was best for Jade. 'I've always wished I could go back and say sorry.'

'So that's why you need to plan ahead? Because you know how unpredictable the future can be.'

Indi didn't know where to look, what to do, what to say. She had never felt so seen, so heard, so understood. So exposed. 'That and juggling A levels with hospital appointments and whatever else Jade needed, running the house, making sure we all ate properly, that bills were paid, food was available. Without a plan, it would have all fallen apart. Maybe I just got too reliant on them, forgot how to be spontaneous. It's hard to remember who I was before.'

'Where was your mother in all this? Surely you weren't alone with your sister?'

'Not physically, but it often felt that way. My mother is a genius, but that comes with its own issues. When she's present mentally, there's no one better and that did relieve the pressures on me. But when she's in a creative phase, she might as well be anywhere else. After she lost my dad, she buried herself in work for months on end.'

'That must have been hard.'

Indi considered. It had been *incredibly* hard, but that was how her mother coped, she understood that. But there had been times when she had wished that someone had allowed her to crumble, to grieve, that she hadn't always had to be the strong one. 'It's how she is. Dad did most of the day-to-day parenting, the house admin, all that kind of thing, then, once he was gone, I did. *Do.*' Suddenly she was tired, of focusing on the past, remembering mistakes, failures, all the things that had led her to where she was now, nearly thirty without a clue what came next.

'And did you take art?'

The question surprised her. 'No,' she said softly. 'In the end, it just felt wrong. I haven't picked up a paintbrush since. Silly, I know.'

The band in the next room who had been busy tuning their instruments for the last few minutes started to play, a decent cover of one of Indi's favourite songs from the previous summer. She twisted round to see that the space in front of the band had been cleared to make a dance floor. It was empty. She tapped her foot in time to the rhythm, eyes half closed. She wanted to dance. To shake off the memories and the sadness and the regret. To expel the emotions and the energy coursing through her. Why *shouldn't* she dance? So, the floor was empty? So, she always waited for someone else to make the first move in this kind of situation? When had she last been spontaneous? Done something just because it was fun? Because she wanted to?

Before she could think better of it, before she could remind herself of all the reasons this was a very, very bad idea, she got to her feet and held out her hand to Mikhos.

'Dance with me?'

He glanced at the empty dance floor, then back at her, eyebrow lifted. 'Alone?'

'Someone has to start the dancing off.'

'And you think that someone should be us?' His eyes were filled with laughter.

'Or I can dance by myself. If you're scared.'

'Is that a dare?' he asked softly.

'Yes.'

'In that case . . .'

For once, Indi hadn't thought ahead, hadn't thought beyond getting onto the dance floor. She hadn't considered what dancing with Mikhos would be like, whether they would be independent, doing their own thing, an awkward shuffle in time . . . instead Mikhos swung her into his arms as if they were in a Fred Astaire film, guiding her so expertly all she had to do was follow.

'Where did you learn to do that?' she asked as the first song came to an end.

'My mother danced, she insisted I learn.'

'Your mother is a wise woman.'

Conversation slowed as they danced, Indi aware of nothing but the sound of the beat and the feel of Mikhos' hand holding hers, his body so close, one centimetre closer and she would be pressed up next to him. It was so tempting, to entwine her arms around his neck, tilt her face up to his, take advantage of the moment, but right now the dancing was enough. She hadn't felt so free for a very long time.

More and more people joined them until the small dance floor was filled with people and, to Indi's barely hidden disappointment, Mikhos let her go to dance more conventionally in the smaller space. Who knew she had Elizabeth Bennet fantasies about being led around a dance floor by a masterful man? There was something dizzyingly sexy about his confident clasp, the steer of his long lean body, his leg against hers. No wonder regency damsels had such heaving bosoms.

Another drink, another dance, another and yet another, and before Indi knew it, it was after ten and her early start and busy day caught up with her. Mikhos saw her conceal a yawn, beckoned the waiter, and started a quick conversation with him in rapid and increasingly voluble Greek.

'Is something wrong?' Indi asked.

Mikhos grimaced. 'It seems we have a problem. I should have checked, I'm sorry. The hotel is full up. There is no room at the inn, which I knew, but what I didn't realise is that the staff quarters are also full because of the storm.'

'Right. Well, looks like it's blankets down here then.' Although down here was filled with guests, who all seemed settled in to ride out the storm with copious amounts of alcohol, even though they had perfectly good rooms to go to.

'There is *one* room, but—'

'I'm sure it's fine. Honestly, I'll take a mattress in a cupboard if I have to.'

He paused, his dark gaze unreadable, before nodding. 'OK then. Follow me.'

The room Mikhos took her to wasn't in the main part of the hotel, instead they went through the hot, bustling kitchens and up a stone staircase at the back until they reached the third and top floor. This corridor was clearly mostly storage, apart from one door at the end which led into a small room, with traditional shuttered windows. Whitewashed with stone floors covered with a rug, it was simple, dressed only with a bed, desk and a narrow chaise. Two recessed cupboards were set in the wall and a small but adequate bathroom opened off.

'This was where I lived,' Mikhos said. 'When we first opened the hotel.'

It was stripped of any personal belongings, but she could imagine him here, working away on the desk.

'It's perfect, thank you. I'll be very comfortable here.' She would, it might lack the luxury of the guest rooms, but there was a homely simplicity she liked. 'Where are you sleeping?'

He didn't answer and realisation dawned.

'This is the last room? That's what you said? And it's your room? Does that mean there's nowhere for you?'

'As you said, there is always the option of a mattress on a cupboard floor.'

'But . . .' Indi looked at the bed. It was a double, but not that big. 'Look, I'll take the chaise.' She regarded it doubtfully. It was very narrow, and actually quite short. Her legs were going to be hanging off it.

His mouth quirked into a half-smile. 'I think a mattress on the floor would be more comfortable.'

'Don't be silly, we're both adults. We can share.' She tried to sound nonchalant, as if jumping into bed with practical strangers was something she did every day.

Not a stranger. A man she had opened up to in a way she had never opened up with Will.

A man she had laughed with, danced with, come close to crying with.

A man she had fantasied about having a holiday romance with.

And there was only one bed . . .

It was the oldest trope in the book and now she realised there was a good reason for that. Suddenly, she wasn't at all tired, every nerve awake and brimming with anticipation and fear. She was aware of his every movement, even when she scuttled into the en suite with an old shirt of his to change into. She checked her phone again, needing to anchor herself, but there was nothing from Jade yet, nothing to remind herself of the world outside this one small room and her place in it.

She left the bathroom reluctantly, aware the shirt barely covered her bottom, to find Mikhos standing bare-chested in the middle of the room. Indi swallowed. He was wearing more than the first time she had seen him, true, but so much flesh – so much toned, olive, masculine flesh – exposed in the intimacy of the bedroom felt like a whole other level.

God, he was handsome, those compelling long-lashed eyes – good genes, her body approved – his face all sharp planes, a full but not soft mouth. A mouth Indi desperately wanted to launch herself at.

She stood still, her hands curling into fists, her legs weak, and she knew that if Mikhos made just one move, no matter how tiny, she would move with him.

'My friend Priya says that I should have a holiday romance. To get over Will.' Oh, she had definitely had one glass too many.

'Did she?' he said softly. 'Any candidates?'

'She thought you would be ideal.'

What had she just said? Why had she said it? Was she absolutely mad?

For a moment, that move hung in the balance, she could almost see his mind working, the tick at his jaw, a heat simmering in his gaze as he looked at her, very deliberately not looking at the deep V at her chest where the buttons ended or the length of exposed leg. She couldn't move, just stood and waited, until, with a smothered curse, he grabbed his T-shirt and left the room without a single word, leaving her standing alone feeling like the world's biggest fool.

How would she face him again the next day? If this was being spontaneous, then it was a good thing she'd spent the last twelve years not indulging.

But there had been a moment, more than a moment, when she could have sworn that he was tempted, when his eyes had flared with something hot and intense, something that had heated her through.

Yes, he had been tempted. Which left one question. Would they spend the rest of her holiday pretending the last five minutes had never happened or was she going to do something about it?

Chapter Eighteen

Jade

Friday 9 June

The next morning, it was as if the storm had never been, the wind fading to a gentle breeze, the sea serene, the sun warm and in a blue sky. Jade was up early after a fitful sleep and waiting at the jetty long before either Mikhos' or Nico's boat arrived back.

Her signal had been restored at some point during the night and with it arrived messages from both Indi and Nico. Both were brief, almost terse, and far fewer in volume than she had expected. After all, she herself had sent dozens at least. But at least she knew they were safe.

She'd brought a coffee and her notes with her and so passed the time reading up on all Aurelia expected her to do and trying to commit all the influencers' biographies to her memory; who had been in which reality show, who was dating whom, who in a feud with whom, who was vegan, keto, anti-carbs or allergic to what. She was just beginning to despair of ever remembering it all when, with a jolt of relief, she saw a boat on the horizon. Nico was back at last!

She didn't even feel herself get up and run, the precious folder of Aurelia's notes left behind on the beach, bouncing impatiently on her toes as the boat came closer and closer. Nico waved as he drew nearer, but his answering smile was brief, and Jade noticed dark shadows under his eyes. Maybe he too had lain awake worrying about her. It would be just like him.

As Jade waved back, she saw a woman come to stand next to Nico. She was a stunningly beautiful girl of around Jade's own height and age with a heart-shaped face and enviably glossy blonde hair in a ponytail made for flicking. She wore huge sunglasses, a bikini top as complicated and skimpy as anything Aurelia owned and a pair of tight denim hot pants which showcased enviably long, tanned legs.

Jade smiled at her in welcome and was aware of an assessing sweep in return. Her skirt suddenly felt dowdy, her top crumpled, her hair untidy. It was like being back at school and somehow missing whatever it was that made one person cool and another tragic.

This must be Aurelia's publicist, the social media expert, someone she would be working closely with over the next week. Which meant Jade needed to bury her inferiority complex back in whatever part of her subconscious it had appeared from and get on with being professional. Mikhos had chosen her to do this, not someone from his marketing and PR teams. This was the opportunity she needed to show she was versatile and indispensable.

Nico tossed her the rope and she caught it, tugging it until the boat was close enough for him to start fastening it to the jetty. As he did so, the girl jumped lightly ashore, her large sunglasses still shielding her eyes, although her nose was crinkled adorably and her smile was wide.

'You must be Jade! It's lovely to meet you at last, I have heard so much about you!' She held out her hand expectantly and Jade took it, feeling foolish. Why hadn't Aurelia or Nico supplied her with a name?

'Ah, yes. I'm sorry, I . . . And you are?' How could she

be a guest manager, she wondered miserably, when she so easily felt so gauche and awkward?

'Oh, I'm sorry, I'm Daisee, spelt double e, thanks, Mum!' Even her laugh was adorable, like a trill. She still looked expectant as if Jade should recognise her.

'Right, nice to meet you, Daisee, thank you so much for coming to help me. Aurelia assures me you're the right person to help manage the influencers.'

Daisee's smile widened. 'I'll do my best. Aurelia totally slays, you know? I've learnt a lot from her. Not that I've given up my own influencing career entirely, got to keep my profiles up, but look to the future, that's what my mum said. Reality shows and game shows and endorsements are all well and good, but where will it end if you don't marry a footballer?'

'Good point.' It was a philosophical question Jade supposed, but not one she had ever considered herself.

'Wait! What must you think of me? I haven't said congratulations!' Daisee seized Jade's left hand. 'Oh!'

'We haven't bought a ring yet.' Jade was more than happy to wait and didn't want anything expensive when they did buy one. After all, she and Nico were just starting out, it was silly to waste money they didn't have on jewellery. 'I'm not really a symbols person.'

'How unique! When I get engaged, I want a rock as big as this island! Guess it's a good thing we didn't get that far, isn't it, Niccy?'

That far? Niccy?

Jade turned to Nico, who was standing beside them with the look of a dog found with his paw in the Sunday roast, and her stomach swooped with a sense of impending dread.

I knew this was too good to be true, that he *was too good to be true.*

'Do you two know each other?' Jade asked.

'We hung out last summer.' Nico didn't meet her eye and the sinking feeling turned into a plummeting one – down a chasm a thousand feet deep and imploding at the bottom.

'Oh dear.' Daisee's pout was as pronounced as her smile. Jade always tried to see the best in people, even when, like the girls at school, they made it very hard, but in this case she was prepared to make a very big exception. 'Naughty boy! Haven't you told Jade about us?'

'Nico?' she prompted. 'What is Daisee talking about?'

Nico was still refusing to meet her eye, his own gaze fixed alternately on the horizon or on his feet. 'Daisee spent some time on Naxos working with Aurelia last year,' he mumbled.

'And?'

Before Nico could answer Daisee piped up. 'It was just a little summer fling. You know how romantic these islands can be? A nice sunset, a handsome boy like Niccy, I mean.' Daisee's smile was pure feline. 'Look at him, how could any red-blooded girl resist? *You* didn't after all. But engaged! That's so next level!'

Was Daisee ignorant of the atmosphere or enjoying causing the disturbance? Either way, every word inflamed the situation.

Jade wanted to say that she was different, *they* were different, but the words wouldn't come. She didn't even know if they were true! The certainty that had anchored her, kept her strong in the face of Indi and Mikhos' disapproval, was ebbing away.

Daisee was everything Jade wasn't, confident, gorgeous, experienced, she had a career, aspirations. Jade could see how Nico would be attracted to her. But what she didn't understand was why he had never mentioned her.

He shifted uneasily as if he could read her mind. 'It was before I knew you, Jade. And it was just casual, fun.'

Daisee tapped him on the arm, all she needed was a fan to complete the coquettish gesture. 'That's not very complimentary, Niccy. Jade doesn't mind, do you, Jade? Honestly! Way to break a girl's heart. I bet as soon as I left, you were taking another girl down to our beach, you smooth-talker, you.'

'I . . . It's not . . .' Nico was clearly in a no-win situation here, but Jade wasn't prepared to let him off that easily. She wasn't a fool, she knew he had had relationships before, expected he had even thought himself in love several times, but she had believed him when he told her that she was different. That she was special. But was she or was she actually just one in a long line of summer romances. If she hadn't got pregnant, would he have kissed her goodbye at the end of the summer and headed off back to the Caribbean and his next fling without a backwards glance?

She felt so stupid, as if once again she didn't understand the rules, her teenage years on repeat.

Nico caught her hand. 'Jade, *asteraki mou.*'

But the endearment failed to thrill her the way it always had in the past. Instead, she wondered, nausea churning, how many other women Nico had called his little star, how many other women he had kissed on the beach, in the surf, in the sea, how many others had been seduced by soft words and lips?

'You should have told me.' It was all she managed to say, but her tone, her expression must have said everything else she was thinking, because Nico stepped away, lips compressed. 'Anyway, what's important is the week ahead,' she said to Daisee as brightly as she could. There was no way she was letting the other woman know just how upset she was. 'There's a lot we need to go through and plan. Let me show you to the villa and get you settled in before we talk about work.'

'No need, I know my way around. I spent some time out here last year with Niccy.' If Jade heard her call Nico that one more time, she would be sick. 'Do you remember . . . Oh!' The giggle was as fake as her suspiciously full pout. 'I'd better not say in front of Jade.'

'Oh, don't mind me, I don't want to get in the way of your reminiscing. If you're sure you know where you're going, then I have plenty to do. I'll meet you back at the villa for lunch.'

Jade turned and walked away, head up, resisting the urge to touch her stomach, to look back, to feel anything at all. She was so out of her depth here. Nico was her first serious boyfriend and she had thrown all of her into him.

'Jade! Jade?' Nico was panting by the time he caught up with her, but she increased her pace rather than slowed down.

'I'm busy.'

'Jade, come on, this is silly. I'm sorry I didn't mention Daisee before, but it's because she didn't mean anything. Not like you. You know I love you, right? It's *you* I am engaged to; *you* I am going to marry.'

'Because I am pregnant.' She so desperately wanted to believe that he was marrying her for her, not because of the baby, but now, between the sleeplessness and the uncertainty Daisee had planted in her, she didn't know what she felt. 'That's why we are engaged. That's all.'

'That's not the only reason. Come on, Jade, Daisee was just a summer fling. You and me. We are real.'

Jade skidded to a halt and turned to face him, her heart softening despite herself as she saw the anguish in the dark eyes usually lit by humour and love. 'Nico, I know that you had girlfriends and dates and flings before me. Of course I know that. And you should have had.' Although *she* had reached twenty-two with nothing but a few dates in her past, her heart totally untouched. Maybe if she had had more experience she wouldn't have fallen so fast, so totally.

'But I can't help feeling there's a pattern here. That Daisee is right, days after she left, you were romancing someone new, and that if I left, you would move on just as quickly. That it's the baby giving us a future, not you and me.'

'I can't believe that you just said that.' He was pale, eyes blazing black. 'I am prepared to give up my *dreams* for you, Jade. To be the husband and father you need me to be.'

'I never asked you to,' she said numbly.

'You didn't need to ask. I want to do it. I want to make you happy, to keep you safe. But you think I'm as much a fool as Mikhos does, head turned by the next pretty girl who walks by.'

'No. I didn't say that.'

'Yes. You did.'

Jade's stomach churned. How could things have gone wrong so very quickly? This is what Mikhos meant when he said we hadn't been tested. How can we get married and raise a baby when . . .' she couldn't finish the sentence.

'When you don't trust me.'

He had never sounded so grim, she barely recognised him. How could she tell him that it was her she didn't trust more than him? That she was afraid their families were right, that she was too untested, too naïve, that all this was too new for her? That of course she would mess up.

'When we don't really know each other.'

'I know you, Jade Drewe. I know you spent too much of your childhood on the outside, that you don't trust easily, especially in yourself. But if *you* don't know me, if you don't believe in me, then you're right. We're not ready to get married and have a baby.' He stepped back, face cold. 'I have work to do. I'll see you later.'

Jade opened her mouth to call after him, but the words remained unsaid. She had hurt him dreadfully, allowed her fears and doubts and lack of confidence to drive a wedge between them. And she couldn't shed those doubts now they had been awakened.

Eyes stinging, she headed back to the beach where she had left Aurelia's folder and picked it up, clutching it to her, cold in spite of the heat. As she straightened, her phone rang. Her heart leaped in hope, but it wasn't Nico, ready to tell her everything was going to be OK, but her mother.

'Mum? Are you all right?'

'Jade, darling. I'm fine. I do hope you're not turning into a worrier like your sister.'

'I just wasn't expecting your call.'

'It's the unexpected moments that are the most rewarding, though, wouldn't you agree?'

'Erm, sometimes I guess.' Today had been unexpected and definitely not rewarding.

'Anyway, darling. I woke up this morning and knew I needed a change of scene and so guess what?'

'Erm . . .' The answer could be literally anything.

'I packed my bag and grabbed my passport and I got the tube to Heathrow and found a flight to Athens in an hour's time. I'll spend the night there and come to you tomorrow, my darling. Isn't it wonderful?'

'Yes,' Jade said faintly. 'Just wonderful.'

Jade was pregnant, had just had her first serious row with Nico and was heading into a week of unpredictable work with a woman who made her feel seriously inadequate. Oh, and Indi was about to be unleashed in Jade's office. Now she had to add her mother into the equation. What else could possibly go wrong?

Paradise was currently feeling a lot more like purgatory and Jade had no idea how to put it right.

Chapter Nineteen

Indi

Friday 9 June

I have done something terrible and it is all your fault 😳😳😳

It took Priya less than ten seconds to reply.

????????

I told Mikhos you thought I should have a fling with him to get over Will.

You did WHAT?! Why?

Indi stared at her phone. It was a lot easier than looking at Mikhos, who had been perfectly civilised over breakfast and in the car back to Naxos Town and was now sailing them back to Agios Iohannis in the same polite and distant way. It made Indi want to hurl herself over the side and swim back to Naxos Town and head straight home so that she need never face him again.

Priya was obviously bored of waiting for Indi to reply.

Because you want to get down and dirty with him? 💑😚

I had too much red wine and we had been dancing and talking and it just felt like there was something there . . .

So you propositioned him? Indi Drewe, I have never been prouder. What happened?

He left the room.

🙀🙀🙀*Why did you listen to me? What do I know? I've been married for seven years? I don't understand romance!*

You and me both.

What are you going to do? Pretend it never happened?

Tempting, but I have over a week left. I think I need to apologise.

Good luck! Keep me posted and never listen to my advice ever again.

Indi grimaced at her phone, sitting still for a moment gathering all her courage before taking a deep breath and walking over to Mikhos, who stood at the tiller, face shaded by his sunglasses.

'I think I owe you a very big apology,' she said before she could bottle out of what was bound to be an embarrassing conversation. 'I put you in a very awkward position last night.'

He didn't reply for a long moment. Indi shifted as the tension grew, wishing she had stayed a coward after all.

'No apology needed,' he said at last. 'Forget about it.'

If only! Indi didn't think she would ever be able to wipe out the memory of her first and only proposition. 'I was a little drunk, and what with the dancing and the conversation . . .' She winced. 'I misread the signals. It was really wrong of me to put you on the spot like that and make you uncomfortable when you have been so kind. I really am sorry.'

'You didn't.' He was still looking straight ahead so she couldn't read his expression. 'Misread the signals.'

'I . . .' Indie had no idea what to say. 'But . . .' Her cheeks were blazing, it was bad enough thinking she'd made a clumsy proposition to somebody who didn't want her, but now she was completely discombobulated.

'I like you, India Drewe. I like your company, I like your drive, your sense of humour. I think you're a very attractive woman.'

'Oh.' Was she ever going to be able to speak in anything but monosyllables again?

'And I was very flattered by the offer. But I'm not interested in being anybody's rebound, confidence-boosting fling. If and when you're interested in sleeping with me because *you want* to, not because you want to get back at your ex-boyfriend or because your friend thinks it's a good idea, then let me know.'

'I didn't mean to offend you,' she said in a small voice. She had been crass, she realised. Mishandled the whole situation. Maybe it was a good thing – if they had slept together, then this journey might be even *more* excruciating, hard as that was to imagine.

'I'm not offended.'

'OK then. Good. Let's never speak of this again.'

'Oh, I don't know.' To her relief, he threw her a quick smile. 'I don't want to forget about it entirely. You might even find it funny one day.'

'I sincerely doubt it. I vote for collective amnesia.' Indi felt conscious of every movement, every gesture. Rather than clearing the air, her apology had just made things even more complicated than they had been before.

If and when you're interested in sleeping with me because you want to, not because you want to get back at your ex-boyfriend or because your friend thinks it's a good idea, then let me know. What was she supposed to do with that promise hanging in the air?

She jumped as her phone vibrated and looked down to see a message from Jade.

Just had a call from Mum, she's on her way to Athens. She is coming to join us here, she arrives tomorrow.

'Oh my God.' Indi read the message again in the hope she might have misunderstood the contents, but no such luck.

'Is anything wrong?'

'Depends on your definition of wrong. Apparently, my mother has decided to pay a visit. I'm sorry, the last thing you want is another member of my family on the island.'

Mikhos grinned. 'I don't know,' he said. 'You and your sister have certainly shaken things up, what's another Drewe woman in the mix?'

'She is the most difficult of us all,' Indi warned darkly. 'Nothing is ever boring where Mum is concerned.'

'Like mother like daughter?' The cool courtesy had gone, replaced with something warmer, more intimate.

Indi just laughed and headed back to her seat feeling oddly comforted. She wasn't sure what, if anything, was going to happen between her and Mikhos, but right now his humour was a balm she hadn't realised she needed.

Once they were back on Agios Iohannis, Indi went straight out in search of Jade, who seemed oddly elusive, and quiet once she did find her, helping organise the sunbeds on the island's largest beach. Indi had been wondering whether to confide in her about last night and the resulting conversation but decided to take a rain check until her sister was less preoccupied. Her questions and comments were barely replied to and Indi couldn't help but notice that Jade was paler than usual, huge shadows under her eyes.

'Are you nervous about next week?' Indi asked. 'I know you hate to be the centre of attention. Hopefully the publicist Aurelia sent can take over most of the public-facing work. Let me know anything I can do to help. I've got a login onto the system, so anything you need at all, just ask.'

'Don't fuss me,' Jade snapped.

The feeling that something was wrong intensified. It wasn't like Jade to be so irritable. 'What's wrong?'

'Why does anything have to be wrong? Maybe I'm just tired of you babying me all the time. This is my job, I don't need you interfering.'

Indie stepped back, trying not to let her hurt show. Last night must have been very stressful, with Jade here alone on the island and the storm raging, no wonder she looked like she hadn't slept. 'You're right. Sorry. How is Aurelia's replacement? Do you think you two will work well together?'

Jade's face twisted. 'Oh yes, we've got loads in common. Turns out she's one of Nico's exes, isn't that nice?'

Oh. Now Jade's snippiness made sense. 'Have you and Nico fallen out over it?'

'Yes, we're not talking and he's furious with me. Happy now?'

'Oh, Jade, of course I'm not happy. What happened?'

'He thinks I don't trust him, and I'm wondering if I'm an idiot to have ever believed him when he said I was different, that he had never been in love before me. Maybe we don't know each other as well as I thought, maybe we *are* rushing into things. You and Mikhos can congratulate yourselves on being right all along.'

Oddly, Jade's words didn't give Indi any relief or hope, instead she ached to comfort her sister. '*Do* you trust him?'

Jade's mouth trembled. 'Right now, I really don't know what I think. I mean, I didn't expect him to have lived like a monk before me, but Daisee is so different, she's my polar opposite in every way. And he dated lots of girls, probably all just like her. Where do I fit into that?'

'How long were they together?'

'What does it matter? They met, they fell for each other, she left and he fell for someone else. It was last year on Naxos. She worked with Aurelia for a bit, hence the job now.'

'So Mikhos knew her? Knew that she and Nico had history?'

Jade shrugged. 'I guess so.'

Only yesterday Indi had admitted that she needed to allow Jade to fight her own battles, but it was hard to step back when Jade was so upset, and even harder to step back when she couldn't help wondering if Mikhos had engineered the whole situation. His concerns about the engagement stemmed from Nico's propensity to fall into relationships after all. Was it so far-fetched to believe he had invited an ex here to see how Nico reacted? It seemed cruel, manipulative, at odds with the man who she had come to know, but they had only spent a few hours together after all. Her instincts about him could be way off base. Much as Indi wanted Jade to see sense about marrying Nico, she didn't want her sister hurt.

Indi stewed over the situation as she returned to the villa. It was almost a relief to bump into Mikhos and Nico, the two having what was clearly a heated conversation.

'Did you do this on purpose?' She marched up to Mikhos, not caring that she was interrupting. 'Did you deliberately invite one of Nico's exes here to upset my sister?'

'I was asking him the same question,' Nico said tight-lipped.

Mikhos' eyes narrowed as he turned to her, clearly displeased with her questioning. 'Daisee was Aurelia's choice, her appointment had nothing to do with me. I trust Aurelia's judgement.'

'But you knew she was coming?' Indi challenged. 'Why didn't you give me a heads-up?'

'I didn't think it was important.' Mikhos sounded as calm as ever, but there was a steeliness about him that Indi had not seen before. 'It's *not* important. As I was just telling Nico. My concern – his concern, Jade's concern – should be focused on nothing but getting this place ready for the first guests. All I care about right now is getting the best reviews from the right people and I will employ whoever I need to in order to achieve that. If Jade can't work with Daisee, then she needs to reconsider whether she's in the right job, and if Nico can't convince Jade that Daisee means nothing to him, then he needs to reconsider whether they are ready for marriage.'

'But—' Nico broke in.

Mikhos held up a hand in clear dismissal. 'Nico. No more. This is a professional environment and it's about time the people working on this island remember that.'

Much as Indi wanted to push the subject, she had to concede that he was right. This was a crucial time for his business and she had promised to help in any way she could. Joining in whatever conflict Daisee's arrival had stirred up wouldn't help anyone. 'You're right, I'm sorry. I'll talk to Jade.'

'No, *I'll* talk to Jade.'

Indi looked at Nico, surprised. She had never seen him so fired up, so resolute, and for the first time she began to wonder if maybe she had been wrong, if he did have what it took to make Jade happy long term. 'OK.'

He nodded at her and turned and went without acknowledging his cousin, clearly still furious.

'I think Jade is going to be pretty busy for the rest of the day, so I'll head into the office and see if there's anything that needs to be done.' It was Indi's way of apologising and Mikhos' rigid stance softened a little.

'Thank you,' was all he said.

'OK then. I'll see you later.'

'So long, India Drewe.' He paused and then leaned forward, kissing her very lightly on the cheek. 'I *was* tempted, you know.' And with that he turned and walked away, leaving Indi staring after him with a mixture of embarrassment and longing.

Chapter Twenty

Jade

'That Mikhos of yours is a marvellous man.' Tabitha linked her arm through Jade's. 'He had a car waiting for me at the ferry and a boat just for me, with lovely Nico as my captain. He said it was an honour to welcome such an artist as me to his home, which is most gratifying. So handsome as well. I would like to see him as Ares, or maybe Achilles?' Indi, walking on her mother's other side, choked. 'There is something rather deliciously ruthless yet vulnerable about him, don't you think?'

Jade squeezed her mother's arm. 'He's not *my* Mikhos, Mother.' And right now, she wasn't sure she could claim Nico as hers either. Not only had they not made up, they had barely talked since Nico had informed her that Mikhos had made it clear that all personal issues were to be put on the back burner until the launch week was over. Jade had been furious that Nico had mentioned the quarrel to Mikhos at all and put her professionalism in doubt and by the time he had left her, the two were further apart than ever. She'd slept alone last night too; Nico had spent the night on Naxos and returned this morning with their mother and what looked like a monster hangover.

But she didn't want to think about that now. 'Come on, let me show you some more of the island.' Jade started along the path leading to the restaurant. 'Isn't it paradise?'

'It's heavenly to be spending time with both my girls.'

'It's a lovely surprise, thank you for coming,' Indi said. Their mother's arrival had seemed to smooth the odd tension that had sprung up between Jade and Indi since yesterday. Jade hadn't meant to snap at her sister, but she was tired of being babied, of being treated as if she couldn't cope. As if she were still a permanently convalescing adolescent.

'Now, darling, you must let me know if I am getting in the way,' Tabitha said. 'You and Nico are both so busy and it is important not to let the romance slip, especially in the early days. Your father and I always made time for each other. A healthy sex life means a healthy marriage, girls.'

'Eurgh.' Jade pulled a face and Indi clapped her hands over her ears.

'La, la, la, I am not hearing this.'

'How did I raise such a repressed pair?'

'Walking in on Mr Greene modelling for you repressed me,' Indi said feelingly. 'I could never look him in the eye – or anywhere else – again after that. It made buying sweets from his shop very awkward.'

'Lovely pecs.' Tabitha's eyes glazed reminiscently. 'And such strong thighs.'

'Moving on!' Jade said. 'Very quickly.'

Tabitha drew in an ecstatic breath. 'Oh! This air smells like nectar. So invigorating for the mind and the body. Maybe I'll stay a while, refill the creative well.'

'You might change your mind when you see the fee – one night costs more than I have ever spent on a whole holiday,' Indi warned, but Tabita just smiled.

'I'm sure dear Mikhos would see the value of an artist in residence. I really require very little.'

Dear Mikhos indeed! Jade raised her eyes at Indi, who flushed. What was *that* about?

'OK.' Jade gave Indi a sympathetic smile. 'This is the restaurant and bar area.'

'Wow.' Indi stepped into the glade and looked around. 'You've done loads. It was all still so bare when I was here on Monday. This is rather spectacular.'

'It does look good,' Jade said. 'It's come together nicely.'

It was an understatement, she was bursting with pride at what had been achieved in the two days since the storm. The outside met the inside seamlessly. Wooden dining tables surrounded by an eclectic mix of benches and chairs, heaped with sheepskin rugs, throws and scarves, were carefully placed in nooks around the edge of the space, whereas in the middle, sofas and armchairs surrounded lower tables, in a way that allowed for both intimacy or a livelier group. Fairy lights were entwined around posts and in trees. A pizza oven and prep station were on one side, a firepit surrounded by chairs and sofas on the other.

The bar itself was in the inside space, a polished wooden semicircle with inviting-looking bar stools at intervals. Plants climbed over beams and shaded tables, flowers creating pops of colour. Art complemented the whole, from the huge abstract on the back wall to the wooden and stone sculptures carefully placed throughout.

'When people holiday in Greece, they want to be outside, but nights can get chilly, and as you know we do get some formidable storms, so we have essentially replicated the outside seating inside. The glass roof and walls are retractable if we want to use the whole space. It makes it super-flexible.' Jade couldn't have been prouder of the space if she had designed it herself. 'The restaurant can seat all the guests, although obviously there is a twenty-four-hour delivery service as well, but we've used the sculptures, plants and movable screens to create smaller, intimate areas. It might be because a couple want privacy or to stop two people dining alone in a big empty room.'

'And when do your first guests arrive?' Tabitha asked.

'Two days.' Jade grimaced. 'Obviously they are why all this exists, but at the same time it will feel strange sharing this space with new strangers every week.' She flopped onto one of the sofas. 'Everything is going to change. It already has,' she added softly, thinking of the coldness between her and Nico, the tension with Indi, Aurelia's departure and the addition of Daisee, who, she had to admit, did know her stuff and was prepared to work. Jade was making a huge effort to be professional at all times and not allow herself to be drawn into any personal conversations.

Indi leaned against the nearest table. 'Talking of which, did Mikhos mention that he has asked me to help look at new booking systems? The one you use is a little outdated.'

Jade felt herself tense and made herself breathe. Indi couldn't help trying to get involved, it was how she was made. 'No, he hasn't.'

'And I hope you don't mind, but I redid your task lists yesterday. They were a little haphazard, so I just put them in a chart, along with KPIs and dates. It'll make everything much smoother.'

Another deep breath. Then another. 'You are un-fricking-believable.' OK, maybe she should have counted to ten. 'This is my *job*, Indi, you can't just go into my office and change how I organise things.'

'But it wasn't organised, that's the point. Just wait until you try my way. It's much better.' Indi sounded amused. As if Jade was throwing a tantrum. Did she not realise how disrespectful she was being? 'I've a lot more experience than you. Honestly, you'll thank me tomorrow.'

Jade hadn't even realised she had got to her feet, but somehow she was standing, hands on hips, glaring at her sister. She couldn't remember the last time she had lost her temper, but right now she was riding on a wave of anger and frustration, with Indi, Nico, herself, with everyone, and she had no idea how to stop, or if she even wanted to. She was sick of people treating her like she was an incompetent child. 'Are you *serious*?' Of course she was. It was Indi after all. 'It may surprise you, Indi, but I am not completely useless.'

'I never thought you were.' Indi's smile had disappeared. 'I was just trying to help.'

'You were trying to take over. To meddle. Just like you always do. Why are you even here? Things haven't worked out with Will, so you decided to come and mess up my relationship instead? I know you don't approve of the engagement.'

Indi flinched as if she had been slapped and Jade took a step back, horrified by what she had just said. First Nico and now Indi, why was she trying to sabotage relationships with everyone who loved her?

'It seems to me that you are doing a decent job of messing it up by yourself,' Indi snapped back. 'You admitted yourself you don't trust Nico. One bump and the two of you aren't even speaking. I have done my best to be supportive, but, of course, I think you are rushing into this – because you are!'

'Girls.' Their mother laid a hand on each of their arms. 'All emotions are valid and letting them out can be very cathartic, but be kind to each other, hmm? I am just going to take a little walk until all this negativity has been expelled. Remember you love each other.' Neither sister acknowledged their mother's words or paused as she floated away.

Now she had started, Jade had no idea how to stop. 'I'm sorry, Indi, I am really sorry that you felt like you had to give up your freedom to look after me, that you sacrificed so much, that you can't cope when people deviate from the plans you make for them, but you have to allow me to make my own mistakes.'

Indi just stared at her, hurt clouding her grey eyes. 'So what? You are going to rush into marriage to prove a point? That's very mature, Jade.'

'I'm rushing into marriage because I'm pregnant! Satisfied? An unplanned pregnancy with someone I've known for just a few months? I guess that proves you right, huh? Your little sister is a screw-up.'

'Pregnant?' Indi half whispered. 'How far along?'

'Eleven weeks.'

'And you didn't *tell* me?'

'Because I knew you would be disappointed and then you would try to take over.'

'Right.' Indi's mouth twisted and Jade realised she was close to tears. 'I'd try to help, because that's what sisters *do*. Jade, how *can* you have a baby here? This isn't real life. You live rent-free in paradise. What will happen when you can't work? Look, I'm not saying never marry him. I'm saying wait. Make sure it's right. Come home and have the baby there . . .'

Every word was so typical Jade could have predicted Indi's speech word for word. 'You can't help yourself, can you? Can you even hear yourself? My baby, Indi, my life! My choices. God, no wonder Will . . .' Jade was breathing hard.

Indi's face tightened. '*No wonder Will* what?'

'No wonder he is dreaming of a world away from you.' The words were spiteful, bitter, and as soon as she said them, Jade wanted to take them back. How could she have been so cruel to the sister who had never done anything but care for her? Remorse flooded through her, but it was too late. The words were out there, and she had no idea how to put things right.

Indi

Indi stood stock-still, trying to control her breathing. For one long, awful moment, she thought she might crumple, but she managed to force the threatened tears, the pain back. Again.

'I see. Because I am so controlling, you mean? Such a martyr?'

'I . . .'

'Well, Mum was right, this has been cathartic, hasn't it? We both know where we stand. My God, Jade. I had no idea you hated me so much. I'm with Mum, I don't need this negativity right now,' she managed to say steadily before she turned away, blinking rapidly, marching out of the restaurant almost at a run.

What had just happened? Was she really so overbearing? Up until now, Jade had always wanted her advice, her approval, had listened to her. When had she lost her little sister? When she met Nico? When she left for the Caribbean? Before that?

Jade was pregnant and she hadn't told her.

Lost in thought, Indi had no idea where she was heading, barely taking in her surroundings as she stumbled along the path, ending up, inevitably, by the water. Kicking off her borrowed sandals, she stepped onto the sound, walking slowly to the very edge of the water until the small waves kissed her toes.

If you must wallow, make it short, then regroup, replan. That's what her father always said when Indi had faced challenges she didn't know how to overcome. The mantra had served her well. She wasn't sure how she would have managed in those bleak days and weeks and months after his death without those words guiding her. Not that she had had time to wallow. Someone one had to step up after all. Someone had to plan the funeral, take care of the admin, cook the dinner.

Someone had to comfort her grieving mother.

Someone had to listen to the doctors and nurses, make decisions.

Someone had to visit the hospital twice a day, help Jade process her pain and her own grief.

It had to be Indi. There was no one else.

There was still no one else.

And keeping busy had stopped Indi from thinking. From wishing things might have turned out differently.

No, she wasn't going there. She couldn't.

Breathe, Indi. Concentrate on the here and now. She inhaled deeply, repeating the words until she could focus again. *Replan. Regroup.*

OK. Regroup: her relationship was over and she was losing her sister as well.

Replan. Indi stared blindly out to sea, for once her calculating brain refusing to do its tricks. Where was her Plan B? Her Plan C? Where was her soothing to-do list, her targets and KPIs?

She had nothing.

Maybe it was time to do some of that wallowing.

She stood there and tried, reliving every one of Jade's words over and over, remembering every detail of her so-called celebration dinner. But it wasn't sorrow Indi felt, not misery coursing through her veins, but fury. Her family, Will, had been more than happy to let her take care of every practical detail. She was the one who managed both her flat and the family home, who made sure insurances were up to date, there was food in the cupboards, bills were paid, gardens weeded and paintwork touched up. Not everyone had the luxury of floating through life. But those skills made her the boring, unadventurous, rigid one? Someone they took for granted. Whose own dreams were unimportant.

Indi looked out at the sea, indignation and fury warring inside her. Did they think she never wanted to be selfish and impulsive? That she hadn't had to *learn* control?

What would happen if she just let go?

Indi didn't stop to think as she began to strip. In her mind, she was going to peel off her clothes in one smooth motion, but her vest top clung to her slightly sweaty skin and she had to wrestle it over her head, temporarily blinded until she managed to wiggle free. Her shorts seemed to have contracted in the heat and she hopped around the beach, in danger of toppling over, until she finally kicked them off and stood breathless but triumphant in her new bra and pants.

She wavered for one moment, but the fury was still strong and so she straightened her back and unclipped her bra, pulling off her pants and leaving them in a heap with the other clothes. It almost physically hurt not to pick up the pile and fold it nicely, but Indi resisted, instead striding boldly into the sea.

It was warm at first, then, very suddenly, she found herself up to her waist, the water cold enough to make her stop and reconsider, until a wave roared in and over her, submerging her, leaving her breathless and gasping and yet gloriously alive, every nerve tingling with the cold salt water, her whole body light and free. Laughing to herself, she faced the next wave, diving under, emerging to shake her hair back.

No more martyr, no more living for everyone else. It was time for a change, starting right now.

Once she'd figured out how.

Chapter Twenty-One

Jade

Sunday 11 June

Jade looked out of her office window, but for once she didn't notice the stunning view and the sea failed to calm her. She had never gone to sleep not speaking to her sister before, yet over twenty-four hours had gone by since their argument and Jade and Indi still hadn't made up.

Nor were she and Nico talking.

The way she was going, she would be at outs with Mikhos by sunset and with her mother by morning.

'Your mama is a shrew,' she muttered, touching her tummy. Since telling Indi about the pregnancy, it had felt more real, and despite her sadness, she felt a shiver of excitement. The baby might be unplanned, but it wasn't unwanted. Whatever else was going on in her life she didn't regret this. It had been a shock to realise she was pregnant so young, but with every day her decision to have the baby felt more right, with every day she loved it more, became more determined to be the very best mother she could. Which meant growing up and fixing all her broken relationships, owning her role in the arguments. Dealing with her own insecurities. She wandered over to her laptop and as she touched the screen, it flickered into life with Indi's plan on screen. Jade looked it over and grimaced. She hated to admit it, but it *would* make planning her days easier. Now she would have to be grateful – once they were talking again.

Jade wanted – needed – to make up with both Indi and Nico, of course she did, but she didn't want things to be the way they had before. She loved her sister and she was grateful to her, but she was very different from the girl who had left home for the first time this winter. She didn't need protecting anymore. She didn't need directing and could make her own decisions.

But her stomach twisted with remorse and unease as she remembered the blank shock in Indi's face, the very real hurt in her eyes at Jade's words. It wasn't going to be as easy as a simple sorry for either of them.

And she had to stop being so grateful that Nico had chosen her and remind herself that she was an equal partner in this relationship if they were going to have any chance of succeeding.

Why did change have to be so difficult?

Jade sighed, but pushed her worries to one side, picking up her to-do list as she headed out of the door. Every villa had to be checked to ensure that it was personalised for the recipient, with romantic gifts for the couples and luxury items for the rest, that there were lights and microphones and everything else available that the influencers would need.

'Darling!' Her mother was in the courtyard, sketch pad in hand and charcoal by her side.

'Hi, Mum.'

'What's wrong, darling? Are you and Indi still arguing? Remember I always told you not to let the sun set on your anger.'

Despite everything, Jade couldn't help laughing. 'That wasn't you, Mum, that's Marmee in *Little Women*. Just before Amy falls through the ice, remember?'

Tabitha's forehead creased. 'Are you sure?'

'Absolutely. But for all that, it's wise advice.'

'Your sister means well, Jade, she loves you. Remember that.'

'I know.'

'She is so like your father.' Her mother's voice was wistful. 'In looks, in temperament. I used to drive him mad too.'

Jade really didn't want to dwell on the argument any longer. 'What are you working on?'

'I'm not sure yet. The sea is calling, but I don't how. Maybe naiads. Would you like to pose?'

'I would love to, but, you know, work.' Jade held up the folder and her mother nodded sagely.

'Of course. I am very proud of you, darling. You are going to be brilliant with these impacters.'

'Influencers, Mum.'

'That's what I said. Have fun, darling. Don't work too hard.'

'I won't, make sure you take a break too.'

The day flew, Jade feeling more and more stressed as the sun headed towards the west. Tomorrow, the first guests would be here and her job would change. If she didn't prove to Mikhos she could handle anything he threw at her, then her chance of a permanent role would disappear.

Between them, she and Daisee had checked every villa to make sure the champagne was chilling, the fridges stocked with goodies, that appropriate flowers and gift baskets awaited each guest. What next? Jade ran a finger down her list. Sampling the bar and restaurant service. It didn't sound much fun alone.

She headed past the spa, only to stop in her tracks as her sister emerged looking polished and glowing, her hair tamed out of its usual riotous curls into soft tumbling waves. 'Hi.'

'Hi. I was just . . .' Indi gestured towards her hair. 'Mikhos mentioned that the beautician was new to the company and asked me to try her out. Not part of my usual skill set, but it felt rude to say no.'

'You look great, you always do.'

'Me?' Indi touched her hair with a self-conscious scowl. 'My hair is too wild, I'm too tall, too curvy, too *much*.'

'I know it drives you mad that your hair is the one thing you can't control, but you're not, you know – not too much, I mean. Do you *know* how gorgeous you are? I always wanted to look like you. Hoped I would grow another few inches, get proper boobs rather than these bee stings.' Jade looked down at her chest and sighed.

'*You* get to walk around without a bra. I envy that. If I tried it, there would be mayhem, accidents, I'd be knocking out random passers-by with out-of-control nipples.'

'You get to wear shorts.' Jade didn't mean to let her voice quaver as she said the words, but somehow it did.

'If I could bear your scars . . .'

'I know.' Jade paused. 'I'm sorry. I said some really horrid things yesterday. I had no right. Especially about Will, I didn't mean it.'

'You had every right, I shouldn't have interfered. And I'm sorry. I guess I'm just not ready for you to grow up. But don't think I'm not proud of you, Jade, never think that. Whatever you do, you are going to be amazing.' Her gaze dropped to Jade's tummy. 'You're going to be a wonderful mother.'

Jade felt a rush of love for her big sister. 'I used your planner today.'

'You did?' Was Indi looking nervous? Jade wasn't sure she had ever seen that expression on her sister's face before.

'I hate to admit it, but it was really good.'

'I'm glad. How are you? You know, with everything? The baby.' She whispered the last two words, and despite everything, Jade couldn't help laughing.

'Good. I was really tired, then a little nauseous, but so far really good. I'm booked in for a scan just after you leave, we'll know more then.'

'Who knows?'

'No one apart from you, and Nico of course.' Jade sighed. 'He's still not speaking to me.'

'If I was going to butt in and offer you unwanted advice, then I would suggest you make the first move. He's proud and you hurt that pride.'

'I don't know what to say to him.'

'Tell him how you feel.' Indi paused. 'How do you feel?'

'Like I need a drink? Oh, not alcohol!' Indi was looking nervous. 'But the bartender is famous for the mocktails he creates. Join me? You can try the real thing and I'll have the fake one and we can compare notes.'

'I'd like that.' Indi pulled Jade close and Jade folded into the embrace, glad of her sister's strength. 'I love you,' Indi whispered against her hair. She brushed her back, touching her scar, and Jade flinched. Indi pulled back, her expression serious. 'Jade, I know you hate them and it is absolutely up to you whether you're happy to wear clothes that reveal your scars, but the only person who cares is you. Well, you and me. Your scars are part of *you*, Jade. They are testament to how brave you are, how resilient. How strong. You dress in whatever way makes you comfortable, but I hate that you feel you have to hide. You don't.'

'I know. I'm starting to realise that.' And she knew that a lot of her new-found confidence was down to Nico and his belief in her. How she wished she could turn the clock back to the morning of Daisee's arrival and start again.

They had reached the bar and Jade waved at Aris the barman, who was rearranging the drinks and glasses, before she slid into a nook and picked up the menu.

'OK. Are you going straight in for a classic porn star martini or do you fancy being hipster with a dirty negroni? You *could* try one of Aris's signature Greek cocktails, a basic but always pleasing Aperol spritz, or dare we risk a margarita?'

'Not tequila this early,' Indi protested.

'Early? It's practically evening. But, in that case, a dirty negroni it is for you and a clean one for me.'

The sisters curled up on one of the comfortable leather sofas and soon fell into an orgy of reminiscing and *do you remembers*, reliving past holidays Jade barely recalled. She loved these times, Indi painting pictures of the family they had once been, retelling stories of the hearty British cottage adventures their father had favoured, their mother usually disappearing to paint, but sometimes, unexpectedly, throwing herself into the hikes in the rain and cold sea swims. After he died, they always went abroad, to houses owned by artist friends, where their mother would paint to her heart's content while the girls wandered around hazy hot French villages, eating fresh bread and sunbathing by lakes.

'What's Mum up to?' Indi asked after a while, then rolled her eyes. 'As if I need to ask!'

Jade laughed. 'She's inspired by the sea apparently. We're in the charcoal exploratory phase now. I give it a week before pencils.'

'A month before paints and then out comes the clay. You can't have her here all that time, she'll drive you mad.'

'And who will feed the cat?'

Indi sighed. 'I'm probably going to move back in while I figure some things out. Thirty and living at home, single with a cat. I am every sad cliché.'

'Not thirty yet, there's three days until your birthday. You still haven't told me what you want to do.'

'Forget it's happening. Seriously. It is horribly mistimed and you'll be busy anyway. Maybe I'll join Mum and charcoal the day away.'

'You should! Miss Tate was always telling me how talented you were and it was a shame you didn't carry on with art. Why didn't you?' Jade had never quite believed her teacher, Indi had shown no interest in art that she could remember, she didn't even doodle.

Indi blinked. 'Dad and I were arguing about my A-level choices that last evening. I just couldn't after that. It felt like a betrayal somehow.'

'Oh, Indi!' It was a shock to hear Indi mention the accident, she so rarely did. Was this why? 'Dad would want you to be happy more than anything. What did stopping art change?'

'That sounds very much like something Mikhos said.'

'Does it?' Interesting. Jade was aware her sister and Mikhos seemed close, especially since their unexpected night on Naxos, but she didn't know they were confiding-in-each-other close. This needed further interrogation. She signalled to the bartender. 'OK, I'm getting you the Greek Surprise.'

'What's the surprise?' Indi asked.

'That you won't remember drinking it in the morning? Ouzo, Tia Maria and coffee . . .'

'Wake you up, then send you unconscious? OK, what about you?'

'Elderflower and mint. I know it's dull, but drinking fruit juice without the alcohol gets a bit sickly after a while.'

Jade waited until the drinks were in front of them and Indi had taken a first cautious sip before she went in for interrogation.

'So, talking of Mikhos . . .'

'I don't believe we were.'

'What happened in Naxos?'

'Nothing much. Why?' Jade watched Indi's cheeks turn red and grinned, enjoying her sister's discomfort.

'I just thought I detected something between you. A *frisson*.'

'A what?'

'Like a connection, something charged.'

'You really want to know?' Indi grimaced. 'I told him I wanted to have a fling with him and he turned me down.'

Jade stared at her sister, trying to figure out if she was joking. She looked serious enough. 'You did *what*?'

'You heard me.'

Jade sat back, aware her mouth was hanging open in astonishment. Her sensible sister suggesting a one-night stand! 'India Rose Drewe. You never fail to amaze me. What on earth made you do that?'

'We talked, really talked, it felt intimate, you know? And we danced and then we got to the room and there was only one bed and we were both being super-polite and lots of you have it, no you have it, I insist, and then I said we should both have it and then . . .' She trailed off.

'And then what? You propositioned him?'

'Priya thought it was a good idea. A holiday fling, I mean, not the proposition.'

'Oh well, if *Priya* says so.'

'I'm sorry, Jade, it is so inappropriate. He's your boss and Nico's cousin. I should never have done it.'

'*He* should not have turned you down.'

'I don't blame him, what a terrible position to put him in . . .'

'Or not put him in, as the case might be.' Jade giggled.

'Jade! Anyway, what he said was that he was tempted but didn't want to be any woman's rebound fling.'

'Oh. Fair enough. I suppose.'

'Absolutely. I clearly need to work on my seduction skills. Less blurting out embarrassing statements is a good start.'

'He's tempted, though, clearly. Does that mean at some point in the future you two might actually get together?' Would it be awkward? Maybe a little, but there was an undeniable energy between Mikhos and Indi. Who was Jade to deny them? And if mere attraction to Mikhos was making Indi behave unpredictably then maybe a fling with Mikhos was exactly what her sister needed to help her relax.

'I'm thinking of renouncing men and embracing my cat lady status.' Indi was slurring now. Well, she was four cocktails in!

'A valid choice too.'

'So.' Indi eyed her meaningfully. 'Enough about me. What's Daisee like to work with?'

Jade rolled her eyes. Daisee wasn't the topic she would have chosen but Indi had answered all her questions about Mikhos, it was only fair she was honest in return. 'You know when I get past the perfect hair and that kind of slinky eyeliner I can never do, she's actually all right,' Jade said grudgingly. 'She's a hard worker, knows her stuff. She told me that she's looking for a career in case she doesn't marry a footballer, but actually she's a lot shrewder than she lets on. A lot of it is a carefully honed act. Honestly, if it wasn't for the Nico thing, I might quite like her. I can see why he fell for her.'

'Jade, you know Nico had girlfriends before you. Why have you gone so deep over this one?'

'It's irrational, I know. Do you think it's hormones?'

'I couldn't possibly comment.'

'She's just so unlike me. It's not Daisee exactly, it's all the Daisees he's been with. What if he gets tired of me? Of being a dad? He's talking of giving up the boat, of getting an office job, of changing his whole life for me. What if he has regrets? I'm not outgoing and confident and glossy. What if I'm not enough?' And there they were, the doubts that had been plaguing her ever since Nico had proposed.

'But the difference is that he wasn't in love with her, Jade, he wasn't in love with any of those girls he may or may not have had flings with. But he does love you. I might think it's a bad idea for lots of practical reasons, but I can see it a mile off. He loves you, Jade, and you love him and you are going to have a baby together. Why does it matter that he had a summer romance last year?'

'You've changed your tune.'

'I'm adapting to my newly single status. I need to believe in happy ever afters.'

'I don't know, Indi. It's like I've been living in this romantic fantasy and I've just woken up. As soon as I saw Daisee, I knew it was all too good to be true.'

'Talk to him, Jade. Give him a chance. There's always a home for you and the baby in London, but if your heart is here, then this is where you should be. Don't let pride stand in your way.'

'Four cocktails.'

'Four cocktails what?'

'To bring out your romantic side. I'll make sure Mikhos knows that!' Jade sighed. 'But you're right. I will talk to him. I promise.'

Chapter Twenty-Two

Indi

Indi opened an eye and immediately closed it again. The light was bright – far, far too bright. Her head throbbed like someone was marching up and down on her temples and her insides were in full-on washing-machine mode.

How many cocktails had they got through? Correction, had *she* got through? Jade's mocktails didn't count, the only hangover her sister would be suffering would be sugar-comedown related. All Indi knew was that she'd lost count after the fourth. She didn't even remember getting back to the villa or to bed.

She opened half an eye again and spied a glass of water on the bedside table. Blessing drunk Indi for her foresight, she downed it and sank back into sleep.

When she woke again, she felt marginally better. It only took three attempts to sit up and five to get out of bed.

Somehow she made it to the shower to spend a good twenty minutes under water as hot as she could bear. It took another half-hour to dress in one of the outfits she'd bought in Naxos Town, pull her hair back into a ponytail and do her best to repair some of the damage to her face. She still looked slightly green when she had finished, but at least she wouldn't scare small children and animals. Probably.

Well, she had promised herself she would start to live more spontaneously and, to be fair, not one of those cocktails had been planned. Although getting blind drunk wasn't quite what she'd had in mind.

The problem was, she didn't know what she wanted. Things clearly had to change – *were* changing, for her, for Jade, she couldn't fight it, she had to embrace it. She just had to figure out how.

Indi laughed, a small hiccup closer to a sob. Look at her, planning how to be less rigid!

Live in the moment, Drewe, she told herself. For the rest of the week at least.

Cautiously and slowly, Indi descended the stairs. The villa was humming with activity, busy with people all filled with an alarming sense of purpose. Of course! Today was the launch, the influencers due to arrive any time.

An old, familiar worry for Jade seized her, but Indi forced herself to push it away. If Jade wanted her help, she would ask.

The scent of coffee lured her into the courtyard. Jade was sat at a table, papers and laptop spread before her, while Mikhos was glued to his laptop typing frantically. Only Nico wasn't giving off frenetic energy vibes, although he was clearly deep in thought, his gaze fixed on the distance, brow furrowed. Indi remembered Jade's words from yesterday, that Nico was going to give up his dreams for her and the baby. Indi knew what that was like and it made her soften towards him. His instincts and heart were clearly in the right place.

'Hi.' If only she could remember how she got back to her bed last night. Or what she had said to who. Hopefully she and Jade had made their own quiet way back and not seen or spoken to anyone.

Mikhos looked up, his smile wry as he nodded. 'Take a seat. How are you feeling?'

'Like I drank the bar dry.'

'You almost did. It took Jade and me an hour to get you to bed.'

Indi chilled as she took in Mikhos' words. '*You* put me to bed?'

'I couldn't exactly leave you to sleep it off in the sand. Don't worry, you were tucked up and snoring by eight thirty.'

Indi tried to remember what she had woken up in. A long T-shirt. Her underwear . . . *Thank God*!

'Thank you then, that was above and beyond any hosting duties.' She slipped into the seat Mikhos indicated without looking at him, gratefully accepting the coffee a maid she hadn't met before brought her. She took a sip, ignoring the churning in her stomach, and smiled across the table at a sympathetic-looking Jade. 'I'm sorry, I hope I wasn't drunk and obnoxious.'

Jade grinned. 'You are a very sweet drunk. Until you got the karaoke urge, that is. Having said that, you did a very nice rendition of "Flowers", followed by "Driving Licence". What you were lacking in tune and sometimes lyrics, you made up for in attitude.'

Indi went cold. 'Ha,' she managed feebly, she had never done karaoke before, but to her horror Mikhos nodded.

'Sadly, you didn't manage the promised rendition of "I Will Survive".'

'Oh God, I am every sort of pathetic cliché.' To go along with her thumping head and churning stomach.

'An adorable, pathetic cliché,' her sister said kindly. 'And look on the bright side, you got it all out of your system before the influencers arrive. There are no videos on TikTok, not even a photo. Just beautiful memories.' She grinned, looking annoyingly chirpy, a glowing advert for teetotalism.

Indi did her best to recover her shredded dignity. 'I don't usually drink very much, I am so sorry. Do let me know how much I owe. For the cocktails.'

Mikhos' lips twitched. 'I did ask you to try out the facilities, you were just following instructions. The drinks are on me. I look forward to your review of each one later.'

Indi thought about arguing but remembered in time the price per night of the resort. One cocktail was probably her weekly going-out budget. 'Thank you. I can just about remember the dirty negroni and the Aperol, but after that I could have been drinking anything. My poor liver. Detox time for me for the next week, maybe month, possibly even the rest of my life.'

'Not Wednesday,' Jade said firmly. 'You can have today and tomorrow to recover, but Wednesday is your birthday and you are going to celebrate. And, speaking of, stop not answering the question – what do you want to do?'

'I did answer. All I want is to pretend it's not happening. Seriously, Jade. I don't want a fuss.'

She didn't. Not anymore. She'd had all these dreams for her birthday, but now with just two days to go, she had no idea what to do apart from pretend it wasn't happening. She'd always thought she'd spend her thirtieth with her friends at her favourite pub and then Will would whisk her away to Paris and propose. She'd dropped enough hints to make sure Will created the perfect surprise party, who to invite, where to hold it, what snacks to order . . .

But while she had been dropping hints, his mind had been elsewhere.

Her thirtieth was going to slip by as quietly as her eighteenth and her twenty-first had. Maybe that wasn't a bad thing.

'We'll see,' said Jade ominously, who clearly wasn't on the same quiet birthday page.

Time for a change of subject. 'Where's Mum?'

'On the beach communing with Poseidon. At least that's what I think she said. She's really in her element now.'

'And you told me she was the wildest Drewe,' Mikhos observed, his placid tone belied by the wicked glint in his eye.

Selective deafness was the only possible defence. Indi sipped her coffee and started to feel marginally more human as the rest of the table gathered their things. Nico was due to head over to Naxos in an hour to collect the first batch of influencers (did influencers come in batches? Maybe a frenzy? There must be a collective noun.) and it was all systems go.

'I'll get to the office in a moment,' she said as Mikhos stood up. 'I won't let you down.'

'You should take the day to recover.'

'I'm fine. Honestly. It's self-inflicted, that's no excuse to—' What must he be thinking? It was launch day and she was suffering with a hangover! No cold or flu usually stopped Indi from working, let alone a hangover.

'No excuse to take the day off when you're on holiday?' He was openly laughing at her, but she didn't mind. There was something intimate about it, warm. 'Indi. Relax. Enjoy the sunshine. I'll see you later.'

'Enjoy the sunshine. Right.'

OK then. She really didn't feel like working on a scoping document right this minute, if she was being honest. So she would, she'd enjoy the sunshine in a spontaneous, relaxed way.

The others darted off, leaving Indi alone. She tilted her head and let the sun warm her. She loved this courtyard, the greenery, the sound of water, the decadence of the swimming pool. If she was rich and lived somewhere hot then she would build one just like it. Maybe she'd fantasise herself an island while she was at it. An island to herself. With a never-ending supply of mezze and a nice, cool *non*-alcoholic drink.

But try as she might to imagine the peace, the solitude, she couldn't help but picture a companion. Tall, dark-eyed, a jawline she really wanted to trace with every finger for comparison. Wrists that, for reasons she really didn't want to examine, she couldn't stop thinking about. A companion who she could talk to about anything, someone who would put her to bed when she was drunk, who seemed to understand her, to like her. It was nice to be liked.

Although she wanted more than just like.

Tell me when you're ready for more than a rebound, he had said. Was that still what she wanted, a rebound fling? Or did she just want *him*, Mikhos?

But now he had put her drunken self to bed, she doubted he wanted her in return.

She looked up at the sound of footsteps and saw Nico walking towards her, smart in his ACR uniform. 'Hi.'

He stopped, his expression a little wary. 'Hi.'

'I just wanted to say . . .' She paused. She wasn't going to interfere in Jade's life anymore, but she couldn't pretend she didn't know. 'Nico, Jade told me. That she's pregnant.'

'Oh.'

'I guess I should say congratulations.' Not that she had said it to Jade, she realised now, nor had she congratulated her on her engagement. She needed to do both.

'Thank you.' He indicated the chair opposite. 'Can I join you for a moment?'

'Of course.'

He sat down, made a clear effort to be his usual relaxed self, but his smile was less easy-going than normal, and she noted dark shadows under his eyes.

'I want to be the best husband and father I can be, I want you to know that.'

'That's good to know, but it's Jade you should be speaking to, not me.'

He pushed a hand through his hair. 'I know, but if she doesn't trust me, then I don't know how to convince her.'

Indi's heart went out to him, he was evidently so sincere. But she had promised herself she wouldn't interfere in Jade's life anymore. 'Look, Nico. It's really hard for me not to jump in here and try to make things right for Jade, whether that's telling you why I think she reacted the way she did to Daisee, or trying to steer her towards the outcome I think is best for her, but she's not just fallen out with you, she was pretty cross with me as well and she was right to be. I've learned my lesson and I am trying to butt out from interfering in her life.'

'So no words of advice? No one knows her like you do.' His gaze was beseeching.

'That's not true, Nico. You know a different side of her to me, and it might be a shorter relationship, still new, but you're the expert on *that* Jade. All I'll say is don't tell her what you think she wants to hear, tell her what's in your heart.'

'Setting up as a counsellor now, is there no end to your talents?'

How did a man as big as Mikhos just appear like that? 'No, no end at all. Project manager, counsellor and very unique singer.'

The warmth in his eyes as he acknowledged her reply heated her through. 'Very unique. Your dancing was special too.'

Oh no. 'Please tell me you are joking?'

'I am, it was more of a sway than a dance.'

'Mikhos,' Nico interrupted, pale but determined. 'I've been wanting to ask you. The job you mentioned, the trainee manager one. Is it still available?'

'It's not so much a job, Nico. It's more bringing you properly into the company. And of course it's available, I always wanted you alongside me, but what about your boat? Your plans?'

'I'm going to be a father. And I need Jade to know that I take that seriously. I need to give her a proper home and security, a steady income. A husband she can believe in, trust. And that means a proper job, not dreams.'

Indi watched Nico, her heart squeezing. He loved her sister. *He really loved her.* He loved her enough to put her first, to put the family they were going to be first. He loved her in a way she knew Will had never loved her – and if she was painfully honest, nor she him. She thought Jade was too young, too inexperienced, to make such a big decision, but her little sister had found a man who would do what it took to make her happy. She could learn a lot from Jade, she just hoped that her sister realised just how lucky she was and didn't let her insecurities push Nico away.

But whatever she did it was Jade's choice and Indi would respect that, however hard doing so was.

'A father?' Mikhos was clearly shocked, but he recovered himself quickly. 'Congratulations.' He pulled Nico out of his seat, enveloping him in a bear hug. 'My little cousin, all grown up.' He raised an eyebrow at Indi. 'Are you OK with this?'

'Getting more OK with it every day,' she admitted. 'But I know that Jade will be a wonderful mother and Nico clearly is going to be an amazing father. And *I* will be the best aunt I can be.' They weren't just words, Indi realised, she meant it. She was excited for the baby, to being an aunt, to new beginnings and hope for a family that for so long had been defined by tragedy.

Mikhos' gaze was warm and full of approval. 'With an aunt like you on its side, then the baby is lucky indeed.'

Indi watched him walk off, full of emotions she didn't know how to put into words. But one thing she did know was that this might not be how she had seen her life as she turned thirty, but right now she wouldn't change it for a million engagement rings and a tick by every one of those unachieved goals.

Chapter Twenty-Three

Jade

'Attention please!' Jade had had no idea that her voice was capable of such sergeant major volume and authority, but to her surprise it worked and the chattering group fell silent and turned to face her.

She swallowed. It was an intimidating group. She had never seen such polished perfection in such numbers before, nor a group so obsessed with their phones, their backdrops, their poses, their filters. In the half-hour they had been here, they hadn't stopped photographing, videoing, dancing, hashtagging, accompanied by a soundtrack of exaggerated compliments, shrieks and exclamations.

The majority were female and in their twenties. Ethnicities and dress seize varied, but the glossy sheen, perfect make-up and camera-ready hair were ubiquitous. The handful of single men were less varied looks-wise, all overly sculpted in a way that left no doubt they spent most of their time in the gym, hair short and ruthlessly arranged. There were also six couples, all but one heterosexual, nestling close to each other in complementary if skimpier than skimpy outfits designed to create the perfect picture.

Jade had never seen such an array of glowing good looks and utter narcissism in all her life and she was acutely aware of the unfashionable length and fit of her skirt and how much of her carefully applied make-up she had sweated off already. As for the couples, they made her realise just how much she missed Nico, the reassurance of his smile, the way he made her feel like she could do anything, feel completely desirable. If he were with her, she would find the group entertaining, not intimidating.

She drew her shoulders back. What was she thinking? She did *not* need a man to give her validation. She was in control here. She had this.

'Welcome to Agios Iohannis and the newest and most exclusive member of the Angelos Cycladic Resort family,' she said, proud to hear her voice stay steady. 'You are all the very first guests here and I know you are going to have a wonderful time. In a minute, Daisee and I will direct you to your villas, each with stunning views . . .' She continued through her prepared speech, reminding them of the itinerary, their contracted obligations and the hashtags and tags they needed to use, telling them about the restaurant and bar, how to order room service, sign up for activities, and ensuring she shoehorned in some of the eco-friendly credentials of the island.

To her relief, the end was greeted with a smattering of applause and smiles. Her first task had gone as planned. It was a good sign. She had this.

It still took several hours to get all the influencers settled into their villas. Daisee had gone through the plans with military precision, reassigning roommates where necessary, knowing where there might be problems. This one had got another's sponsorship, that one had slept with someone else's boyfriend, one expected couple had broken up and were now dating new people. It was a complicated jigsaw, but somehow they had got there and the two women reconvened on the beach, knowing their charges were safely occupied unpacking and exploring their villas for the next hour.

'All this for just a few days.' Jade collapsed onto a handy sunbed with a groan.

'Between them, they have a reach of over twenty million,' Daisee said, curling herself up on the next sunbed with a grace that had eluded Jade. 'Most of that audience can only ever aspire to a place like this, but that doesn't matter, they'll ensure that this is the last word in luxurious cool. The journalists have a very different audience, we need the combination of the two.'

'But is it necessary? We're practically booked up for nearly two years already without a single review.'

'Thereby adding to its allure. Bookings can be cancelled, the work we're doing ensures that they won't be.'

'I guess. So, let's go through the itinerary.' She had to give it to Daisee, she knew exactly what she was doing and she was a hard worker. While Jade had been curled up in the bar with Indi, Daisee had been busy tweaking the itinerary to make sure their guests didn't have a single moment to feel bored. Or to get up to mischief.

'OK, so we've done the welcome tour, briefing and settling in. This afternoon is an activities one, followed by cocktail hour here at the bar. Then everyone will return to their villas for their dinner. Deliveries start at seven thirty.'

That was a change. 'Isn't that a lot more complicated than feeding them en masse here at the restaurant?' Jade asked.

'They've all pre-ordered and this way they get to showcase how luxurious it is to eat in the villa and we get plenty of dining-on-the-terrace pictures. We've got especially romantic meals for those here with their SO.'

SO? Special one? Significant other? Safe option?

'And hashtag me-time for the rest,' Daisee finished.

Jade could only nod, biting her lip – had Daisee actually said hashtag non-ironically?

'Tomorrow evening, there's the party and that's a hot and cold buffet showcasing local cuisine. Wednesday dinner here with the option of eating in Naxos if they take advantage of the organised day trip.'

'Let's hope most do,' Jade said feelingly. 'Then they are the tour guides' problem.'

'We'll still need to accompany them.'

'I'll feel like a teacher on a school trip. I thought nothing could be worse than thirty four- and five-year-olds at the Science Museum, but I think I might have underestimated forty influencers set loose on Naxos.'

The influencers had been given five activity slots, one for this afternoon, two on Tuesday and two on Wednesday. Sunbathing and using their private pool counted as an activity, as did spending a few hours on any of the island's beaches – that was the kind of activity holiday Jade could get behind! Other options included a few hours at the spa – another very appealing option – a trip out on the boat to swim or, more likely, pose, with paddle-boarding or jet-skiing available for the more active. They also had the option of the day trip. Each influencer had to pick five different activities – four if they chose Naxos – to ensure that all the island had to offer was highlighted equally across all their different platforms. It was completely eye-opening. Jade still didn't quite see how influencing was an actual job, but she had to admit her charges must be doing something right if they got to sample all this luxury for free.

'I'm going to wander around for the rest of the afternoon and take pictures for the ACR's social media channels,' Daisee said. 'Do you want me to take the radio?'

'No, I'll stay on call and I need to check in with the restaurant about tomorrow as well. There's a lot of pieces to this party.' Aurelia had arranged for a DJ, entertainment and yet more goody bags, as well as a lavish buffet focusing on sustainable, local food. With every aspect needing to be shipped to the island, it was a logistical challenge and Jade wanted to triple-check every detail. This was the kind of thing Indi thrived on. Maybe she could ask her to help.

And there, she admitted, was the irony. Two days ago, she had said terrible things to her sister and accused her of butting in on Jade's space. Now Jade would welcome her interference with open arms.

Underlying the whole was the niggling worry of Indi's birthday. Jade didn't believe for a second that Indi really wanted her birthday to be forgotten. Indi loved birthdays and especially loved notable ones. Hadn't she taken Jade to Euro Disney for her twenty-first for an over-the-top few days of nostalgic girl time? Will – she allowed herself an extreme eyeroll – had enjoyed a surprise party and a weekend in Barcelona complete with football tickets. And Indi would get what? Jade didn't even have a cake.

No one else was going to be able to sort this out, it was down to Jade. She might just need to pull in a couple of favours.

'Great!' Daisee smiled, flicked her ponytail and walked away, even her walk was jaunty.

Jade watched her go and found that the jealousy that had eaten away at her had gone. Her reaction to Daisee, to finding out that she and Nico were last year's news, was just that, *her* reaction, *her* insecurities, *her* worries over the future.

She'd made up with Indi, now she had to figure out how she and Nico moved forward.

She sighed. Mikhos had been right. She had been naïve and believed that they were heading into a happy future just because they wanted it. The disagreement over the apartment, her jealousy over Daisee just proved how far she had to go. Turned out growing up wasn't easy, but Jade had no choice. She was going to be a mother, and thanks to her sister, she knew exactly what kind of mother she wanted to be.

She started to walk back to the villa in search of Indi, but veered off to the jetty where she knew Nico was readying the jet skis and paddleboards for anyone choosing an active afternoon. He stood on the beach, bare-chested and bronzed, hands on hips as he gave a moored jet ski the once-over and her heart jolted painfully. She missed him, missed the surety of him, of them.

He must have heard her because he turned, his smile professionally welcoming, only for it soften and deepen as he realised it was her.

'Jade, is everything OK?'

'Every influencer accounted for.'

'Indi told me that she knows – about the baby, I mean.'

Jade sank down into the sand beside him, wrapping her hands around her knees, and he joined her. 'I should have cleared it with you first, I know. After all, I was the one who said to wait before we told people. I'm sorry.' She sighed. 'The worst part is that I said it in anger to shock her.'

'She didn't seem shocked to me.'

'She's had a couple of days – and a lot of cocktails – in which to process it.'

'Mikhos heard us talking about it too.'

'So now he knows? That's fair. But if he and Indi both know, then I really need to tell Mum. I don't want her to hear it from anyone else. You might want to set up a call with your parents too.'

Nico turned to her, taking her hand in his. 'I spoke to Mikhos about the job. I told him I wanted it.'

Jade's heart sank. 'Oh, Nico, no! I don't want you to change all your plans for me.'

'I want to,' he said firmly. 'I *need* to. You're right, Jade. Not that bit when you thought I don't really love you – you couldn't be more wrong there – but I've done a lot of thinking recently. I guess I *have* drifted through life, from boat to boat, relationship to relationship, happy with the lack of commitment, dreaming of a future but never in a hurry to get there. I liked that you saw me as steady, wanted a life with me. You made me want to be the man you saw. Daisee . . .' He paused.

'I know,' she said softly. 'I know that my anger over Daisee has more to do with me, than you. I have a lot of insecurities, Nico. I guess *I* hid those from *you*. I liked that you saw me as free, and confident, not as poor Jade with her scars and operations who missed out on so much. It's like I reinvented myself with you, but I couldn't shed my old self entirely. I looked at Daisee and thought, well, of course he fell for her, look at her.' She looked down at her clasped hands.

'Hey, look at me.'

But before she could respond, the sound of voices alerted her to the arrival of two of the couples, all impossibly gorgeous, glowing and toned and radiating *hashtag blessed* vibes. The girls were in bright, teeny bikinis, the boys in surfer shorts and shades, competitively jesting as they neared the jet skis.

'I had better go,' she said quickly. 'We've both got work to do.'

'Jade . . .'

She leaned over and gave him a quick, fleeting kiss, realising as she did so just how much she had missed him. How much she had wanted to talk over her argument with

Indi with him, how much she had wanted him to hold her and tell her that everything was going to be OK.

'We'll talk,' she promised. 'Let's just get through the next few days, OK?'

'It's a deal.' He got to his feet with the careless grace she loved and held out a hand to help her up from the beach. 'Just remember one thing. I love *you*, Jade Drewe. And that's not going to change.'

'Me too.' Jade squeezed his hand quickly, then turned to walk away. Things weren't back to normal, not just yet. She had to process his news about the job for a start. Before that, she had to find a way to tell her mother and Nico's parents about the baby, which would change things once again. They would never again be the carefree couple who had kissed in the Caribbean surf. But maybe that was OK. Jade had never felt as strong, as focused as she did right now, which was good because she still had three days of influencing influencers to get though. She was going to need every ounce of her new-found strength.

Chapter Twenty-Four

Indi

Monday 12 June

Despite feeling more alive than she had just an hour ago, Indi didn't think she could face many people, especially groups of strangers – and glamorous strangers at that – which meant she needed to stay on this side of the island. Nor could she hide away in the office, Mikhos had been quite clear that she should take the day off, and if she was being honest, her hangover was still making itself a little more at home in her temples and limbs than she was comfortable with. Maybe it was time to try relaxing.

To think was to act. Well, normally to think was to open a spreadsheet and make a plan, but even Indi could manage to sunbathe without KPIs and objectives. Returning to her room, she grabbed the beach bag she'd picked up in Naxos Town and added a couple of towels and a book Priya had lent her with strict instructions to enjoy. Sunglasses, sun cream, a hat, chilled water from the mini-fridge . . .

Indi picked up one of the swimsuits she'd also bought on Naxos, a pretty blue-and-white-striped number, and looked at it. Yes, it was as pretty as she remembered. And modest, low-cut on the leg, high on the neck. Sedate and sensible. Exactly what she'd been looking for. Only, was it maybe just a little bit boring?

The two bikinis Aurelia had left her were hanging in her

wardrobe, tiny colourful scraps of material. They wouldn't cover *one* boob, let alone two, surely. They would probably look ridiculous on.

But she'd never know if she didn't try . . .

She picked up an orange one, and looked at it. 'Here goes nothing,' she muttered.

It took a few attempts to figure out which was the front and which was the back and where all the straps and strings went. The end result was a little too reminiscent of chicken trussed up for roasting for Indi's comfort and she spent the next ten minutes trying to wriggle out of it.

The second was more traditional in shape, if still scantier than anything she had ever worn before, and when she stood in front of the mirror, she was fully prepared to laugh, wince and discard it for her one-piece. Only . . . she stared at herself. It really wasn't too bad. In fact, it looked rather good. The bright pink suited her far more than she had anticipated. She would never have picked the colour herself, but it brought out the chestnut glints in her hair, made her grey eyes look more silvery. It was, of course, a size too small, but the tight fit wasn't unflattering. The bottoms were a tiny triangle held together with string, the top barely contained her breasts, but somehow it worked. Even with the hangover, she felt – well, she felt *sexy*.

Indi threw a sundress over the top of the bikini, pulled on her flip-flops, making her way down the stairs and to the front door remembering Jade's description of the small cove behind the villa, private and sheltered. It sounded perfect.

Just a few minutes later, Indi emerged from the olive groves to find an idyllic, if small, semicircle of soft sand. She stood for a moment and breathed in the fresh air, taking in the unadulterated view out over the sea, feeling her head clear and her stomach settle.

It *was* the perfect spot. Trees nearby offered shade for when the sun got too overbearing and the sea shelf was high at this point, so the waves lapped rather than roared onto the shore. Looking around, all she could see was sea, sand, trees and sky, as if she were all alone in the world. All she could hear was the gentle rumble of the water.

Indi had applied her sun cream before donning the bikini and so she spread out her towel and lay down in the heat of the sun, her book forgotten beside her, eyes closed under the ridiculously sized sunglasses Aurelia had also left her. The warmth soaked into her body, into her bones, and somehow she knew she would be OK. She'd sort out her living situation, she'd figure out life on her own. She'd work out how to be the best aunt she could be, even if she was in a different country. Life would go on, different maybe, but on.

It was all too much introspection for such a beautiful day and Indi resolutely pushed the thoughts to the back of her mind and concentrated on feeling the sun seep into her bones, her mind drifting, until the sound of footsteps alerted her to the fact that she was a) not alone, and b) in a bikini at least a size too small, and one which hadn't been exactly all-encompassing to begin with.

Indi opened her eyes, but she knew who it was before she saw him. Mikhos.

'I took your advice,' she adjusted her sunglasses. 'Look. I'm relaxing.'

'Wonders will never cease.' She could hear the smile in his voice. 'How is it?'

'Nice. I mean, I wouldn't want to do it all the time, but nice.'

She popped herself up on one elbow, then remembered the brevity of her bikini and tried to rearrange herself, painfully aware that if she wasn't all cleavage, she was all bum.

Mikhos didn't move, she couldn't see his expression under his sunglasses, but she knew he was watching her. That he was aware of every shift, every centimetre of flesh exposed, and the sudden surge of heat she felt had nothing to do with the sun.

She searched for something to say. 'So, you must be pleased that Nico wants to come and work with you properly?'

'I think we have spent more than enough time talking about Jade and Nico.'

'Right.'

The silence stretched, but it wasn't uncomfortable, more anticipatory. Mikhos still didn't move, preternaturally still.

'I've been doing a lot of thinking,' she said after a while. 'About what I said in Naxos. You were right. It was really rude of me.'

'That's not what I said.'

'It's what you meant. Telling you I wanted a fling to get over my ex. It was rude. And . . .' she swallowed. 'It wasn't entirely true. It was an excuse. Because if my life had been so perfect and my plans so foolproof and I had been so certain of Will, then how could I want another man so soon after he left me? It had to be a rebound, that was the only thing that made sense. That's what I told myself. I was wrong.'

'You were?' She still couldn't gauge what he was thinking, there were no clues in his tone, his expression still hidden by his sunglasses.

'Yes. Because I wanted you not as a rebound, but because you're you.' There it was. She'd said it. And she'd never felt so vulnerable in her life.

He didn't answer, instead he shifted his gaze out to the sea. 'Have you been for a swim yet?'

'Not yet,' she confessed. Where was this going? Had he heard her, because she didn't think she'd ever find the courage to repeat any of that.

'Right then.' Mikhos removed his sunglasses before sliding off his shirt in one easy gesture.

'What are you doing?' she half-squeaked.

'Swimming.' He unzipped his shorts and stepped out of them gracefully. Indi couldn't tear her gaze away from toned, olive flesh, a reassuringly broad chest covered with a smattering of dark hair which traced an intriguing path down over his nicely muscled stomach to disappear under the waistband of his short, snug swimming shorts. Shorts that left about as much to the imagination as her bikini.

Indi swallowed, her mouth suddenly dry.

'So, are you joining me?'

She looked down at herself doubtfully. 'I'm not sure this bikini is actually meant to be swum in.'

'Then take it off.' His eyes gleamed. 'I promise not to look.'

'Liar!' But she accepted the hand he extended to her and allowed him to pull her up, his grasp strong and sure. 'I'll risk it.'

'It suits you.'

She tugged at it self-consciously. 'Do you think? It's a little small.'

'Don't do that.' His voice was harsh and she looked up at him in surprise, aware that when they were this close, he was a good few inches taller than her, something she wasn't used to. She liked it.

'Don't do what?'

'Don't put yourself down. You look magnificent.' His voice lowered. 'Good enough to eat.'

Indi's body warmed by at least ten degrees.

'This is nothing . . .' Her voice was unnatural, high. 'The other one was all straps. I looked like a turkey ready for Christmas, or as if I were wearing a bondage outfit.'

His eyes darkened even more. 'Now that I would have liked to see. Maybe you can give me a private showing later.'

Indi stared up at Mikhos for a long charged moment. 'Maybe I will.'

She swayed towards him, almost but not quite touching, her breasts aching for the hard planes of his chest, for touch, for release, aware her breath was coming in shallow pants.

Mikhos hadn't even touched her and she was ready to explode.

'You look warm.' He reached out and brushed an errant curl back behind her ear, his fingers brushing her neck as he did so. Indi quivered and she saw his acknowledgement of the effect he was having on her by the flare of heat in his eyes. 'Like you have a fever.' He lazily traced his finger from her ear, across her jawline, curving along her half-open mouth. 'Do you need cooling off?'

Probably. *No.* That was the last thing she needed, thank you very much. Indi was quite happy to stay in this hazy, not quite real fug of desire and need. But before she could even attempt to formulate an answer, Mikhos had swung her up in his arms and was striding towards the water's edge purposefully.

'Put me down.' She was aware she was bleating like some kind of clichéd heroine. Next thing, she would be beating her fists on his back. No one had picked her up since . . . well, she couldn't remember when. 'Mikhos, seriously you'll break your back!' Generously curved Amazons weren't exactly easy armfuls, but Mikhos didn't seem fazed by her length or weight as he waded into the sea, ankle deep, knee deep, thigh deep, waist deep . . . Her feet were submerged, the water at this depth colder than she had expected, deliciously fresh on her heated skin.

'You want me to put you down?' he said teasingly.

'Not here!' Now she was clinging on, despite herself laughing at the absurdity of it all, feeling his solid chest shake, hearing the rumble of his laughter too.

'No? How about here?' He took a step further into the sea, then another. Now her bikini bottoms were soaked, her calves.

'Mikhos . . .' It was half an entreaty, half an acknowledgement of the inevitable as he swung her down to face him.

The water came up to the top of her ribs, swirling around the bottom of the bikini top, cold and shocking and welcome. Her arms were still around Mikhos as she found her balance and she realised that his were still firmly clasped against her waist, holding her close so she could feel every hard sinew, every muscle and . . . She swallowed. There was no doubt he wanted her too. Wasn't cold water meant to shrink things in that area? If so, no wonder Mikhos was so confident. He had nothing to compensate for.

'I thought you were going to drop me,' she accused him.

'Never. You need to learn to hold on, Indi. To trust people to have you.'

'I trust you.' It was true. Truer than she was comfortable with. She had accused Jade of jumping in too fast with a man she had known for six months and here was Indi jumping all the way in after little more than a week.

No more waiting. Indi was used to taking control and Mikhos had had things his way for far too long. She slid her hands up to his shoulder and stepped even closer, enjoying his sharp intake of breath. 'That was naughty.' Her voice was breathy and she watched him swallow with satisfaction. 'Bad boys need to be punished . . .'

His eyes flared and while he was still clearly processing that statement, she shoved, not too hard but enough to unbalance him, and Mikhos was down in the water, totally submerged with a yell of indignation. Indi's sense of victory was short-lived as he emerged, spluttering, hair slicked back, body gleaming, to grab her by the waist and pull her down on top of him. Indi twisted, sliding out of his grasp as she set off in a fast crawl, along the shoreline, hearing the splash of water, his ragged breath as he raced towards her, overtaking her, stopping her, pulling her close – and yes! Thank God! Finally! His kiss was everything she had been doing her best not to dream about, sure, strong, practised and yet intimate, as if he was exactly where he wanted to be and she the only person he wanted to be with.

Somehow Indi was on her feet, still chest deep in the water, entwined around him, kissing him back with all the weeks of pent-up strain and stress needing release. She entwined her hands around his neck, pulling him closer, loving the surety of his hands splayed on her waist, possessive and yet tender, his fingers caressing as they held her there. Her legs were entangled with his, her body pressed so close to him, it was if she were dissolving into him.

She had no idea how long they stayed there, the waves washing around them, the sun beating down on their heads, she only knew now. Mouths hot and urgent, soft and sweet, lips trailing tantalising kisses, hands exploring, roaming, discovering. She could have stayed there forever, for the first time in a really long time not thinking ahead, not planning, or worrying, just being, until Mikhos, still kissing her as if she was the only important thing in the world right now, began to slowly but meaningfully back her through the sea up to the shore.

'What?' she managed as she reluctantly tore herself away, her lips swollen, feeling completely unlike her own mouth, her hair wet and tangled, bikini half undone. But she didn't care.

'I want to see you,' was all he said, but the meaning, the intent in his eyes was so clear, her legs shook with anticipation.

'Here?'

'Anywhere.'

Indi tried to muster her lust-addled thoughts. The cove was hidden but not private, the island no longer a secret paradise for just the lucky few, but a busy bustling place. The chances that no one would come exploring were slim.

But at the same time she didn't want to wait, didn't want to run the risk that heading back to the villa reality might reassert its grip on her, that she would literally come to her senses. Because she deserved this, didn't she, after a lifetime of always being the sensible one? She deserved no-holds-barred, reckless, lust-driven, no-thoughts-of-tomorrow sex with someone who made her feel like the most desirable woman on earth and who made her clench with just the glint in his eye.

'Here,' she said, unable to articulate much more, but the word was enough, as Mikhos was kissing her once again while slowly but surely guiding her to the towel she had lain out on the sand, lowering her to it, somehow untying the few strings that still held her bikini together as he did so. It was so like Mikhos to manage what could have been an awkward, fumbling moment with nonchalant ease, but Indi didn't have time to spare more than a moment on the thought as he slid beside her, his eyes exploring every inch of her with a hunger that took away the last of her embarrassment and doubt. She knew she was ready as she pulled him to her.

She'd been waiting long enough.

And then he bent to kiss her again and she could think no more.

Chapter Twenty-Five

Indi

Wednesday 14 June

'Happy birthday!'

A chorus of greetings met Indi as she made her way into the courtyard, looking around her in surprise. She'd told them she hadn't needed anything and had (sort of) meant it. Besides, she knew how busy everyone was. When had Jade had time to manage this? She knew her mother wasn't responsible, the decorations were far too conventional for her to have been involved. There were no nude statues for a start. Instead, colourful balloons and garlands festooned the flower-filled table which was set with a dizzying array of pastries and fruit, a satisfying heap of parcels and cards piled up at her place.

Indi's breath caught as she looked around at the smiling faces; Jade, her mother, Nico, Demeter . . . and Mikhos. He wasn't smiling, not exactly, but there was a warm glow in his eyes, something soft, almost tender. Heat rose through her and Indi could feel her cheeks bursting into flame as she remembered just how tender he could be. Had been.

More than once. On more than one occasion. On consecutive days.

Did everyone here *know*? Surely they must have guessed, although she was trying hard for discretion.

'Thank you,' she managed. 'I didn't expect . . . shouldn't you all be at work.'

'Yes!' Jade bounded over to envelop her in a massive hug. 'We should and we will be, but Antinous and Daisee are covering for now, so we can breakfast with you.'

'Happy birthday, darling.' Tabitha kissed her. 'My beautiful grown-up girl. I am so proud of you and the woman you have blossomed into. A glorious bud bursting into full flower.'

'Thank you, Mum.' Indi kissed her mother's cheek, her own glowing. At least Mikhos and Nico were used to her mother by now.

'I will make you anything for breakfast,' Demeter promised as she also embraced her. 'Eggs, pancakes, French toast?'

'I'm not sure there is anything else I need.' Indi returned the hug. She had got very fond of the older woman over the last few days, her organisational skills and ability to juggle twenty tasks put Indi to shame – *and* she never wrote a single thing down. Indi could learn a lot from her.

'Happy birthday. I have been very busy arranging your birthday surprise.' Nico's hug felt less boyish than previously, there was something more steadfast in his expression. He and Jade still had a lot to figure out, but although Indi would do anything to spare her sister pain, she knew this test of their relationship had matured them both.

'Oh no,' she protested. 'It's just a day after all. You're all needed here, today is too important. I'm not going home till the weekend, we can celebrate on another day.'

'I've arranged cover, so no arguing.' Mikhos' mouth curved into a slow smile. 'It's all taken care of. Be ready by three.'

'Yes, sir.' Their eyes met and held and Indi's whole body tightened. This was not the time or place to remember just what they had been doing during snatched moments and stolen hours over the last two days, but it was very hard to forget when he looked at her like she was infinitely desirable. When he made her feel infinitely desirable, not too much but somehow just right.

'This looks fabulous!' she exclaimed, self-conscious and over-enthusiastic in response. 'Let's eat.'

'Let's open presents,' Jade responded. 'Come on. Here's mine!'

Indi always preferred giving to receiving presents, found opening them in front of a crowd embarrassing, but not today. This morning, she felt loved, special. 'OK then.'

She knew how much it frustrated her sister when she carefully peeled back the paper on a gift and grinned wickedly as she slowly undid the tape, taking her time as Jade vibrated with excitement.

'Oh, Jade!' She held up the box to examine the pair of shell-shaped silver and turquoise earrings nestling within. A small card informed her that they had been handmade by a jeweller on Naxos. 'I love them, they are beautiful. They will always remind me of here, thank you.' She jumped up to kiss her sister, holding her still-slender body tight. It still seemed impossible that there was a baby growing inside there, that this time next year, her little sister would be a mother, taking that huge step before Indi. But Indi didn't feel jealousy. It wasn't her time, not yet, not for motherhood anyway. But she was ready to embrace being an aunt with everything she had. 'Love you.'

'And I love you. I am so glad you like them.'

'This is from me.' Nico proffered another wrapped gift.

Indi smiled up at him as, equally carefully, she unwrapped it. 'Nico, you really shouldn't have. Oh! A matching bracelet, this is too much, Nico.'

'You're family.'

'I guess I am, but even so, it's far too generous. But I love it, thank you.'

'This is mine. Happy birthday, darling.'

Tabitha's gift was fabulously wrapped as ever and Indi genuinely enjoyed taking her time opening it as much for the act itself as watching Jade try hard not to explode with impatience. 'Oh, Mum!' She held up a beautiful scarf and examined it. 'This is perfect.' The designer was a school contemporary of Tabitha who was now a famous print designer. Indi adored the scarf, but she equally loved the knowledge that her mother had gone out and bought it, wrapped it and brought it over, the care and thought and planning as appreciated as the gift itself.

'And this is from me.' To her surprise, Mikhos also handed her a brightly coloured parcel.

'You didn't have to,' she muttered, unable to look directly at him like some latter-day Psyche confronted with her immortal lover, not sure she wouldn't burst into flames if they made eye contact.

'I know.' He was leaning back, seemingly indifferent to her reaction, but his fingers were drumming on the table as she started to open it.

Carefully, Indi undid the ribbons, and peeled back the tape to reveal a wooden box. She opened the catch and swung the top open to reveal— 'Oh!' She started to lift the contents out, all beautifully packaged inside. 'Look at these. Paints! Pencils, paper, brushes. Thank you.'

'Gorgeous quality,' was all her mother said, but her voice was husky and her eyes bright. 'Very thoughtful.'

'They are. Too good for a beginner like me. I haven't picked up a paintbrush since school.' She looked up at him now, a question in her eyes. She'd mentioned her old dream to pursue art, why she had stopped. Had he remembered?

'If you are going to start again, you should have the best tools. And I thought you might want to start again. One day.' He paused, seemingly unsure for the first time since she had met him. 'But tell me if I'm wrong, if I overstepped.'

Indi swallowed hard, her throat tight. 'No, you're not wrong. I might, you're right. Thank you.'

'You are very welcome.'

Indi ate the eggs Demeter had insisted on preparing for her and some of the delicious spinach and feta pastry, but she barely tasted anything as she looked at the box of art supplies still open, filled with bright colour and possibility, her hands itching to explore them, to touch them despite all the years she had pushed her passion away. How could Mikhos get it so right after so short a time? How could he understand her so well?

Once breakfast was over, Mikhos, Nico and Jade dispersed to their duties. Indi had been offered the run of the whole island and the spa, activities, anything she wanted, but now she'd started enjoying sunbathing and swimming, she decided she might indulge herself for a few more hours. After all, she was on the countdown clock now, her return journey just a few days away, and who knew when she'd get the opportunity to be so lazy again? No, she wasn't going there, there was no point spoiling such a wonderful day by thinking about leaving. Mikhos' look when she announced her decision was so full of knowing humour she almost choked on her pastry, but by the time she had recovered herself, he had gone.

'That man has depth,' Tabitha announced, helping herself to another pastry. 'Formidable depths, with a quiet strength of character. Fascinating.'

'You don't build up a business like this without strength,' Indi pointed out, but her mother just smiled serenely.

'Anyone can be successful in business, darling,' she said inaccurately. 'I am talking about his soul. He is the sort who doesn't give his heart easily, but when he does, it's forever.'

'Right. Have you ever thought of going into fortune telling?' Indi got up and dropped a kiss on her mother's head. 'What are your plans for this morning? Join me for a swim and sunbathe and a generally lazy morning?'

'Thank you, darling, but I still don't know what form the sea should take, I can't quite pin it down, which is, of course, just as it should be. I must commune with my muse.'

'Sounds like fun. You know where I am if you need me.' Indi escaped thankfully. She loved her mother, but when she started prophesying, it was time to run away. *Give his heart forever, indeed.* OK, she hadn't had any kind of *where is this going* conversation with Mikhos because there was no need! He lived here, she lived in London, they both had busy lives. It was what it was and that was good for her, to be able to live in the moment. It was a holiday romance, just as Priya had advised, no more, no less.

Indi headed back to the hidden cove, knowing it was the one place on the island where she was unlikely to encounter influencers in the wild. They seemed to have multiplied, spreading over the island in their too short shorts and giant sunglasses. She stopped, confused, when she reached it, thinking that someone had found their way there after all, only to realise that the cove was free of people, but that someone had clearly predicted her arrival. One of the poolside sunbeds had been set up under a tree, draped with several thick towels. An ice bucket was filled with bottles of water and a propped-up note simply said *Call when you want champagne.* Fresh fruit, crisps and pistachios were set out in little bowls and a pile of glossy magazines were piled in a wicker basket. The note on them said *Relax.*

She took the scene in, her heart full. 'I am so spoilt,' she said out loud, realising that she was perilously close to tears. She couldn't remember the last time someone had anticipated her needs like this.

Indi moved the towels and stripped down to her swimsuit – her own sensible one-piece this time – and lay down on the sunbed, trying to concentrate on relaxing. It was a shame that her brain would insist on thinking, would dwell on the present Mikhos had bought her. The thoughtfulness of it. She'd only mentioned that she'd wanted to carry on art briefly, part of a much bigger conversation. He must have purchased it before they had even slept with each other.

At that moment, her phone rang and Priya's name lit up the screen. Indi instantly accepted the videocall.

'Hello?'

'Happy birthday to you!' Instead of her friend, Indi saw two identical four-year-old girls who immediately launched into a high-pitched rendition of 'Happy Birthday'. Indi's whole jaw ached by the time they came to a ragged finish with her attempts to keep her laughter in.

'Meera, Amara, that was the best "Happy Birthday" I've ever heard. Thank you!'

'Happy birthday, Aunty Indi,' they chorused.

'Thank you so much, my poppets.'

'Did you get nice presents?' Amara asked and Indi nodded.

'I really did, including a new painting box with all the colours.'

'Oooh!' they chorused.

'Hand the phone over,' she heard Priya tell them. 'Stop hogging, Aunty India. Ooh!' Priya's mouth fell open as Indi turned her phone around to show off her surroundings. 'Look at your bougee set-up. Birthday beach babe!'

'That's me.'

'So where are the other guests? Have you met that guy from that survival show yet? I reckon he is all muscle, no courage. I bet if you sneaked up and said *boo*, he'd fall off his sunbed. Easy on the eye, though. What about that annoying dance one, the one who's always making up routines in her kitchen? What's she like? Does she dance when she's talking to you too?'

Indi laughed. 'You know more about who's here that I do!' Indi had done her best to avoid the very young and very beautiful guests. Luckily Mikhos had proven the perfect distraction.

'It's all over social media. I've been looking out for you on the 'gram but not a glimpse. How are you managing to stay invisible? I've seen Jade a few times, the sun and beachside living suits her, she's positively blooming.'

Indi decided to wait to tell Priya just how blooming Jade really was until when she got home, once the first scan was done.

'I'm at the other end of the island. Sorry, not a muscle or dancer in sight.' Well, maybe a few muscles . . . her whole body heated at the memory of just how many of Mikhos' muscles she had explored.

'Maybe later. Happy birthday, Indi! So? How is it going? Have you heard from Will? Has he grovelled for forgiveness yet?'

'Not exactly, but I did get an email from the letting agent acknowledging he'd handed in notice on the flat, so I've got the joy of flat hunting or moving back into my bedroom at home to decide between. But I'm fine, over it. Over him,' she said quickly over Priya's expostulations and colourful curses. 'Pri! Not in front of the girls!'

'They've run off to watch TV and they've heard it all before. Oh, Indi. What an arse.'

Indi thought for a second about refuting Priya's statement but not strongly enough to actually do it.

'I never trusted him.' Priya was in full flow. 'His hair was always just that bit too perfectly tousled.'

'He did spend a lot of time on his hair.'

'You're better off without him.'

'I am. I really am.'

'You will be fabulous, flirty and thirty!'

'I'm not sure I know how to flirt.' But as she said the words, she remembered Mikhos' darkly amused look and could hear him saying: '*Are you flirting with me, India Drewe?*'

'It's never too late to learn, you're nowt but a lass.'

'If you take that accent anywhere near Scotland, you'll be arrested.'

'It was *Yorkshire*! And the principle is the same. I know you think you need life all sewn up by a certain age, but you don't, Indi. You only left home two years ago. You spend your whole life worrying about other people. Maybe it's time to figure out who *you* are.'

'Maybe. But I hope my future includes what you and Dev have – a home, kids, someone to be with. You're so lucky, Pri, you have two gorgeous daughters, a doting husband you adore. You have the whole package.'

'Now maybe, but when I met him, I told myself I would never marry Dev.'

'*What*? How did I not know this?' Indi sat up so quickly, her sunglasses fell off. 'What were you thinking? He's perfect for you!'

'I know that now, but then he was *too* perfect, my parents' dream made flesh. Tall, handsome, Hindu, a doctor . . . *I* wanted a poet, or a boy with a guitar, someone who made me a rebel. Instead, I am married to exactly who my parents wanted for me and, as much as I thought I wanted something different, I love my life. I love him. What I'm saying, Indi, is that love can be unexpected. Not everything can be solved with a spreadsheet.'

'Blasphemy!' Indi pretended to gasp in outrage. 'And you a project manager! They'll take away your accreditation if you carry on like this.' But Indi knew what Priya meant. She'd been reaching the same conclusions herself over the last week.

'So . . .' Priya sounded super-casual. Indi was instantly on guard, she knew that tone and it usually meant trouble. 'You're officially single.'

'It's too early to set me up with any of Dev's friends. I still haven't forgiven you for the foot guy and that was four years ago.'

'He owns a chain of foot clinics and a flat in Marylebone and a manor house in the Cotswolds *and* he's still single. He asks about you sometimes . . .'

'Not even if I'm still single at forty!'

'But I *wasn't* planning on setting you up, not yet anyway. I was just thinking . . . you need an adventure, Indi. To do something unexpected, daring. What about Mr Half-naked? You've still got a few days, there's time for you to make a move. Oh! Indi, don't, don't cry. I didn't mean to be insensitive. It's far too early. I am so sorry.' Priya's distraught tone switched to accusatory. 'Hang on! You're *laughing*?'

Indi wiped her cheeks, wet from semi-hysterical tears of laughter. 'About Mikhos,' she said. 'There's something you should know . . .'

Chapter Twenty-Six

Jade

Wednesday 14 June

'Oh, darling, this was a marvellous idea.' Tabitha turned onto her back to float lazily, eyes half closed.

'Mmmm.' Jade tilted her head back, loving the soothing feel of the water on her limbs. 'There is something about swimming out in the open sea, isn't there? Crazy to think that somewhere beneath us is a volcano.' She turned her head to watch her sister floating several metres away looking more relaxed than Jade had ever seen her look before.

Jade had been at her wits' end at how to make Indi's birthday as special as it needed to be with all her work pressure. She should have organised something the moment she knew Indi would be with her on the day but had expected some kind of steer from her sister. When it was clear that said steer wasn't materialising, she had realised that she was going to have to take matters into her own hands somehow. It was Mikhos who had offered both a boat and someone to sail it, and a solution: an afternoon sail to Santorini, a swim off the boat, then transport to the picturesque, much-photographed village of Oia for a wander during sunset, followed by dinner and an evening sail home. It was perfect, sophisticated, bespoke and, for the first time in months, all three Drewe women were spending time together, just the three of them.

'I thought Santorini would be too far away for just an afternoon and evening.' Jade turned onto her back as well. 'But, of course, sailing across is part of the experience, especially when you see dolphins on the way. Mikhos pulled all kinds of strings to get us a table in the restaurant as well.'

'It's a shame he couldn't accompany us.'

'Someone has to run the actual resort, Mum, and Mikhos does own it!'

'Yes, but at Mikhos' level, surely there are people to do it for you.'

'Plenty of them, but this is the very first time he has guests there, he wants to supervise himself.' Jade grinned at her mother. 'You're just disappointed because you hoped to see him in his Speedo's, admit it.'

'Oh no, darling. That wouldn't be at all appropriate. Posing for me is one thing, but it would be undignified for me to ogle. Especially when . . .'

'When what?'

'That was a very thoughtful gift he bought your sister.'

'She's just split up with Will, Mum.' Jade shared her mother's suspicions that there was something brewing between Mikhos and Indi. They were so very careful not to look at each other. But it was Indi's business and she would tell them if she wanted to.

'Even so. I bet I'm right, darling. And how are you?'

'Fine, I'm fine. I feel a lot better, not at all sick, more energy, thank goodness.' Jade had told her mother about the baby a couple of days before. Tabitha had reacted predictably with tears, libations, and a lot of advice, some of it even practical.

'You're blooming. But I meant your soul, not your body. I know things have been difficult.'

'My old insecurities. Nico offered me everything, and I mean everything, Mum. He's going to use all his money to build a house, not start his business, take a job he doesn't want. I worry that one day he'll resent me for it.' Things were a lot better between them, but they still hadn't had the time to sit and really talk. The idea that he was giving up his dream still preyed heavily on Jade's mind.

'Have you spoken to him about this?'

'Yes, a bit. He says I'm overreacting, that this is what he wants, but it's been so fast, Mum. Then I met Daisee and saw how different his past relationships were to me and don't know why I got so angry. Frightened, I guess.'

'Your father was nearly engaged when he met me. To a girl from his village, she was all Laura Ashley dresses and head-bands – well, it was the eighties – and his parents loved her. He had a future planned for himself – a job in his father's firm, a suitable marriage, life in the town he grew up in. He gave it all up for me. And I worried, Jade. I knew I would never be a conventional wife or mother. I thought he might resent me, that he might come to hate all the things he said he loved about me. I nearly called the whole thing off several times.'

'But he didn't. Resent you, I mean?' Jade held her breath. She remembered so little about her dad, she drank up every story.

'He got frustrated with me plenty of times. But no, he was proud of me, supported me. And I supported him, even attended those horrid corporate drinks parties.'

'What made you fall in love with him?'

'He made me laugh.' Her mother sounded far away. 'No matter what, he made me laugh. I miss that most of all. And he was kind, truly kind. Not a pushover. People mistake kindness for weakness, but it's not, it's a real strength. And he was full of strength.'

'Like Indi.'

'And you, Jade. I see your father in both my girls. It makes me so proud.' Her mother's voice was thick and she paused. 'Darling, if you love your Nico for reasons that will be true in five years and fifty years, then you have a good chance, no matter what. Hormones fade and attraction changes, but the qualities that make a person unique, they endure. Trust your instinct, Jade.'

It wasn't often the Drewe women indulged in mass beautification and so it felt both strange and special to be crowded together in the downstairs galley helping each other with zips and necklaces, admiring dresses and fighting for mirror space. Tabitha had opted for a long silk kaftan in greens and blues, her still dark hair piled up in the kind of messy bun that Jade used to spend hours trying to achieve before conceding that it was one of those things her mother just did. Indi had chosen a simple dull bronze dress, the colour enhancing the red glints in her hair and her slight tan. She'd left her hair loose and it coiled around her shoulders.

'I've always loved your hair,' Jade said enviously and Indi touched it self-consciously.

'I spend so much time trying to make it behave. But recently I've been thinking I need to stop apologising for my hair, my boobs, my height. To embrace it.'

'You should definitely embrace it. What did Mikhos call you? Magnificent? He was right.'

Jade was watching for the tell-tale signs and, sure enough, Indi immediately went red.

'Your father always adored your hair, he would spend hours helping tease out tangles, remember? So much more patient than me.' Tabitha paused, her eyes so full of sadness and memory, it was almost more than Jade could bear to see.

'More champagne?' she asked brightly, quickly filling her mother's and sister's glasses. 'To Indi,' she said, raising her own elderflower fizz in a toast.

'To my precious oldest girl. I thank the gods every day for you,' Tabitha said and Indi's mouth wobbled.

'You'll make me cry.'

'I do,' their mother insisted. 'Don't ever think that I don't see all you do, know what it's cost you, because I do. Your father would be so proud if he saw the woman you have grown into.'

'Do you really think so?'

'I know so. All he ever wanted was for you to be the person you wanted to be, whoever and whatever that was. His parents spent so long trying to make him into the kind of man they wanted him to be, he swore never to do that to his girls.' Tabitha set her glass down and crossed the narrow galley to take Indi's face in her hands. 'Oh my darling. I let you carry too much when you were younger. I knew that you wanted to be busy, that managing everything helped you with your grief, and so I stepped back, but I kept stepping back until it became engrained and I find it hard to forgive myself for that.'

'I never minded.'

'You *should* have minded – and I should have minded for you. Grief is so complicated, there's no template, no right way to be, but selfishness is never right. Your father would have told me to get out of the studio and make sure you went out and had fun. He would never have let you stay at home so long, especially not during your university years. I just got so used to having you there, I didn't want to lose you as well.'

'You'll never lose me. Besides, I may need to move back home for a while until I get a new place. You'll be begging me to move out.'

'Never! Not until you find the path that's right for you. Whatever that path is, whoever may accompany you on it, for the whole journey or part of the way. Your father always said I gave him the gift of laughter, the freedom to be himself. And he gave me the stability to be *myself.* That's why we worked. That's all I have ever wanted for you two. That you find the happiness we shared.'

'The gift of laughter,' Indi said softly. 'That's beautiful.'

'Well, of course we argued, bickered all the time. He said I never could put things in their right place . . .'

'You still don't!' Indi interrupted with a smile, eyes bright with tears.

'*Or* see why it mattered. And your father was very tiresome about fulfilling obligations and timekeeping, but we loved each other very, very much and I was very lucky.'

'So are we,' Indi said. 'You might not be the most conventional of mothers, but I wouldn't have you any other way.'

'Let's make our libations for your birthday, and then go and explore this delightful island.' Tabitha's smile was strong and proud as she kissed first Indi and then Jade.

Jade clung onto her mother for a moment. 'I hope I am as wise a mother as you are.'

'You will be a good deal wiser, Jade. I don't need to prophesy to know that.'

'One more toast before we do.' Indi held up her glass. 'As you know, I had big plans for this birthday. But all the planning and projecting and targets didn't prepare me for waking up single at thirty and for spending my birthday with just my mother and sister. But I want you to know that there is nobody I would rather be with. To the Drewe women.'

'The Drewe women,' Tabitha and Indi echoed and held their glasses up before heading up to the deck to make their libations to the obvious bemusement – and amusement – of Nico and the deckhands.

Tabitha stood at the prow and held her glass up high. 'To laughter.' She tipped it and watched the liquid hit the sea.

'To change.' Indi did the same.

Jade thought long and hard. About her mother, widowed too young, Indi facing a future so different from the one she had hoped for, about Nico. The baby growing bigger and stronger every day. 'To choices. May we always make the right ones.'

'And to us,' Tabitha added. 'To family. I love you both so much. You're the most perfect things I ever created. And the most painful.'

'Oh no, here she goes . . .' Jade groaned.

'Do we have to?' Indi pleaded. Tabitha smiled serenely while she topped up their glasses. 'It was bad enough before, but Jade really doesn't need to hear it right now.'

'I was sick throughout my pregnancy,' Tabitha started the familiar tale.

'Weak by the time I got to hospital,' Jade continued.

'But nothing could have prepared me for the first labour pangs.' Indi struck a dramatic pose.

'It was like being torn apart!' Jade copied her.

'Wicked girls,' but Tabitha was laughing.

Jade took another sip, watching Indi laugh as she teased her mother, and she knew that whatever happened, she and her baby would be OK. She had her family, she was loved and that was a gift she would remember never to take for granted again. She glanced over at Nico and saw he was watching her, love in his eyes, and she held up her glass to him in a silent toast.

'OK,' she said. 'I'm hungry! Let's go explore Santorini!'

Chapter Twenty-Seven

Indi

Wednesday 14 June

As the boat neared the jetty, Indi saw a tall figure waiting for them. She didn't need the light to fall on his face as they pulled alongside to know who it was.

Mikhos caught the rope the deckhand threw him and helped secure the boat before extending his hand to help first Tabitha, then Jade and finally Indi ashore. He held onto her hand a fraction longer than needed.

'Thank you,' she said softly as she stepped onto the jetty. 'That was the most amazing evening. What a beautiful town, and the food was exquisite.'

She loved the barely there smile which flickered across his face when he was pleased. 'You are very welcome.'

'I just know you're all so busy, I hope it didn't take up too much of your time.'

'Indi, if it had been a lot of trouble, it would still be fine, you deserved to have a good birthday, but it was no problem, all I needed to do was provide a boat and call in some favours. That was all.'

'Just like that?'

'Just like that.'

'Well, you might say *no problem* and *just like that*, but I want you to know that tonight means a lot. I had a wonderful time.'

'Mikhos, darling, what a wonderful experience.' Tabitha came towards them, hands outstretched. 'It is many years since I trod the hilltops of Santorini and bathed in its beauty, but it has by no means lost its charm, although it is infinitely busier. Thank you.'

'Any time.' Mikhos shared an amused grin with Indi. She liked his easy way with her mother, the evident respect and liking he held for her. Will had always been clearly uncomfortable with Tabitha's extravagant manner.

'Yes, thank you, Mikhos, the restaurant was fabulous.' Jade joined them.

'It was a success, then?'

Her sister glanced at Indi. 'I hope so.'

'It really was. How has it been here?'

'Forty influencers are well and truly influenced. That was a good idea of yours, Jade, to put on entertainment tonight as well as last, most of them are in the bar and restaurant and a good time is being had by all. The band is about to start its second set if you would like to join in?'

'Oh music!' Tabitha flung her hands up towards the sky. 'Dancing under the moon.'

'I take it that's a yes?' His eyes crinkled with laughter and Jade nodded.

'I want to check in with Daisee anyway. I'll walk over with you, Mum. Indi, music and dancing? Or another drink?'

Indi inhaled deeply, the sharp tang of the sea and the fresh green scent of olives. 'Maybe in a bit. I'll come and find you. I fancy a walk.'

Jade nodded. 'Don't be long. We still have plenty of celebrating to do.'

Mikhos waited until Jade and Indi's mother had headed out of sight before turning to her, face shadowed in the lamplight. 'Do you want company on your walk or is this a private commune with nature?'

It had been a long time since Indi had experienced the thrill of butterflies taking wing in anticipation, but right now her stomach felt like the insect house at London Zoo.

'I already poured libations with my mother and swam in the sea, so all rituals duly covered. Company would be nice.'

'Yes.'

One word, but every butterfly fluttered its wings at the tone in which it was said. Grave and with intent.

They fell into step, hands swinging, barely touching, but each time they did, a shiver of anticipation shuddered through Indi. 'If you'd told me just a couple of weeks ago that I would be spending my birthday with my mother and Jade and no one else and that it would be one of the best evenings of my life I would have scoffed,' she said as they began to walk, by unspoken design, away from the resort and towards the villa. 'I mean, we have spent lots and lots of time alone, the three of us, spent many special occasions together, but in the last few years I have always found the big days easier if diluted – by Will, my friends, Jade's friends. But today was really special. It feels like we were exactly where we needed to be, even if it's nowhere we expected to be, if that makes sense?'

'It does. Not too heavy for a celebration?'

'A little,' she admitted. 'There were tears from everyone, more than once, but not anger or pain. It felt right somehow, to start a new decade, a new era, in a new place.'

'A new era?'

'For Jade, a whole new life; for Mum, adjusting to Jade being gone; for me, returning home to a life without Will. And that's fine, I've more than come to terms with that. I wouldn't have him back if he begged.' She meant it as well.

Somehow, the time away, the soul-searching, the time with Mikhos had helped her see that she had outgrown Will, as he had her, she just hadn't wanted to admit it. 'It's just the whole being single thing and other people . . .' She pulled a face. 'I give it a month before well-meaning friends and colleagues start nagging me to sign up to apps or try to set me up with successful foot doctors.'

Mikhos took her hand, lightly, casually, but like everything he did, with intent. 'That's oddly specific.'

'I never enjoyed dating. I was so relieved that being with Will meant being out of that world. No first dates or ghosting or unsolicited dick pics. No game playing. Now I am back at Go and the rules have changed; time is no longer on my side. I still want a family of my own someday.'

'You are the expert at writing the plan, Indi, adapt it.' They had come to a beach Indi hadn't visited before, a twist of sand lit only by the huge moon hanging low in the sky, casting a silvery path across the water.

'Do you even wonder where it goes?' She stared out at the path. 'I love the way it looks like you could just run right across it, a bridge over the sea.'

'There's more of your mother in you than I realised.' She could hear the laughter in his voice.

'That reminds me, thank you.'

'I believe we have already covered this.'

'For the paints, the pencils, all of it. It was so thoughtful.'

'I didn't overstep?' Again that hint of doubt in his usual confident voice. 'I know it's a sensitive subject for you, but it seemed a shame to just stop something you once loved.'

'No. Not at all.' It was true. She had been taken aback when she realised what was in the wooden box, but the most prominent emotion had been anticipation followed by joy.

'Besides, now I can put art as a hobby on my Tinder profile, next to spreadsheets and colour-coding my underwear.'

'I'd swipe right.'

'That's good to know.'

'Indi.' His voice was husky and she put a finger up to hush him, pressing against the firm warmth of his mouth.

'It's OK. I know what this is.' There were just a few days left then back to reality. She was grateful for these moments out of time, but she wasn't going to start kidding herself that there was more to this than a summer romance, beguiling as the thought was.

'Then you are two steps ahead of me.'

'The stars have aligned, that's all, and I for one am very glad that they have. But don't worry. I haven't substituted an M for the Ws in my life plan. I am not plotting a proposal and a wedding and a baby. Your life is here and it's a wonderful one and my life is far away and I need to figure out how to make it wonderful without seeing it as a series of tasks to tick off. Wish me luck?'

'You don't need luck. You have this.'

'I have known you for less than two weeks.' She was figuring it out as she spoke. 'That's no time at all. And I literally just broke up with someone, and although I now know that was right for me, I still need to process what that means, who I am now. I like you a lot, Mikhos. I fancy you even more. But I am too grown-up and sensible to mistake those feelings for something deeper. If I lived here, if you lived in London, then who knows, maybe we would mature into something, maybe we would stay right here, but we'll never know and that's OK.'

Indi knew that every word she was saying was true, but she couldn't deny that part of her disbelieved them. She ached for Mikhos, craved him. It was just a crush, but wasn't the beauty of crushes that they felt so much *more* until the day you woke freed from their weight and realised that the object of your desires was just ordinary after all?

His mouth twisted into a smile. 'Less than two weeks? I think our paths were always supposed to cross, India Drewe.'

And then he bent his head to kiss her, sure and knowing and sweet.

Indi made herself forget tomorrow and her journey home, what awaited her at the other end, any fears about the fallout from this brief fling, how much she already knew she would miss this island, this man, and made herself concentrate on the feel of his mouth against hers, the taste of him, his strong, solid body, which made her feel small, delicate, wanted, desired.

'I don't want to join the party,' she breathed against his mouth. 'I just want you.'

'You're wish is very much my command,' he murmured, the kiss intensifying. 'It is your birthday after all.'

Saturday 17 June

Once again, Indi was woken by the sun dancing on her face. She was going to miss this! The London sun was brasher, harder, unpredictable.

She rolled over and felt something – someone – warm and firm.

Mikhos. She was going to miss this too. Miss him.

Ridiculous! she scolded herself. It had been less than a week since they had got intimate. That wasn't enough time to get to *missing*.

But that wasn't entirely true, because in many ways they had been intimate from the start. She'd told him things she had never told anyone before and she suspected the reverse was true.

As for the sex . . . She stretched, luxuriating in every sweet ache and twinge. She definitely was going to miss that. If only there was a way to carry on for a little longer. But no, for once, Indi resolved, she was not going to plan ahead, scheme and plot anything. She might not see Mikhos ever again. More likely, thanks to the relationship between Jade and Nico, they would stay friends. Who knew, maybe even hook up sometime. But one thing was for sure. His life was very much here and hers was not. She had a job to return to, friends. The next stage, whatever that might be.

As for Jade, it was time she stepped back and let her sister make her own mistakes – or not – as difficult as that was going to be. Her role was no longer caretaker, but big sister, friend and aunt. It sounded glorious.

'Morning.' Mikhos rolled over, trapping her under him, and she wound her arms around his neck. 'I can hear you thinking. All OK?'

'More than OK. I just can't believe my holiday is over already.'

'Ah.' His eyes glinted. 'I believe we have a few minutes before we get up. Any idea how we can fill them?'

'Yes, actually. Hold on.' Indi reached over to her bedside table and extracted a file. 'I will email it to you as well, but I wanted to give you a parting gift.'

'What is it?' He took it, his expression filled with curiosity. 'Take a look.'

Mikhos squinted at the first page and started to shake with laughter. 'India Drewe, have you given me a scoping project as a parting gift.'

'A completed scoping project with recommendations, including a shortlist of three. Like it?'

'Like it, I love it.' Mikhos set the folder down on the table on his side. 'It's as unique as you are.'

'Let me know if you have any questions.'

'Oh I have plenty . . .' With one swift movement, he had her pinioned her underneath her. 'Like just how many freckles do you have and have I kissed them all?'

An hour later, Indi started to pack. It didn't take long to put the handful of clothes she had bought into her carry-on case. Indi lingered for a long while over the tiny bikinis Aurelia had bequeathed her, then, at the last minute, shoved them into the bottom of her bag. They were a souvenir after all, a symbol of this time of change, although whether she'd ever actually wear them again was another matter. Bag packed, she made her way down to the courtyard with a heavy heart for her last island breakfast. She wasn't ready to leave just yet, didn't want to leave her sister. Nor, if she was honest, did she want to leave Mikhos, but she pushed that thought away. Holiday romance, remember?

Nico, Mikhos and Daisee were at work, but Jade had been given an hour to breakfast with her family before they departed. She stood up to kiss Indi as her sister entered the courtyard and Indi stopped, shocked and moved.

'You're wearing shorts.' Not just shorts but bottom-hugging tiny shorts that perfectly showed off Jade's slender limbs, her scar clearly visible down one side of her thigh. Indi couldn't stop her gaze dropping to it, before she forced it away. 'Look at you.' Her voice was thick with emotion and she tried to sound more normal. 'You look great.'

'I thought maybe it was time to stop hiding,' Jade said simply, and Indi nodded, blinking back tears. Somehow, over the last week, Indi had turned into a perfect Niobe and she used to pride herself on never crying.

She held her sister close for one moment and then sat down at the large wooden table, smiling up at Demeter as she brought in a laden tray. 'Demeter, I am going to miss your coffee, and your pastries and I am really going to miss you.'

'Come back soon, you hear?' Demeter replied and Indi nodded.

'For your coffee, I'll swim here.'

Jade sat back on her chair, coffee in hands, dark hair in a glossy ponytail. 'I've got used to you being here,' she said, lip wobbling. 'Both of you. The island is going to feel empty without you.'

'Not when the first real guests arrive , it won't,' Indi teased her. 'Right, I want the first pictures as soon as you have had the scan, and daily pictures of every sunrise and sunset. Oh and please send me these weekly.' She brandished her favourite spinach and feta pastry. 'Along with the baklava, of course.'

'I'll do my best.'

'So, what was the final influencer tally?' They had headed over to Naxos on Thursday to spend a night there in Mikhos' Naxos Town hotel before making the journey home. They'd all arrived back in London late last night and more posts were dutifully pinging onto their various platforms today.

'Eventful. One couple split up, two more coupled up, one involved the resolution of a love square . . .'

'A *what*?!'

'He had been stringing along three of them, slipping into DMs and goodness knows what else, so when he finally picked one Thursday night, apparently the fallout was not pretty. But Daisee is very good about keeping control and reminding even drunk and furious influencers of their contractual obligations. Their feeds are all #wellness and #authentic and #blessed with not a catfight to be seen.'

'Sounds messy.'

'The journalists seem like a breeze in comparison. And then the real work begins!'

'But you like it still?'

'I love it. So far, it doesn't seem that different from corralling a room of four-year-olds, but I do.'

'Then that's all that counts.'

Jade's eyes narrowed. 'Who are you and what have you done with my sister?' She grabbed another pastry from the dish in the middle of the table heaped with golden baked goods, fruit and fresh bread. 'Speaking of corralling, are you looking forward to chaperoning Mum home?'

Indi waved her clutch. 'I have her passport and ferry ticket here and I printed out her plane ticket. I have booked a taxi from the ferry terminal to the airport and a taxi from Heathrow home. Now I just need to put a tracker on her and we're all good.'

Jade's eyes were bright with laughter. 'Good luck.'

'I'll need it.'

'And you'll be OK?' Jade's tone turned serious.

'Going back to my childhood bedroom?' Indi's stomach swooped despite her determinedly cheerful face. 'I've survived worse than Will Talbot's thirty-something crisis. Don't worry about me.'

'It only seems fair,' Jade said softly. 'Considering all the times you've worried about me.'

Indi reached out and gripped her sister's hand, searching for the right words, but before she found them, her mother's voice broke the moment.

'Girls! I have been inspired! The sea was the wrong direction entirely. How about the modern social media star reimagined through Ovid. Or do I mean the other way round? Starting with a bacchanal frenzy for the cameras.

Indi, what time is our boat? I don't want to lose a single moment! I need my studio.'

'Not for an hour, Mum, so have some coffee and eat something. You can make notes all the way home.' She winked at Jade and mouthed, 'That will keep her quiet.'

Indi looked around at the beautiful courtyard, the blue sky up above, the sound of the sea always present, her sister, growing up, her mother, who in many ways would never grow up but was so very much herself, and knew how very lucky she was. She loved and she was loved. The rest would take care of itself.

Chapter Twenty-Eight

Jade

Jade stood on the jetty, shifting from foot to foot. 'Do you have everything?' she asked.

Daisee nodded. 'I didn't need much for just over a week.'

It took some effort, but Jade managed to keep her face neutral and her eyes unrolled. 'Exactly.' She slid a glance at the three large suitcases, which contained the multiple outfits Daisee had changed into every day. If this was travelling light, goodness knows what she needed for a full holiday.

But then Daisee had been happy to be centre stage, photographed and videoed over and over, always smiling, always friendly. There was a skill to what she did, Jade knew that.

'It was a long way to come for just a few days. We're very grateful.'

'Worth it, though! It was a lot of fun. And the job's not ended, I'll be chasing up reposts and flashbacks for weeks yet. We need to squeeze every bit of exposure out of them.'

'Of course. Well, thank you. I would never have managed by myself. It's been a real education.'

Daisee laughed. 'I know it's not your world, and it probably seems ridiculous . . .'

'No, no,' Jade protested, not entirely truthfully.

'It *is* ridiculous. But it's my world and it's given me opportunities to travel, to experience things I would never have experienced if I'd taken an office job. Aurelia is a real inspiration, I want to be where she is one day.'

'I'm sure you will be.' Jade looked over at the beach and saw Antinous with some relief. 'Looks like your ride is here. Don't want you to miss the ferry.'

'Stay an extra day in the sunshine? No, that would be terrible.' Daisee paused. 'Jade, I just want to apologise. For that first day.'

'You don't have to . . .' Embarrassment curled through Jade.

'Oh, I think we both know I do.' Daisee looked down, all her usual swagger gone. 'I was deliberately stirring things. I wanted to make you uncomfortable. Not my finest hour.'

'Oh.' Jade had no idea how to respond to such candour. 'I see. No, actually I don't see. Why on earth would you do that? You don't even know me.'

'The thing is.' Daisee stared at her feet. 'I was with Roman Jones?' She said it like the name should mean something. 'The singer? Finalist on *Star Search Britannia*?'

'I think I know who you mean.' Jade vaguely recalled a gelled-haired, beefed-up singer who specialised in crooning ballad covers.

'We'd been together for months, official and everything. It was great for my profiles and my business. And I thought he really liked me, you know. But first he says he needs some time and then he's photographed with Lola Linford.'

'The model?' Even Jade knew who Lola Linford was.

'I was so humiliated. I thought if I could get back with Nico and show I'd moved on, it would prove to Roman that I didn't care. Nico is so photogenic,' she said with a sigh. 'And his muscles are from work, not the gym. He's the real deal. When I realised we were going to have to ride out the storm on Naxos, I was delighted, it felt like the perfect opportunity to rekindle that old flame, but all he could do was talk about you. How it was love at first sight, how cool you are, how clever, that you were soulmates. It was cute actually.'

'Right.' Despite everything, Jade couldn't help smiling at the thought of Daisee hitting on an oblivious Nico who could talk about nothing but Jade. But, on the other hand, Daisee's meddling had had real consequences. She and Nico had fallen out, but not because of his past, not really, but because in the end Jade hadn't trusted in them, in him, the way she needed to.

If she and Nico were going to make a go of it, then she had to learn to trust, not naïvely as a lovestruck girl, but properly, maturely. Learn to disagree, to cope with insecurities, to ride out the storms. Because there would be more, there always were. One thing she did know, it wouldn't be as simple as waving Daisee off and picking up where they had been before.

'Keep in touch,' she said as they neared the boat. And she kind of meant it, but it was still with some relief that she watched Daisee sail off into the horizon.

Jade remained lost in thought as she returned to the villa and her desk in the office. She'd personalised it since she had moved here, a framed photo of Jade with her mother and sister, a photo of her with Nico. She picked it up and stared at it for a long moment before replacing it on her desk and switching on her computer.

As hoped, the last few days had generated a lot of publicity and the inbox was full. Generic enquiries were dealt with by the team on Naxos, but anything more specific was directed to Jade and she was kept busy sending details of villas that met specific needs, packages for anniversaries and honeymoons, and all the other queries that found their way to her. In between, she was checking the rota; all twenty villas needed to be spotless, ready for the journalists who were arriving later that afternoon.

'Hey.'

Jade jumped as Nico came up to her desk, so absorbed she hadn't noticed him come in. 'Hey yourself.'

'Mikhos said to tell you that you're not needed this evening. He's handling hospitality tonight with the Naxos press team. He says you are going to be busy enough for the rest of the week, so take some time.'

'He already gave me Indi's birthday,' Jade protested and Nico grinned.

'And now tonight. You know the rules of hospitality.'

'Grab your time off while you can, yes I know.' Jade looked up at Nico as he leaned against her desk and her heart turned over. 'What about you?'

'Me?'

'Are you off this evening too?' She felt ridiculously shy as she asked the question, as if they were back on the yacht, dancing around that first attraction.

'I am.'

She looked down at her hands. 'Want to do something?'

'Always. And I know just the thing.'

An hour and a half later, Jade and Nico were at their favourite table in their favourite restaurant, overlooking the harbour at Naxos, drinks in front of them and food orders in.

'You know,' Jade said, leaning back with a sigh of contentment. 'I love the island, I really do, but it's nice to be among people who aren't colleagues or guests and not always adding things to a never-ending to-do list.'

'Agreed.' Nico raised a hand to greet a couple walking by, calling out something in fast, voluble Greek, and Jade remembered guiltily that she hadn't opened her language app in days. 'Indi and your mother OK?'

'Yes, they managed to get all the way back to London without Indi going too mad, even though Mum is in a full-on creative phase.'

'Mikhos has seemed a little preoccupied since she left, don't you think?'

'Just a bit.' They shared a conspiratorial grin. Indi and Mikhos had been discreet, but there had definitely been something going on there and Jade was determined to quiz her sister sooner rather than later.

Jade took a sip of her drink and looked out at the idyllic scene. Boats of all sizes bobbed in the harbour, their lights twinkling in the dusk, people sat outside tavernas and bars, a mix of tourists and locals. It was a nice mix, she thought, enough tourists to create a buzz, but not so many the island felt overtaken. This was the island she was going to be making her home on. She loved it here – and she loved the man sitting opposite her. Somehow, she knew that everything was going to be all right.

'Daisee left OK as well,' she said.

Nico stilled. 'Oh?'

'She was an amazing help in the end. I was really glad she was here in an odd way. She really knew what she was doing.'

'Aurelia trained her,' he said matter-of-factly, and Jade nodded.

'I could tell. And, of course, she is of that world. I still don't understand it. It feels so alien.'

'That's because it's a world of pretend and gloss. You're real, that's what I love about you.'

'You should know that Daisee told me that she tried to stir up trouble on purpose. She'd just had a break-up and was hoping to console herself with a fling with an old flame. She apologised, which was something.' Jade looked down at her drink. 'I need to apologise too. To you. I overreacted. I said some horrible things.'

'I get it.'

'You do?'

'You're pregnant, Jade. Everything is changing and it's all happened so fast. Then I tell you I am selling my flat, giving up my business dreams, taking a job I had told you I didn't want.' He sighed. 'I thought that's what a man does, he takes care of his family. But a marriage is a partnership. I should have discussed it all with you properly, not just made all these decisions and expect you to agree with me.'

'I know you did it because you care, it just felt too much too soon, you know?'

'I do.'

'We don't have the foundations we need yet. And that's OK, we're still building them.'

'What are you saying? That you don't want to marry me?' His voice was full of emotion and her heart squeezed painfully.

'Not at all. But let's wait a year. Let's meet our baby, let's figure out who we are as a family first. Because when I stand up next to you and say I do, I want to know it really is for ever, that we have the strongest of foundations. I believe it will happen, Nico. I believe in us. I am so confident, I can afford to wait. Can you?'

Nico stared down at his beer for a long, long second before looking up and taking her hand. 'Yes,' he said at last. 'I can. You, Jade Drewe, are worth waiting for.'

'You'd better believe it.' Jade's heart was somehow both lighter and fuller than it had been all week. 'And so are you, Nico Angelos, so are you.'

She leaned over the table to kiss him, knowing she had made the right decision, that not yet wasn't giving up or giving in but growing up. And she couldn't imagine a bigger adventure than doing so with Nico by her side.

Chapter Twenty-Nine

Indi

Saturday 22 July

Indi checked her watch. *Right on time.*

To her surprise, Priya was already there. Her getting to work early habit was an anomaly, she was usually chronically late, due to the complexities of getting out of the house without one of the girls or the dog still attached. Tonight, she had neither and looked glowing in a glittery pink maxi dress.

'You look gorgeous.' Indi kissed her cheek. 'Have you done something different to your hair?'

'I had a blow-dry. Thank you for noticing, Dev couldn't see any difference and Amara cried because I didn't look like Mummy anymore.'

Indi laughed, but she was conscious of not jealousy exactly, but an ache of envy. There had been no one to comment on her appearance as she left her house – her mother had gone out and the cat had just given her a disdainful look.

'But look at you!' Priya stepped back to give Indi a full once-over and whistled. 'Indi, you look hot! I am going to have to be your bodyguard tonight to fend off all the men falling at your feet. Look at your legs! Why on earth have I not seen their full glory before?'

'Don't be ludicrous.' The green, silky, mini slip dress was unlike anything Indi had worn out before and had required a great deal of bra googling to find one that supported her, was comfortable and allowed for the thin dress straps. The dress fell to mid-thigh, showing off her still tanned legs and she'd left her hair down, in a mass of curls and spirals.

It was hard not to feel self-conscious, Indi had always been the kind of tall girl who tried to fade into the background not boss her height, and she had been ultra-aware of double takes and head turns as she made her way to the Stoke Newington pub where she and Priya had arranged to meet.

'This is a treat.' They stepped inside and Indi looked around the busy pub for a table. 'Thanks for suggesting it. I wasn't looking forward to a Saturday night alone on the sofa wondering where it all went wrong again. I did enough of that last week. And the week before. I thought it might be weird moving back in with Mum, but she's barely there.'

'It's a belated birthday treat and, believe me, I am just as happy to get out as you are. I love Dev's parents, but a three-week stay is two weeks and three days longer than I am comfortable with. Which makes me super-ungrateful, as they are here to help out with summer childcare and I am immensely thankful to them, of course.'

'Of course.' Indi grinned at her friend. 'But we all need some space every now and then. Let's find a table and I'll get a round in.'

'Good plan, shall we try upstairs?'

'Upstairs, isn't that usually reserved for private functions?'

'Not all the time and it's really noisy down here.'

The noise level seemed normal to Indi, but she couldn't see any tables and so she followed Priya up the stairs leading to the big room on the first floor sometimes used for gigs or comedy nights, and occasionally as an extension of the downstairs space. The door was open, but she couldn't hear anything from within.

'Pri, I'm not sure . . .'

'Go in and check.'

'If you insist, but I am telling you . . .' Indi pushed the door the rest of the way and set foot inside.

'Surprise!'

'Happy birthday!'

'What on earth?' Indi whirled round to glare at Priya, who was leaning against the door laughing.

'Your face! Happy birthday, Indi!'

The room was filled with Indi's family and friends, her mother, uncles and aunts and cousins, a few of her mother's artist friends, who were a collection of honorary uncles and aunts, as well as school friends, college friends, university friends, her team and other colleagues. There must have been over sixty people in the room, all dressed up and smiling at her.

A table at the back was heaped with enticingly wrapped presents, and one on the side filled with a delicious-looking buffet. A DJ booth was set up next to the present table, with Dev looking very pleased with himself, headphones around his neck, happily ensconced behind the decks.

'Don't worry,' Priya whispered. 'I have given him a very strict playlist.'

'But how . . .' Indi was lost for words. 'How did you get hold of all these people?'

'Your mother and Jade and one giant WhatsApp group. I know it's over a month late, but by the time we realised that Will . . .' She stopped.

'That Will's birthday surprise really did fit the surprise criteria . . .'

'That Will had failed spectacularly, it was already too late to organise anything sooner. We had to find a date, get a room.'

'Pri, it's perfect, thank you!'

*

Over the next half-hour, Indi was busy greeting her guests. It was amazing, and a little incongruous, to see so many parts of her life come together. Watching Alesha and her gorgeous husband in earnest conversation with her Uncle Graham was intriguing. Graham was a small-town lawyer who was almost a parody with his handmade, pinstriped suits and pocket squares, whereas Alesha and Daffyd ran a community wildlife reserve and spent most of their lives in fleece. The incongruity was reflected throughout the room, with artists chatting to lecturers, project managers to actors, all to the background of tunes from the noughties, complete with a heavy dose of Spice Girls, of course.

Finally, Indi had a moment to catch her breath, a glass of champagne in one hand and a home-made samosa in the other, courtesy of Priya's mother-in-law, and she stood back to take in the room, her heart full. If only Jade had been there! Her little sister hadn't breathed a word in any of their calls and WhatsApps and yet all along she had been planning this. And how she had managed to stop their mother from letting any details slip and ensuring she turned up during her current creative frenzy from 2,000 miles away was a complete mystery. Clearly Indi wasn't the only project manager in the family.

Pulling out her phone to send a thank you to her sister, Indi saw a new message alert and went to open it, mind still far away in Greece with her sister, only to snap back to reality when she saw it was from Will.

What on earth? Apart from a brief confirmation that he could have the flat until he left, she hadn't heard from him at all. He hadn't been there when she had packed up her stuff.

Do you have five minutes? I'm outside.

Indi swelled with righteous indignation. Was she only worth five minutes after four years? And he had just shown up on the assumption she had nothing better to do but jump when he commanded?

I'm not at home.

She sent the message with a tingle of satisfaction. That would show him she hadn't spent the last six weeks sitting waiting for him to get in touch.

I know. Rich didn't know we had split up and mentioned the party. I'm outside the Rose and Crown.

Dammit. This was her *birthday* party. She wanted to catch up with people who were here to celebrate with her. But, on the other hand, she wouldn't be able to relax now until she knew just what it was he wanted.

'Bloody Will,' she muttered.

She looked around, everyone seemed happy. She could probably slip away for a few minutes.

I'll meet you outside. You have exactly five minutes. I will be using a timer.

Indi's heart sped up as she headed down the stairs, her palms damp with nerves. She had loved Will, had hoped to spend the rest of her life with him, and then he had left her.

But it wasn't Will who kept her awake at night with longing, but Mikhos. Which was ridiculous. She had loved Will, she was merely infatuated with Mikhos. Another week with him and she would probably have been well and truly over him.

But what a week it would have been!

Snap out of it! she ordered herself. *You can't go and see Will thinking about Mikhos.* Not that she owed Will anything.

It was a hot evening and the air hit Indi with a blast as she stepped outside the air-conditioned pub. She looked around and saw him immediately. He looked just the same, tousled hair, strong and capable, in a blue short-sleeved shirt she had bought for him and a snug pair of jeans. She folded her arms. 'Hi.'

'My God, Indi, you look incredible.' Will looked her up and down, appreciation clear in his expression. 'Is that new?'

'I don't see that it's any of your concern. I don't have long and if you want to waste the five minutes by commenting on my clothes, that's up to you.'

'No, sorry. It's just, you seem like a new person.'

'It's just a dress, Will.'

He shook his head. 'No, it's more.'

'A break-up will do that to you. It makes you assess your life, your past.'

Will looked down at his feet, 'I am sorry, Indi. For how I approached everything. If it's any consolation, my parents are furious with me. They send their love by the way. They have told me several times that I am an idiot and that I will never find anyone like you again.'

'I always loved your parents.' She took a breath. 'Is that what you wanted? To apologise? Only I'm busy.'

'I just wanted to let you know in person that my ticket is booked. I leave next week.'

'Right.'

'Indi, it's not too late. You could still come with me.'

Indi half closed her eyes and allowed herself to just feel. To feel grief and anger and nostalgia and regret and irritation and the last vestiges of love. 'We both know you don't really want that, and we both know I am never going to say yes, but thank you for asking. Look, I had better get back. I'd ask you to stop for a drink, but every single person at the party wants to tear you limb from limb and I don't think that's in Priya's party plans. She might not get her deposit back either if the room is splattered with your severed body parts.'

'Understood.'

'Bye, Will.' At least she was getting the chance to say it. 'I really hope you find whatever it is you are looking for out there.'

'Bye, Indi. Be happy.'

'I intend to.' And she did. More, as she stood and watched Will walk away, she knew that she was going to be OK.

Jade

Jade broke into a skip of delight as she left the house and guided Nico and Mikhos down the road. 'That's where we went to school.' She pointed out the old Victorian building. 'And this is the old cemetery, I used to play hide-and-seek here.'

'How quaint,' Mikhos said and she smiled at him.

'It's really a great space, you must visit it tomorrow.'

She still couldn't believe Mikhos had accepted her invitation to accompany Nico and herself to London for Indi's surprise party. But then he hadn't been quite himself over the last few weeks, a little more introspective, a little distracted.

The resort seemed to be going well, with glowing reviews and bookings more than healthy, so it seemed easy to deduce that Indi was the reason for his subdued demeanour and his acceptance of this trip. But maybe that was just wishful thinking. Mikhos' grandparents lived in Surrey after all and he was taking the opportunity to visit them while he was here. Maybe he just fancied a weekend away and the party gave him the excuse he needed.

'It's so busy.' Nico looked pained. 'So much traffic.' Nico had never been to London before and it was increasingly clear he was not a big fan of cities or anywhere where he wasn't within a half-hour walk of the sea. 'Did you like growing up here?'

'It's all I knew. And it was pretty cool having all the theatres and museums on our doorstep.'

'And the cemetery,' Mikhos said drily and she laughed.

'Of course. But I'm not sure I would want it for my kids. I do miss London and I am very happy to be back, but I wouldn't want to live here again.'

It made her a little sad that less than a year away could do that; she had always been such a proud Londoner. But there was a lot to be said for waking up to the sound of the waves crashing, to the feel of sand between your toes, and any sudden sounds a squawk of gulls and not a car backfiring.

'Right, here we are.' She took Nico's hand. 'Baptism of fire, are you ready? All my family are in that room. My dad's brother, his wife and their two children. His sister, her wife and their son. My mum's two sisters and two brothers and various spouses and children. Plus friends of Indi's who have known me since I was a baby. It's not too late to cut and run.'

Nico straightened his shoulders. 'I have to meet them some time.'

Over the last six weeks, Jade had become increasingly sure that her decision to wait to get married until after the baby was born was the right one. She and Nico were busy with their jobs, but together they had been to visit an architect to discuss the villa Nico wanted to build, and she had persuaded Nico to keep the apartment as an investment for now and take out a small mortgage instead to make up the rest – and contributed her own yachting earnings to the land purchase. Mikhos had come through with a job offer for her as well so they could afford it – and maybe one day Nico could sell the apartment and buy his boat. A baby shouldn't mean giving up on dreams, just postponing. And strange as it seemed, their argument brought them closer together. She was surer than ever of him, of them.

The pub was busy, filled with couples and groups enjoying a summer Saturday night out. Jade recognised a few friends and acquaintances and waved at several people as she manoeuvred her way through the room to the stairs at the back. As she neared the top of the stairs, she could hear voices chattering, accompanied by the sound of the Sugababes, and she grinned at the thought of Dev's face when he had opened the playlist she and Priya had painstakingly put together. No boys with guitars or achingly cool obscure bands here, just poptastic hit after poptastic hit.

She opened the door, flanked on either side by the two tall, broad Greek men, and looked into the room, her heart swelling with happiness as she took in the fruits of several weeks of planning. Priya had done an amazing job! *Happy birthday* banners and colourful streamers decorated the walls, along with photos of Indi at all ages, from a beaming round baby to a recent shot of her on the beach in Greece. Jade spotted a picture of Indi stood next to her father, identical shy smiles on their faces, and blinked. How she wished he was here, that he could meet Nico and see how Indi, Jade and their mother had grown even closer over the years. How proud he would be of Indi, for taking care of them all for so many years, for not breaking down when her dreams shattered. Jade just hoped he would be proud of her too, that she would be as good a mother as he had been a father.

The room was rammed, with groups of people drinking, talking and eating, with several already on the dance floor. In the middle was Indi, statuesque and gorgeous in a dress Jade instantly coveted. She hadn't seen them yet and Jade waited, full of anticipation.

She didn't have to wait long. Priya tapped Indi on the arm and pointed and her sister turned, standing stock-still, disbelief on her face for one long moment before she let out a cry and hurtled across the room to grab Jade.

Jade held her sister close, half laughing, half crying, as if it had been years since she had last seen her, not just a few weeks.

Indi stepped back, still holding Jade's hands, her face full of happiness. 'You're here! How? When?'

'Our plane landed a few hours ago. We changed at home, then came straight here.'

'How long are you here for?'

'Just Monday, a literal flying visit, but it's peak season so we couldn't stay away any longer.'

'I am just so happy you made it at all. Thank you. I know you organised this, along with Priya . . .'

'Priya did all the hard work. Indi, you look amazing, that dress is utterly lush.'

'So do you.'

Jade pulled at the red halter neck dress, an old engrained habit. Her arms were bare, her back bare, the dress left half her thighs exposed, her scars clearly visible to anyone who cared to look, skimming over her rounding stomach. 'It's not too bright?' But she didn't really mean bright, she meant too much – or, in her case, too little. It got easier every day, but she was still getting used to feeling so exposed, to the vulnerability of it.

Indi understood perfectly and her eyes softened. 'Absolutely not. It is perfect. You are perfect. My grown-up little sister.' She turned to Nico. 'Nico, thank you for coming. How are you finding London?'

'Big and noisy.'

'That just about sums it up. I am so happy to see you. Go get a drink, you probably need one.' Indi dropped a kiss on Nico's cheek, and as she turned to Mikhos, Jade grabbed Nico.

'Come and meet the family,' she said. She wasn't sure how her sister would feel about Mikhos being there. Would she have preferred her summer fling to have stayed firmly in the past or was she secretly glad he was here? Either way, Jade knew her sister would want to greet this guest alone.

Indi

It was almost too much. The party, the final farewell to Will and now Jade's surprise appearance. Mikhos on top of it all was like some kind of delirious dream, but whether that was a daydream or a nightmare, she wasn't quite sure. Not that he didn't look as sexy as ever, but she had convinced herself that he was just a fling, that she had moved on. Seeing Mikhos in the flesh made her realise just how much she had been fooling herself. She hadn't moved anywhere.

'Hi.' She didn't know whether she should kiss him, shake his hand or give him a hug, so in the end she didn't do any of them, just stood there looking at him, a smile playing shyly on her lips. 'I didn't expect you to be here.'

Ouch. Awkward sentence. Did that sound like she *didn't* want him to be here?

'Of course you are very welcome.' Worse, she sounded totally pompous.

But Mikhos didn't seem in the least offended, his eyes crinkled with laughter. 'I believe that's why it's called a surprise party.'

'Of course.' She could feel herself start to smile as well and allowed herself to meet his gaze. His expression was warm, intimate, and she immediately felt more at ease. 'Did you come all this way just for this?'

'I'm fitting in a visit to my grandparents tomorrow, but yes, just for this.'

'OK. Right. Why?'

She couldn't believe she had just asked that question? Indi had never felt quite so gauche in any of her thirty years as she did right now.

Mikhos' grin widened. 'The stars seemed to align.'

Did that mean he fancied a hook-up? But coming to London for a quick shag seemed excessive, even if the last one had been as epic as their last night together. Maybe not excessive then. But Indi wasn't sure she was ready for a series of hook-ups. As a one-off, it had been perfect, but she wasn't really a casual sex kind of person. And if she was being honest there was nothing casual about sex with Mikhos.

'You look very serious.' His voice broke into her thoughts.

'Sorry, overthinking as usual.'

'I don't want to spoil your party.'

'No, you're not!' Indi was painfully aware that Priya and Alesha at least were openly watching them, Priya giving her a far from surreptitious thumbs up when Indi caught her eye. 'Not at all, but I could do with some air.' She paused. 'Come with me?'

It was still light outside, still hot and sticky, as she led Mikhos over the road to Clissold Park. As usual, the park was busy with picnicking groups and families, dog walkers and joggers, enjoying the late sunset and balmy summer evening. Almost automatically, she started following the path round and he fell into step beside her.

'You haven't even had a drink yet,' she said, struck by the omission. 'I'm a terrible hostess!'

'I didn't come for a drink. I came to see you.' Hope swelled in her chest. That had to be a good sign, right? Unless he just had some questions about the tendering document of course.

'I saw Will earlier. He wanted to say goodbye.' Indi wasn't sure why she was telling Mikhos this, but it seemed urgent to be clear about where she stood.

'How does that make you feel?'

'Mostly relieved it's done, to be honest. It feels as if all that belongs to another time. So much has happened.' She forced herself to add, 'We happened.'

'Yes.'

Another silence. Indi was half relieved, half frustrated, although she had no idea what she wanted him to say.

No, that wasn't true. She wanted him to say he had spent the last few weeks thinking about her the way she had spent them thinking about him. That against both their inclinations they had somehow connected on a level deeper than sex. That they had been more honest with each other than with any other person. That there was something real, something tangible there if they were just brave enough to reach for it.

'I miss you,' he said at last, so low she almost didn't hear him. 'I wish we'd had more time. I don't want to wait to see you again, to leave it up to fate, I want to take fate into our hands. I want to get to know you properly, India Drewe. To see if this is the start of something.' He looked a little lost. 'I have never felt this way before. I probably sound like an idiot.'

Indi couldn't believe what she was hearing. 'You want to get to know me?'

'I also want to kiss every inch of your body,' he added with a wicked grin that made her insides dissolve. 'But yes.

And I know your life is here and mine is in Greece and you have a career and—'

Indi stopped walking and pulled Mikhos round to face her, putting a stop to his words with a kiss – a soft, gentle kiss, tender and sweet, a kiss she never wanted to end, oblivious of joggers tutting as they ran around them and the jeers of a group of teenagers drinking under a tree.

'I want to get to know you as well. We don't have to have it all figured out.' She was aware she had never said those words before in her life. She liked saying them. 'We can take it as it comes. I can visit you, you can visit me, we can call . . .'

'Phone sex?' he said with an anticipatory grin that made her stomach swoop.

'Maybe,' she teased.

'I like the sound of that.'

'We'll need to be organised.' She started heading back to her party, her hand firmly in Mikhos' hand, her mind busy planning. 'Time differences and busy schedules. How do you feel about spreadsheets?'

It was Mikhos' turn to stop and pull her close for another lingering kiss. 'I love them,' he said. 'The more formulas, the better.'

'Then I'll create one just for us,' she promised.

It should have been Indi's worse nightmare, an uncertain future with a man she'd known for just a short while, but as she entered the room to introduce Mikhos to a beaming Priya, Indi knew that, for now, she was allowing the stars to align. The rest was up to them.

Chapter Thirty

Jade

One year later

This time, Jade wasn't taking any chances. She was going to be here to meet her sister's boat right on time. Just as she had been for every other visit Indi had made back to Agios Iohannis over the last year. And there had been several. Not solely to see her, of course, but the two sisters always spent plenty of time together. It was amazing to see Indi so happy, so relaxed, alive in a way Jade had never seen before.

She didn't have to wait long. Within minutes, the boat was visible on the horizon and soon Indi was jumping onto the jetty to fling her arms around her sister.

'Indi, you're here! How was your journey?'

'Really good. Hello, Jade baba.' Indi stepped back and looked around. 'You're alone? Where is my niece?'

'Way to make it clear I am second best.' Jade rolled her eyes. 'She's at the villa with her grandmama finishing her nap, so she is not too grouchy for Aunty Indi.'

'And how's Mum?'

'She's like a creative one-woman whirlwind, I've never seen her work at such a rate. It was so kind of Mikhos to build a studio for her.' Tabitha had spent increasingly long periods on the island, finally making a permanent move the previous month, partly driven by creativity but mostly by her adoration for her new granddaughter.

'A kindness I hope he doesn't regret.' The sisters shared a smile.

'It must be strange living back in the house without her.'

'It feels so big and empty, I can't believe she didn't even leave me the cat! Is it strange having her here?'

'I love it,' Jade said. 'She's so happy and she's actually a huge help. She adores Ariadne and Ariadne adores her. What with Nico's mum, Mikhos' mother and Mum that daughter of mine is being completely spoilt!'

Arm in arm, the sisters started the walk towards the villa. 'Have you given moving out any thought?' Jade asked.

'Not yet.' Indi was decisive. 'I might be thirty-one and back in my old childhood bedroom, but I have money in the bank for when I am ready to buy and it's better for someone to be living there now Mum has gone. It's a practical move, not a backwards step. Besides, it's easier to find my way with my painting without Mum hovering!'

Jade slanted a glance at her sister, was Indi protesting a little too much? It must be odd for everyone else to be moving on – Jade with the baby and now about to be married, Tabitha's move to Greece – while Indi was in the house she had lived in for almost all her life.

'Life is good,' Indi continued. 'Not much has changed over the last six weeks. Work's going well. Oh! Priya is pregnant again. She swore twins were enough, but I think now they're six, she's forgotten all the reasons why she said no more. I keep telling her twins often reoccur in families and maybe it will be triplets this time!'

'One is enough for me!' Jade said feelingly. 'Why do parents get competitive about crawling? Ariadne is only scooting and I can't turn my back for one minute.' But she was aware of the pride in her voice as she said it. Jade had been excited about being a parent but she hadn't realised how all-encompassing her love for her daughter would be – nor had she known how Ariadne would bring her and Nico even closer together, both besotted with their small daughter.

'Already?' Indi sounded suitably impressed. 'She's a genius, just like her aunt. How's work going? You're coping with it all?'

'I am so lucky. Mum has her one day, Nico's parents twice a week, and Nico and I share the other two days. Who would have thought that Mikhos was a progressive flexi-time employer?'

'He's also a doting whatever kind of cousin he is.'

'True! I've never seen him look as scared as he did first time he held her, but he adores her now – and she him.'

'I'm still surprised Mum went for Grandmama. I thought she would want something more mystical.'

Jade laughed. 'Not at all! She is very vocal about the feminine power of grandmothers. She'll be in her element this evening.'

'Are you sure this is OK as a hen night?' Indi asked. 'Just you, me and Mum in the villa. And Ariadne of course. Is that exciting enough for you?'

Jade leaned against her sister. 'I can't imagine anything nicer.'

'Then it will be the best hen do of four there ever was.'

The evening was everything that Jade wanted it to be. There were no drinking games or fluffy handcuffs or branded T-shirts, instead the three of them spent an indulgent couple of hours at the spa, while Demeter watched Ariadne, before getting dressed up for a meal of all Jade's favourite food. The three finished up on the sofas around the pool, while Ariadne slept in Indi's arms, reminiscing about Jade's childhood.

'Your father would be so proud,' Tabitha said, tears shimmering in her blue eyes. 'I wish he was here.'

'Me too, but you will do an amazing job of walking me down the aisle. Both of you.' In a change from tradition, Jade would be accompanied down the aisle by her mother and her sister, both of whom had raised her in their different ways.

'And he'll be there,' Indi said softly. 'Watching over you.'

'Do you really believe that?'

Indi nodded. 'I do.'

That night, Jade and Indi shared a room, just as they had when Jade was little and she was too excited to sleep, the night before Christmas or a birthday.

'I just want you to know I am so proud of you,' Indi said just before they fell asleep. 'The amazing woman you've grown into, the incredible mother you've become, the wonderful sister you are, the success you've made here. I love you, Jade. I always will.'

'And I love you. Marriage, babies, that won't change that,' Jade promised, just as she fell asleep to the sound of her sister's breathing, her daughter sound asleep in the same room as her grandmother next door. She couldn't ask for anything more.

Indi

Indi wiped a tear as Jade and Nico smiled into each other's eyes, as they circled around the dance floor.

'Are you OK?' Mikhos slipped an arm around her waist and she leaned against him.

'I'm being sentimental, which is most unlike me, but look at her. My little sister is all grown up. She's a wife, a mother, she no longer needs me.' But there was no self-pity in her tone or her heart. All she felt was pride and happiness.

'She'll always need you.' Mikhos extended a hand. 'Shall we dance?'

Indi took his hand and allowed him to pull her onto the dance floor to join the handful of couples. She felt a little on edge. Usually when she visited Naxos or the island, she stayed with Mikhos, but not seeing him until the wedding had discombobulated her and she felt almost shy as he pulled her close.

'I've missed you, I've hardly seen you all day.'

'It's hard work being chief and only bridesmaid and you were busy enough being best man. I've never seen Nico so nervous, I thought he might faint.'

Mikhos' laugh was low and sent desire vibrating through you. 'You gave a beautiful speech. And you look beautiful too.'

Indi looked down at the blue silk dress as it swished around her ankles. 'It's a gorgeous dress, I feel very lucky, I have seen bridesmaids dressed as everything from Bavarian wenches to ye olde milkmaids to stripper chic. This is elegant and classy. I just need a reason to wear it again.'

'You can wear it for me any time.'

'I thought you liked that bikini I bought last September,' she teased and his eyes darkened.

'You know I do.'

Indi couldn't believe that a year on she and Mikhos were still, well, something . . . They hadn't spent more than six weeks at a time without seeing each other, she coming to Naxos or he to London, even if just for a couple of nights, and in between, there were the phone calls and the video calls. Somehow, over the last year, she had found herself telling him everything, wanting his advice, his input. He was the first person she messaged when something good happened, the first she turned to when she was down.

As for the phone sex, that had been revelatory, both freeing and very, very erotic. Although not as good as the actual in-person sex. Something to look forward to tonight . . .

The rest of the evening was a whirl of dancing, eating and laughter until they waved Jade and Nico off to the honeymoon suite at Mikhos' most exclusive hotel before they headed to Scotland for their honeymoon. Jade was determined to show Nico that there was more to the UK than busy cities. Nico's parents were taking Ariadne for the night, but the baby was accompanying her doting parents on their travels.

Indi was spending a few days on Naxos at Mikhos' villa at the top of the old town with stunning views over the sea.

'Good thing I bought my flats,' Indi said after they had said their final goodbyes as she eyed the steep cobbled path. 'Every time I stay here, I swear I grow a new thigh muscle.'

'I am more than happy to give you a biology lesson later.' Mikhos brushed his hand over her bare back and Indi quivered at the light touch. 'But do you want to walk back via the beach first?'

'Always.'

She kicked her shoes off as they reached the beach, scooping them up and holding them by the straps, inhaling deeply, looking up at the star-bright sky and listening to the waves gently lapping at the beach. 'I miss this when I'm in London.'

'Then maybe you shouldn't go back to London.'

'That's a nice idea,' she laughed a little nervously. Mikhos sounded uncharacteristically serious. 'Shame my life is in the UK.'

'But does it have to be?'

'Well, yes.' But was that true, now her mother and sister were both living here? 'My job is in London. Last I looked, there was no university on Naxos.'

'But you work in project management, not as a lecturer. You don't have to work in a university.'

'No, I guess.' Where was he going with this? Indi had made joking comments before about not wanting to leave at the end of a visit, but not in a serious let's move in kind of way. After all, she was doing her best not to plan for the first time in her life, to enjoy the day to day. But at the same time, she did miss Mikhos, as well as her family when she wasn't here, London feeling increasingly lonely, Naxos more like home.

'Over the last year, you sorted out my booking software . . .'

'I just did the scoping document.'

'You wrote the tender document and took time off to do the interviews.'

'Well, yes, but only because I had experience.'

'You suggested a new phone system, you came with me to look at that small chain on Crete and helped me with the plans.'

'That was all you, I only added a few thoughts.'

'It was your idea that I invest in Nico's boat.'

'You'd have got there eventually. I can't believe it's been such a success already.'

'We work really well together. Don't you think?' Mikhos stopped and turned to face her. 'My business is growing all the time. I need a director of operations, I can't do it all myself anymore. I started to write the job spec and I realised I was describing you. The qualities, the experience, everything. You're already half doing the job.'

'But . . .' Was he *serious*? 'Mikhos, I don't know anything about tourism or building or . . .'

'No, but you understand my business, you demonstrate that over and over. And you do look after a large team, huge budgets. Look, Indi. You're perfect for the role. I promise that I am not asking you to consider it because I like being with you or because I want you with me. If you want, we could live separately and continue to see each other, or you can live with me. Whatever you want. I have thought about this a lot. I know moving to Greece isn't part of your plan, but I am sure being a director is.'

'Of course it is, but when it happens, I want it on my own merits.' But she couldn't deny that excitement was building as he spoke. Stay in Naxos? Allow her and Mikhos to grow, to see if what they had could be permanent, be near her family, have a job that played to her talents and strengths. As Mikhos spoke, Indi realised this was exactly what she wanted, she'd just not allowed herself to dream that big before.

'You know that Cycladic Resorts is far too important for me to offer this on any basis but merit, I promise you that. You have everything I need and want, in business and in life.' His voice hoarsened. 'I trust you with everything in my life and that's not something I ever thought I would say. I know you are the right person in every way. I guess the question is, am I?'

What had he just said? The meaning of his words were slow to sink in, but when they did, Indi was almost overwhelmed by the emotion behind them. She reached up to cup his cheek. 'I love you.' She had never said the words to him before, it made her feel vulnerable to say them now, but he had made the first move and she had to follow. 'I love you, not because you're a ridiculously sexy and successful man, but because you make me feel safe, you make me want to take a risk even though it terrifies me, you make me a better person. I want to see what the future holds, and I want to do it with you.'

She took a deep breath. Was she really going to do this?

'So yes. Yes to the job, to being together, to it all. Yes!'

'I love you too,' Mikhos said. 'The moment you turned up, the stars aligned and didn't move. It terrified me, it terrifies me still, but I know it's right.' He laughed. 'I wasn't sure you would say yes, so I'm not sure what to do apart from promise that you won't regret this.' There was a vulnerability in his voice that was new to her, proof, if she needed it, that he meant every word.

'I know exactly what to do.' Indi grinned up at him. 'How about you take me back to your villa and we celebrate in style.'

'Oh yes?' She was getting fond of that eyebrow lift. 'And what did you have in mind?'

'A bottle of champagne, you, me and very few clothes. What do you say?'

'I say what are we waiting for?'

She leaned in to kiss him, and as she did, Indi knew that this was where she was meant to be. She had come to the island a year ago to bring her sister home, but here she was, wildly off piste, and she had never been happier.

India Drewe loved a well-laid plan. But, it turned out, she also liked it when life was full of surprises and adventure.

And falling in love on the island was the biggest adventure of all.

Acknowledgements

They say writing is a solitary profession. For those of us with full-time jobs, it's half a solitary profession and half wondering who you need to beat out to get a seat on the always overcrowded train to Marylebone. So I would like to start by acknowledging all the stalwart commuters on the sometimes struggling Chiltern line as I write on phone, laptop, and freewriter depending on my seat situation. Don't worry, I haven't descended to dictation software in public (yet).

Huge thanks to the team at Orion, especially the always brilliant Charlotte Mursell, heroine inspiration for previous books, and the visionary Sanah Ahmed. Thank you both for taking a chance on me. Thank you also to Jade Craddock for her detailed copy edit. Any remaining mistakes are definitely the author's own.

Thank you also to a decade's worth of writing cheerleaders. The romance world is full of brilliant, supportive, talented women who seldom get the recognition they deserve. Special thanks to my first crit partners all those years ago, Julia, Maggie and Jane. To Merilyn. To Donna and Pam, I miss you both. And to all M&B True Love authors past and present. What a fabulous bunch you are.

Working full-time and writing almost full-time is a sanity-testing way to make a living and I couldn't do it without Rufus and Clover, always ready with encouraging face licks and to drag me out for mind-clearing walks in the mud. Most of which Clover will wear when we get home, but showering the puppy is a great procrastination tool. Special mention to Rose for making us so welcome in our new home town and a big I Miss You to everyone we left in York.

And finally to Dan and Abby. Living with a (this) writer is never easy but yay! Another one has reached The End. Love you both.

Credits

Jessica Gilmore and Orion Fiction would like to thank everyone at Orion who worked on the publication of *Love on the Island* in the UK.

Editorial
Charlotte Mursell
Sanah Ahmed

Copy editor
Jade Craddock

Proofreader
Jane Howard

Audio
Paul Stark
Jake Alderson

Contracts
Dan Herron
Alyx Hurst
Ellie Bowker

Design
Charlotte Abrams-Simpson
Rosanne Cooper
Nick Shah

Editorial Management
Charlie Panayiotou
Jane Hughes
Bartley Shaw

Finance
Jasdip Nandra
Sue Baker

Production
Ruth Sharvell

Marketing
Brittany Sankey

Publicity
Becca Bryant

Sales
Jen Wilson
Esther Waters
Victoria Laws
Toluwalope Ayo-Ajala

Rachael Hum
Ellie Kyrke-Smith
Frances Doyle
Georgina Cutler
Sinead White

Operations
Jo Jacobs
Dan Stevens